AN UNCONDITIONAL FREEDOM

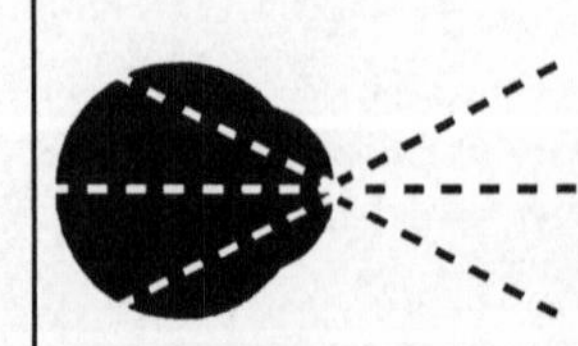

This Large Print Book carries the Seal of Approval of N.A.V.H.

AN UNCONDITIONAL FREEDOM

ALYSSA COLE

THORNDIKE PRESS
A part of Gale, a Cengage Company

Farmington Hills, Mich • San Francisco • New York • Waterville, Maine
Meriden, Conn • Mason, Ohio • Chicago

The Loyal League #3.
Thorndike Press, a part of Gale, a Cengage Company.

Thorndike Press® Large Print African-American.
The text of this Large Print edition is unabridged.
Other aspects of the book may vary from the original edition.
Set in 16 pt. Plantin.

LIBRARY OF CONGRESS CIP DATA ON FILE.
CATALOGUING IN PUBLICATION FOR THIS BOOK
IS AVAILABLE FROM THE LIBRARY OF CONGRESS

ISBN-13: 978-1-4328-6273-2 (hardcover alk. paper)

Published in 2019 by arrangement with Kensington Books, an imprint of Kensington Publishing Corp.

Printed in Mexico
1 2 3 4 5 6 7 23 22 21 20 19

For anyone whose trauma
was treated as weakness:
You survived. You're here. You're brave.

Any human power can be resisted
and changed by human beings.

— Ursula K. Le Guin

Prologue

January 1862
Outside of Richmond, VA

"I want to help my people get free."

That was how it all started.

No, that wasn't true. It had started with Ellen moving into the house next door. Daniel had been seven years old, the free-born child of a seamstress and a blacksmith who did well for themselves.

"You ain't never been a slave?" Ellen had asked him one day as they played, wide-eyed, as if she hadn't known Negroes could be born with their freedom instead of having it given to them by white folks. She'd still had her sweet Southern accent then. Years later — when he'd asked her to marry him and she'd said she wouldn't, that she had to go fight for their people — he'd told her fighting wasn't her place. She'd responded in the crisp tone of a woman educated by Massachusetts abolitionists.

"You haven't ever been a slave," she'd said, her brown eyes so expressive that he'd known she wouldn't change her mind about either fighting slavery or marrying him. War was brewing, changing everything Daniel had struggled and strived for, but he'd panicked at the thought of losing Elle. Elle who he'd seen by his side forever, even if she hadn't been able to see herself there yet.

"You were a child, it wasn't such a hardship," he'd countered, thoughtlessly. No, that wasn't true. He'd had one driving thought: to dismiss her reasoning and make her see that she belonged with him.

Elle remembered everything — *everything;* her mind was strange like that, and it was part of why she'd wanted to join the resistance against the Confederacy. She remembered what it was to be enslaved, down to the detail; she'd remember what he'd said to her, always. She would not look kindly on it, either.

After rejecting him, she'd left for Liberia on a mission to see what life could be had for their people in Africa, whether their country went to war over the slavery question or not. To scout for what life might be built there without the strictures of American society. He'd written letter after letter, not knowing when or if they'd reach her.

> I love you, Ellen. You say that you are not the right woman for me, but I will never believe otherwise. You have had my heart since we were children: I hope that one day you'll see fit to take that which is and will always be yours.

He'd waited.

In the interim he'd studied his law books, scouring the codes and cases for things that might be helpful in securing freedom for his people. The United States prided itself on the rule of law, did it not? He would use that pride as the key to undo the shackles of slavery.

He'd waited.

When he'd heard there were men about his town, men asking for those free Negroes who would aid in the fight for the Union, he'd gone to them. That's what Elle would have wanted, and perhaps if he wanted what she wanted she would come home to him.

"I want to help my people get free."

It had been true. He'd been fighting for the same in his law clerkship, in a more temperate way. He'd always wanted to guide his country toward the path of righteousness, and he wanted to do it with Elle by his side if she ever came back. He'd show her that he understood.

He sought out the strangers.

The two white men had spoken to him about the despicable nature of the slave trade. They'd shared a meal as they figured out the ways in which Daniel could be helpful to the Union cause, with his physical strength and his knowledge of the law.

Daniel had awoken trussed, confined in a wooden box that jolted about as if on the back of a wagon. When the lid was finally pried off the box, days later, Daniel's hands were a gory mess, nails splintered to the quick. The blood from trying to headbutt his way free from the box had congealed on his forehead, and he was covered in his own filth.

"Breaking these uppity darkies sure is something," one of the supposed abolitionists had said cheerfully to his compatriot.

Daniel had always been a hard worker. He'd helped his father with his smithing business, even though his father's goal had been for Daniel to be educated, to be one of the Free Blacks who rose as high as society would allow them.

He'd never known work as he'd found it on the Georgia plantation where he'd been sold. Work that sapped the strength from your body and your spirit and wasn't even to your benefit or that of those you cared for.

Daniel had always been stubborn. Elle had once told him that if a mule brayed at him he'd bray back just to have the last word, and for the mule to understand that it had lost the argument.

The first time he'd been beaten bloody, spitting out a tooth that his hated overseer snatched up to sell, he'd stopped braying back.

It had occurred to him one night, as he lay reeking of sweat and festering wounds, that he'd thought himself above this. He'd thought his freedom was something innate; he'd been born into it after all. God had seen fit to make him free. It was only as he swatted at insects that ran over him in the darkness of the cabin, as he heard the snores and exhalations and murmurs of those who had been born into slavery, many on that very plantation, that he'd understood the lesson he'd missed all those Sundays: blessings were always conditional. His had been rescinded. Had the people sleeping around him, who spoke of the Lord as their savior, too, ever had His grace to begin with?

By the time Daniel arrived on the Virginia

auction block, sold by a master who feared losing his slaves to roving Union soldiers, he was no longer thinking, *I want to help my people get free.* He was trying not to remember anything of his past. That he had been a man, supposedly born with certain inalienable rights. The Daniel Cumberland he'd been would have fought harder, would have stopped that overseer. He wouldn't have let another man stick his hands in his mouth and test his flesh and inquire about his temperament. Daniel let the white man before him do just that. He didn't respond when the potential buyer listed his defects, trying to knock money off of his price. As he was led away, the only thing he thought of was that he was glad Elle had gone to Liberia, though it had cracked his heart in two. He was glad she had left this foul chamber pot of a country, that would make a man love it, then remind him how it despised him at every turn.

The devil who had purchased him was gentler than the last. He helped Daniel up into the wagon and looked at him like he was an equal. Daniel hated him for that. There wasn't much he didn't hate anymore. Only Elle, and he wished he could hate her, too. She could never know how low he had been brought, she who had warned him.

"None of us are free when they might snatch us off the street and say we're a runaway. None of us are free while one of us is enslaved."

He fell asleep in the wagon; he, who used to balk at old, lumpy mattresses. When he awoke, they were traveling down a country road that was more ruts than level ground. He could see the constellations above him, glorious bright kindred spirits, also trapped in the designs of men when all they wished was to be free.

Elle would have told him he was being too poetic. She might have kissed him, too, as she had sometimes when the line between best friend and lover had blurred.

He closed his eyes against the too-human feeling that rose inside him then, and against the pricking heat that pressed at his eyelids.

Weak. You're weak.

The wagon pulled to a stop.

Footsteps crunched on hard-packed ground, but there was silence in the winter night. Was he alone with this man?

I'm weak, but my body isn't. Maybe I'll kill him. It wouldn't be so hard. I know there's no God to pass judgment, and if there is a God I deem Him too cruel to be obeyed.

He shifted, and the sound of his chains

hitting the wagon floor made him reconsider his plan. He couldn't travel far with those. He'd seen a man try, seen how the shackles had made him easy prey for the slave patrols and their dogs.

Daniel sighed and wished he could sink into the wood of the wagon. To curl up into a knothole and disappear. To become nothing in body as he was in soul. The world was too cruel, and he had been forced to receive that truth, to take it in like some awful communion. He didn't care to see what life had in store for him next.

Several additional steps were heard; he wouldn't have been able to kill his new owner, anyway. Or he would have had to kill that man and a few more. The idea didn't disturb Daniel as it once would have. The fact that they might kill him first didn't either.

The back of the wagon dropped down and Daniel crawled out into the darkness to find his new owner standing with men who filled him with shame. They looked like he had before he'd been dragged so low. Black men in respectable dress, their hair glossy with pomade and their beards neatly trimmed.

"You're free, Daniel," the man who had bought him at auction said. "These men are going to help you get back North."

Tears pressed at Daniel's eyes and he struggled to keep his mouth from trembling. Cruel, cruel jest. He wouldn't believe him. Couldn't. What was freedom? How could he be truly free if a white man could arbitrarily decide that for him?

He tried to make an inquiry, but an ugly, pathetic sound came out instead. He slammed his mouth shut.

"Brother Daniel," one of the Negro men said carefully. "We can assist you in heading North, but first I must ask: do you want to help your people?"

Daniel stared at the man, nostrils flared and hands shaking. The chains of his shackles shifted and that seemed to jolt the white man — not his owner? — into action. He rushed forward with a key and undid the shackles.

Daniel clenched his fists around the urge to throttle the man when he smiled proudly and said, "You are free."

Daniel didn't bother to correct him.

"I can't help my people," Daniel said, his voice hoarse. "I couldn't even help myself."

The other Negro man nodded thoughtfully. "If you do not count yourself as fit to help them, what about avenging them? Would that better suit you, my brother?"

"Yes," Daniel said before he could even

fully process the question. The word came out thick and choked by anger. "Yes."

"Good, good. First you must rest, but then I will tell you of the Four L's: Loyalty, Legacy, Life, and Lincoln."

Daniel didn't give a good goddamn about Lincoln or any other L word. He wanted revenge. He wanted someone to pay for his suffering, and if these men would help him achieve that, he would join them.

"Liberty," Daniel said darkly as he ran one hand over the bruise where the shackles had pressed into his wrist. "I think I should like to use my freedom much more constructively this time around."

Chapter 1

Late October, 1863
Cairo, Illinois

Daniel sat in the corner of the main room of the secluded cabin nestled in the Illinois wilderness. His seat was farthest from the door, so he couldn't make a quick escape, but the solid presence of the wall behind him was preferable to the vulnerability of leaving his back exposed, even among his compatriots.

"I would like to bring up the topic of . . . loyalty," the small, dark-skinned man at the front of the room said. Dixon or Dyson or something like that — Dyson, yes, that was it. Daniel forgot things often now, except, of course, the things he desperately wanted to burn from his memory.

None of the men and women gathered looked back at Daniel, but he sensed their collective attention shift to him. He could feel the weight of their judgment coil around his neck, settling into the grooves of the scar tissue there and squeezing.

He sucked in a breath, readjusted himself slowly and deliberately in his seat. He ignored the tightening at the base of his neck and the sweat that broke out on his upper lip, hidden by his beard.

"We swear Four L's in this society," Dyson continued, his voice gathering strength like he was a preacher at the pulpit. "Loyalty, Legacy, Life, and Lincoln. Those are the things we swear to uphold. You'll note that *cruelty* is not among our tenets."

Daniel hauled himself to his feet, running his hand over his grizzled beard. He hadn't groomed with a mirror for days and could only imagine what he looked like to others. Gone were the days when women called him baby-faced and his peers looked to him as an example of a stylish modern man.

The detectives seated nearest to him shifted slightly away — he knew what they said about him. *Addled. Insane. Broken.* They weren't wrong, to his shame and consternation. He had once been happy, carefree, his greatest trauma that the woman he loved hadn't loved him back. Perhaps all that had befallen him had been to teach him some lesson, a Jobian test of sorts. That thought might have been a comfort if his belief in the Lord hadn't been beaten out of him like dirt from a carpet.

"If this is about that Reb I killed over in Tennessee, can we not just be forthright?"

There was a grumbling among the detectives.

Dyson nodded, holding Daniel's gaze. "Very well. Your mission as a detective was to gather information about a Rebel who might have ties to the Sons of the Confederacy, and to use him to find others of his ilk. Instead, he was found stabbed to death, and now the local whites are talking about a vengeful Negro."

Dyson paused, as if Daniel would refute that moniker. It was as accurate a descriptor of him as any of the others given to him since he'd joined the Loyal League.

Daniel said nothing, and Dyson pressed on. "There's been talk of 'stringing up a few darkies' to remind the slaves what happens when they step out of line."

"You provide such a detail to convince me that killing slave owners is something I *shouldn't* do?" Daniel asked, garnering a few muffled laughs from around the room. Dyson opened his mouth to speak, but Daniel had heard enough. "I killed that man because it was necessary. We may not wear the Union blues, but we are at war and all's fair, in case you need reminding." Daniel's face began to grow warmer. "I don't recall being told upon my recruitment that I should value the life of some bastard secesh more than I value my own or that of my people."

"Don't twist my words, Cumberland," Dyson said. Daniel felt like he could have twisted the man's neck, more than his words, but that wouldn't have helped his position. "We are running covert operations here, and wanton killing ain't exactly covert."

"I don't kill wantonly." Some people thought Daniel enjoyed taking lives, but each death was just another stone added to the shame and anger and disgust that bent his back with their weight. He didn't savor killing, but neither did he shy away from what needed to be done.

When he'd seen the slave owner, the burly man had been holding the wrist of a girl barely older than Elle had been when she'd arrived in Massachusetts, pulling her along behind him. The fear, and acceptance, in the girl's eyes had left Daniel with no choice. The fact that some people thought there *was* a choice was the real issue.

"I trust that Brother Cumberland wouldn't do anything to endanger the 4L," Logan Hill, the detective who had recruited

Daniel, said. Logan had been a slave once, too, and though he didn't understand Daniel, he tried to. Given that Daniel didn't understand himself any longer, he appreciated Logan's attempt. "And the loss of one slaver is a boon to us, if anything. We will find other links to the Sons. It's not as if the bastards are few and far between, unfortunately, and they've been stirring up more trouble as the war goes on."

Dyson nodded tightly, but his mustache bristled. "I hope Cumberland will exercise more caution in the future."

Daniel sat down, hands crabbed together in his lap as Dyson droned on, and though the room was filled with his brothers and sisters in arms, he felt utterly alone.

War was a lonely thing he'd discovered. Survival was, too.

He inhaled deeply. That was all right. He needed to be alone. Being around others for too long only reminded him of what he had lost. Even kindnesses grated upon him. He often wondered how he'd been strong enough to survive the cruelties borne upon him, only to feel so weakened by the mere memory of them.

"Daniel?" He looked up at Logan, who was now sitting in the seat beside him. The other detectives were filing out of the cabin.

The meeting had ended and he hadn't noticed.

"I . . ." Daniel shrugged.

Logan knew.

"It's all right. You didn't miss much. Brother Dyson speaking about some of the operations in the area, the new detectives arriving. Things have gotten hot in the field since Chickamauga."

Daniel nodded. The Rebels had won, but the victory was far from a decisive one. Confederate officers ranted about General Bragg's incompetence in front of their slaves, and talked up their petition to Davis to have the man fired. The slaves had passed the information on via the whisper network until it reached the ear of someone sympathetic to the 4L cause. Judging from the number of reports they'd received, there had been a lot of ranting officers.

Logan shifted uncomfortably, and because the detective wasn't prone to awkwardness, Daniel knew what was coming.

"It helps to talk, Daniel," he said. "I'm not saying you have to, but if you ever need to lay down your load, I'm here. Most of us detectives have demons to deal with — demons unleashed upon us by this cruel society. You can't let them fester in you."

Logan meant well. He did. But even the

idea of telling someone else what he had experienced, of his shame and embarrassment and the trouble he had caused, nauseated Daniel.

He couldn't.

Everyone else seemed to manage their demons just fine, unless they overindulged in moonshine as some were wont to do; Daniel alone seemed unequal to the task of everyday living. That was shameful enough without sharing the rest of his pathetic tale.

"A toast to the Union Cause! And to our abolitionist brothers in arms."

Daniel gritted his teeth. He'd been such a gullible fool.

Logan sighed. "That gal Ellen? She wrote to see how you were faring, and sent along another letter for you."

Logan handed him the slip of paper — yet another reminder of all the evils that had befallen him. He took it only to avoid embarrassing himself further. When one of the 4L's top operatives sent you a message, you were supposed to read it immediately. Daniel would store this one with the others. Unopened.

"I know you two go way back. Maybe seeing her would do you some good." Logan raised his thick, arched brows.

Daniel imagined Elle, who he'd thought

would be his wife, sitting intimately with her husband. Her *white* husband — Malcolm McCall, the man responsible for securing Daniel's freedom. He imagined her sharing reports of Daniel's behavior in pitying tones, and both of them knowing him for the sad excuse for a man he was.

"I'll give it some thought," he said, slipping it into his pocket.

Logan nodded and made to stand before sitting back down.

"The man you killed —"

"Which one?" Daniel asked. He drew a dark delight from the way Logan's mouth dropped into a frown, but did not tease him further. "If you mean the man Dyson brought up — I will do many things in the name of gathering information, but I won't allow a man to hurt a child on the chance he's in possession of useful information."

Logan startled, but then nodded and stood. He clapped Daniel on the shoulder, and Daniel allowed himself a bit of pride in the fact that the touch didn't set his teeth further on edge.

"Come along. There's dinner to be had and information to be shared. If there's some way to put this infernal war to bed, maybe we'll happen upon it over a drink."

Daniel had his own ideas on how to end

the war — but he knew better than to tell anyone else. If there was one thing that had been pounded into him — quite literally — since the morning he'd awoken hog-tied and gagged, it was that you could not trust anyone. Or you could, but betrayal always awaited you for such a foolish decision.

"Right," he said, following Logan.

"There's also the business of the new recruits," Logan said. "There's something Dyson asked me to discuss with you."

Of course, Logan wanted more than a drink. Daniel nodded grimly. He had a feeling that whatever this was, he wasn't going to like it.

Chapter 2

Janeta had no idea where she was. Ohio? Kentucky? North Carolina? She'd never been farther inland than Florida until just a couple of months ago, and now she had traveled so much that the states — Confederate and Union both — were beginning to blur. She hadn't realized how truly vast a country could be. From the safety of her father's cane plantation, Cuba had seemed like a place too large to ever fully explore, and America was many, many times larger.

She was exhausted from walking and riding and hiding from Rebel pickets and the few brief but miserable hours of sleep she'd managed. Once night had fallen, she'd silently followed her guide through the wilderness. The hem of her fine dress was filthy, and she hadn't bathed for days. She could just imagine her older sister Maria wrinkling her nose in disgust: *Pero que sucia, Janeta!*

She hadn't seen her two older sisters in weeks. They were still back in Florida, keeping watch over the family home and the Union soldiers who had decided to use Villa Sanchez as a base, seeking entertainment from the *exotic beauties,* as they called them. The presence of those soldiers was what had placed Janeta on her current path — that and her own naïveté. She had thought herself able to read anyone, but she was starting to believe that she'd purposely left the book of Henry unexamined.

Henry.

She'd just wanted to please him. The Florida boy with a bright smile and laughing eyes who'd made her feel beautiful, who surely would have asked for her hand in marriage if the war hadn't started. Wouldn't he have? He'd told her he didn't care about her background, or her accent, or her golden brown skin.

"It wouldn't be fair to marry you just yet; I could be killed by one of these Yankee bastards any day now."

He'd held her tightly as she'd wept in fear of things to come, had kissed her, had made love to her. Janeta had sinned, but if loving Henry was a sin, she wasn't sure what God had made her for. Though now that she was away from him, now that she'd had days on end to examine their conversations, she wasn't so sure if Henry had been seraphim or snake.

When the *Yanquis* had started coming to Villa Sanchez every evening, expecting food and entertainment, she'd hated the intrusion — hated even more that Henry and his fellow officers had been driven from the town after a brief skirmish.

"I miss you so much," she whispered. She was still vibrating with excitement and vindication after having received his letter asking to meet in secret, outside of town. She'd waited so long for that moment, and when it had come, she'd risked being captured by the Union pickets to go to him because finally, finally Henry wanted her, too.

"Mm-hmm." He stroked her cheek with his thumb, then gripped her face and pulled her gaze up to meet his. It wasn't a gentle touch, but he was under pressure, after all. His troops had failed to hold the town, and he was clearly upset. He was upset and had called for her, of all women. Not either of her pale-skinned dark-eyed sisters. Not Camille Daniels, who blushed to the roots of her blond hair every time Henry looked in her direction. Janeta felt warm and like she might float away, the same sensation she got when she

snuck one sip too many of her father's finest rum.

"Tell me, do the Yanks ever talk about things pertaining to the war while you entertain them?" Henry asked. His gaze on her was focused, direct, and hard.

Janeta shook her head, bewildered. She had expected sweet nothings and declarations of love, not this. "Entertain them? We cannot force them to leave."

Henry raised his brows, just enough to show that he was dubious. "I suppose you can't. But if you really care for me, you'll be sure to tell me everything they say while under your roof. Smile prettily at them and get them to spill their secrets."

Her heart sank. "I do not like speaking to them. They presume things that they should not."

"Don't you want to please me?" Henry asked.

They both knew the answer to that. There was only silence after that, and then Henry's fingertip traced against her collarbone. Janeta trembled, and closed her mind against the in-quiet at what he'd asked of her.

Henry had received a promotion when her information helped his regiment win an important victory, and Janeta had felt a fierce pride. She had helped him; he couldn't help but love her now, could he? He'd asked for more information, and more, telling her he cared for her even as suspicions gathered and the danger grew. And when everything fell apart, he'd told her he could help free her father . . . at a price.

Janeta had once thought she'd give him anything, and she'd been right.

Here she was.

She wondered what her life would have been like if this damned war had never started. If Palatka had stayed a calm, tourist town and busy import hub instead of getting stuck in a tug-of-war between the North and the South. Or if a true compromise had been found before Sumter had been attacked, though she wasn't sure what compromise there could be between those who believed in slavery and those who didn't. Those like Papi and those like the detectives in the group she had infiltrated.

And where do I stand in all of this?

She'd learned many things since she'd left Palatka — about the world, and the war, and her place in both. After the move from the Sanchez plantation in Cuba to Villa Sanchez when she was fifteen, she'd thought herself worldly. She knew nothing. She'd been in the invisible enclosure of the Sanchez wealth and her father's beliefs. Beliefs she wasn't sure were right.

Janeta sighed and trekked on. She was starting to think her guide was purposely confusing her, as they had turned and backtracked so many times that the only other option was that the guide was terribly lost, which Janeta knew not to be true.

It didn't matter; if she wanted the information, she would get it. That was how things had always been, and she couldn't see that changing now. That was how she had found herself seeking out the Loyal League, far from the Florida parlor where she had played pianoforte for her father's guests and laughed around spoonfuls of sweet flan. Even farther from the plantation in Santiago, where she had been called *mi princesa hermosa* so often she had forgotten her name was Janeta.

She didn't want to think about what she was now. She didn't have a choice — she had always had to work for her place in her family, and a war wouldn't change that.

"Almost there," the guide said. The woman didn't look so different from Janeta: a complexion that showed she was *mulata,* thick, curly dark hair. "My name is Lynne, by the way."

There was a sharp undercurrent to the

simple statement. *We've been walking for hours and you never asked my name.*

And Janeta hadn't; she'd treated the woman like she was a servant, because in her world, the woman would be her servant.

"I'm sorry, Lynne. It was incredibly rude not to ask. I'm just so exhausted." She thickened her accent, hoping it would cause the woman to take it as some cultural misunderstanding.

The woman made a polite sound of acquiescence and Janeta broke into a sweat despite the cool, late-September air. She would have a reputation now: rude, uppity. Words her American tutor had taught her.

She'd had a reputation in Palatka, too — several depending on whom you talked to. She had been described as overly friendly, standoffish, shy, intelligent, shallow. Any number of things and none of them quite fit her — or maybe, all of them did. That was the way of it when you presented people with what they wanted, as Janeta had done since she was a girl. Since the rumblings of war had started, the descriptions had changed to things like passionate, feisty, and flirtatious. Janeta didn't think she was any of those things, and she certainly didn't try to be those things, but apparently the *Yanquis* heard her accent and saw her skin and made the decision for her. The Rebels, too. It was why she was there, after all.

She glanced anxiously at Lynne, who'd resumed her silent march.

You can't make such mistakes before you even arrive. Too much was riding on this. Her family's entire future. Her own happiness.

"Thank you for guiding me," Janeta said, feeling Lynne out. "I am very eager to meet the others and to help in any way that I can."

Lynne made a sound that somehow conveyed "you're welcome" and "don't worry about it."

"We need all the help we can get. We just lost a few good detectives, and every hit hurts."

Janeta said nothing. She was good at pretending, but not that good. If she achieved what she had been sent to do . . .

Dios, me perdone.

They came upon a cluster of small cabins. It was a good location — remote, not easily accessible, not much to look at. She'd seen more elaborate shanty towns in the countryside of Cuba. This looked like a poor farmer's spread, not the temporary headquarters of one of the North's most important spy rings, which she supposed was the reason they had chosen it.

Lynne led her toward the largest building, what looked like an old farmhouse, and as they got closer the scent of food made Janeta's stomach rumble. A low murmur of voices reached her ears, drowning out the evidence of her unfamiliar hunger. She took a deep breath and tightened her hands into fists, feeling the resistance of her leather gloves.

Dame fuerza.

An image of her father as she had last seen him — thin, filthy, crammed into a cell unfit for even a slave — flashed into her head. She'd remembered the giant crucifix that hung in their church in Santiago. As a child she'd hated seeing how Jesus suffered there, exposed for all to see. Her father, with his stringy hair and kind eyes, had reminded her of the helpless anger she'd felt staring at the crucifix.

"Do not worry over me, Janeta. I have made my peace with the world, and if I am reunited with your mother in the afterlife sooner than later, that is more than fine with me, princesa."

But Janeta had to worry over him. She was the reason he had been pulled from his bed in the dark of night. She was the reason officers put their boots up on his couch, smoked his cigars, and groped Janeta and her sisters in hallways of their villa. He was her father, damn it. She had to make this right.

"You can help your father, Janeta, and me too, if you are brave enough," Henry had pressed. *"Do you think you are, my sweet girl?"*

Janeta took a deep breath as Lynne pulled open the barn door and they stepped inside. The conversation died down until there was only the sound of cutlery against plates and chairs creaking as their occupants turned to look at her.

The room was full of Negro men and women, with skin tones ranging from much lighter than Janeta to deepest brown. Their clothing also represented a spectrum, from rough-hewn and ill-fitting to finely tailored. Their expressions, though, were all similar — friendly curiosity, more or less — with the exception of one man.

He was dark skinned and broad shouldered, a beard covering his jaw but not distracting from the intensity of his gaze on her. There was such anger in his eyes, and his full lips were pulled into a frown.

"Is this our newest operative, Lynne?" a man at a nearby table asked in a friendly voice. "A few others have arrived, and I believe she's the last of them."

Lynne nodded and inclined her head toward Janeta. "She is, Dyson. This is Janeta. She's Cuban, so her accent alone will grant her access to places us *American* Negros would be barred from." The word *American* was spoken with an undertone Janeta didn't understand. "She speaks Spanish and French, too, which should help with some of these European agents crawling around."

"A bit of Italian and Russian, too," Janeta threw in. "And the Russians have implicated that they would help the North should France or England throw their hats in the ring."

Janeta knew there were many other Negros who spoke French, particularly the Haitians who assisted the North, and other Cubans. She hoped that her Russian would make her more valuable to the Loyal League. She needed to be as valuable as possible.

There were murmurs around the room, and Dyson smiled broadly.

"Excellent. We need as many talented brothers and sisters aiding the Union Cause as possible. You'll be paired with one of our seasoned detectives, who has been investigating the European connection."

There was a huff of annoyance and

Janeta's gaze was again drawn to the hard-eyed man.

"Ohhhh, you pairing her with him?" Lynne let out a chuckle. "I guess we could use more dramatics, huh?"

"Is there going to be a problem, Cumberland?" Dyson asked, turning to the man.

"No, sir. Long as she doesn't get in my way."

The derision in his tone chafed at Janeta, the way it always had, whether coming from her sister or her father's business associates.

"What makes you think you won't get in mine?" she asked because her exhaustion had overruled her common sense.

His gaze landed on her and she wished she hadn't said anything. Janeta knew what hatred was; she'd felt it every time she'd visited her father in prison, every time she thought of how a great man had been reduced by these Americans in a war that wasn't even his. The hatred she'd felt was a flickering flame compared to the inferno she saw in Cumberland's gaze.

"Are you sure this accent is to be such a boon?" he asked Lynne, though his gaze was still locked on Janeta. "I have met many a slave with an African accent, even though by law the import of slaves was stopped in 1808. Their foreign accents do not help them. Perhaps our Cuban friend can enlighten us about how such accents still exist?"

The hair at Janeta's nape raised under his scrutiny, and that of all the other operatives. She chose her words carefully. "Ships still import slaves from West Africa, and Cuba is a place where they are sold — sometimes to American buyers."

Cumberland nodded grimly. "I was friends with a Cuban man on the plantation where I was first enslaved. He told me about your country, and how the color of one's skin wasn't always an indicator of one's allegiances."

Janeta had not expected to be met with immediate suspicion.

What have I done wrong? Will I fail Papi already? And Henry?

She kept her face impassive. "Yes, social castes are different in Cuba, but both America and Cuba are slave societies that must be dismantled. Right now, slaves are transported on ships that are allowed to carry out this barbarous trade because they fly the American flag as protection against investigation by British antislaving patrols. If slavery is abolished here, that flag's protection means nothing, and Cuba must soon follow suit, no?"

"And is that your reason for joining the Loyal League?" Cumberland pressed. "Abolition?"

Janeta was searching for the correct deferential response to his parry, examining each word to be sure she wouldn't reveal herself, but then paused and took in the body language of the people around him. Dyson looked annoyed, as did several other operatives. The man beside him wore an expression of chagrin. A few people rolled their eyes, and she heard at least one suck of tongue against teeth. It seemed Cumberland was not well loved.

How surprising.

"Is that not your reason?" she asked, letting steely challenge hone her voice. It was a risk, but if standing her ground against Cumberland endeared her to her fellow operatives, it would be worth it.

"No," he said baldly. "Abolition is a welcome byproduct, but I have a much more sensible reason to fight."

"And what greater cause is there than freedom?" she asked boldly, thrusting her chin up. Henry would be proud of her. Papi would, too. She would tell him about this moment when he was released and her family was reunited.

Cumberland's hand went to the blade

sheathed at his side. "Retribution."

A shudder went through her at the word because there was no longer hatred in his eyes as he said it. There was nothing at all. A sinkhole had once opened up in her small Florida town: sudden, inexplicable, leading down to a fathomless darkness. She felt the same looking into Cumberland's eyes as she had staring into that dark abyss.

"Enough, Daniel," the man beside him said. "I know distrust comes natural to you, but every new detective is thoroughly vetted."

Cumberland grunted, finally tearing his gaze from Janeta. She released the breath she'd been holding and resisted the urge to lift her hand and cross herself. Daniel was a man, not a demon. She needed only her wits to best him.

"Of course. Of course," he muttered. "I'll do as I'm told, Logan. We all know how to do that here, don't we? Who needs a lash when propriety dictates our actions just as well?"

Daniel stood suddenly; Logan didn't flinch, but others around him did.

"I'll go for a walk now," he said abruptly.

"But —" Logan began. Cumberland stormed past him and out the door.

Janeta schooled her face to timid fear as

she moved into the seat he had abandoned. She took in Logan's frustrated expression. He was obviously a man who cared about people; others were annoyed, but he seemed more worried than anything.

Janeta pitched her voice soft and tremulous. "I didn't mean to upset him."

"It's all right," Logan said. "Cumberland has had a hard go of it."

"Haven't we all?" Lynne asked, settling into another empty seat at the table with two plates. Her frostiness toward Janeta had all but melted away. She handed her the dish of cold chicken. "I'm sorry you got stuck with him. You're in for a rough road. Dyson, maybe you should pair her with someone else."

Lynne turned in her seat as if to call over the man in charge.

"No, it's all right," Janeta said. "He'll warm up to me."

Another woman beside her laughed.

"Darlin', he ain't got nothing inside him to warm. I don't know what he was like before, but that's a man that been turned hard as stone."

Janeta knew what that was like, to lose the soft parts of yourself. Maybe she'd get along with this Cumberland better than she imagined. Either way, it was clear he wasn't liked or seen as trustworthy.

He was exactly what she needed in a partner.

"I'm sure we'll get along just fine," she said with a polite smile. "Thank you for the food."

CHAPTER 3

Daniel glanced up at the night sky, visible through knotty branches shedding their many-hued leaves. He remembered the autumn in Massachusetts, rivers of gold and fire above his head. He remembered lying in a pile of leaves with Elle in the forest behind their homes, kissing her with the youthful certainty that she was the only one he could ever love, a certainty that had never left him.

When he'd returned home to visit his family after his rescue, the trees had been as bare and spindly as he'd felt standing before his parents. He'd reconsidered his pledge to join the Loyal League — after all, hadn't he dreamed of nothing more than returning home? But when he'd tried to return to work, the lawyer training him had caught Daniel sitting in the courtroom with tears streaming down his face and gently told him to take some more time to recover. His mother had been unable to stop staring at him pityingly, buying him several new cravats to hide the scarring at his neck, and had doted over him as if he were a foal taking its first awkward steps. Worse, Daniel had felt like one, uncertain that his legs would hold up beneath him as he struggled to move forward. His father had been worse — the man he'd so admired had been unable to look at Daniel at all, sharing his observations about the war with some specter over Daniel's shoulder. Telling Daniel's left bicep that, really, other Negroes had it worse, and he needed to be strong and forget what had happened.

Daniel had considered leaving the Loyal League too many times to count. On his first mission, he'd been posing as a server during a meeting of influential Confederate officers. One had grabbed him by the arm to ask for another glass of wine — innocuous, as far as those things went — and Daniel's body had gone taut as a bow, his mind blank save for the memory of his overseer grabbing him by the arm.

"You think you can come stir up trouble? You think you smarter than me, boy? I'm gonna show you what your meddling gets you and these pickaninnies."

Daniel had nearly been sick on the table,

though he'd managed to wait until he could run out behind the restaurant to retch. He'd claimed to have eaten spoiled meat and no one had known what had really happened — that his past had risen up to claim him, as it did so often since he'd gained his freedom. His shackles had been unlocked, but the ghost of them remained, tightening against his stomach or throat or heart at the most inopportune moment to remind him that he would never, ever be rid of them.

He'd thought about quitting every time he heard the names Burns and McCall — which was often, as they were the League's most celebrated detectives. It seemed that, even when undercover, they couldn't evade the eventual accolades. Last he'd heard, they'd stolen troop movement plans from an officer on a train, and, when cornered by Rebs, Elle had grabbed Malcolm's hand and jumped, pulling him after her from the moving train. Some thought the story to be greatly exaggerated, but it was her bravery and stubbornness that had made Daniel fall in love with her. It may not have really happened as reported, but it certainly *could* have.

He sat on a fallen tree in the dark forest, away from the noise and annoyance of the barn, and fingered the letter from Elle —

his best friend, once. The woman he had thought would be his wife. He'd been so *sure.* But everything he'd been sure of had proven to be a lie given enough time.

Tension gathered at his neck as stared at the rumpled rectangle of low-quality paper. He couldn't bring himself to open it; he'd once called Elle hard-hearted, but she wasn't in truth, and that was why he couldn't read her words. He couldn't bear to see whatever kindness she had sent him. Worse — whatever pity might be hidden between the lines.

It was best he didn't respond; her letters were being sent to the wrong man, anyhow. The Daniel Cumberland she'd known had died in the bed of a slaver's wagon. Elle wouldn't like the new Daniel. No one did.

He considered quitting whenever a fellow detective tried to engage him in discussion of the bright future that lay ahead for America, once this war was over. Daniel had been optimistic once, too. He'd been two years into his clerkship with a local abolitionist lawyer when he'd been kidnapped. He'd thought he could change things from within the system; he'd thought the American system *could* be changed. Then he'd awoken in a coffin with manacles around his wrists. He'd seen how casually white slave owners and overseers doled out the most humiliating and painful punishments — punishments for the simple crime of having been born a Negro and not showing proper shame in that fact.

His hope for America had died many brutal deaths; stripped nude and lashed with leather straps, choked by fusty hemp rope against his throat, crushed by the weight of bales and bales of tobacco.

Elle had once scoffed at his idealism.

"You think you can fix everything with a suit and tie, in a courtroom. Slaves probably built that courthouse, but white men crafted the laws, and changing them will take more than a fine suit and a quick tongue," she'd said.

"Someone has to try to change the laws," he'd replied, agitated by her calm dismissal.

Elle had looked at him with the queerest expression. "I'm not talking about changing the laws, Daniel. I'm talking about changing the white men who craft them. Show me how to do that and we'll solve the problem of America."

Daniel had to laugh bitterly at that now, given her choice of husband.

But just because he didn't believe in his country anymore didn't mean he didn't have ideas about how to save it. There were other fools who hadn't yet awoken from their dream of freedom and equality, and even if America didn't deserve such citizens, those fools deserved some reward for hope in the face of such insurmountable evidence. His ideas were best enacted alone, however. And now he was stuck with a bothersome distraction of a partner; he was sure this was punishment of some sort to rein him in.

He tucked Elle's letter into the pocket of his jacket.

Janeta was lovely, to be certain. She had large brown eyes framed by long lashes, a wide, pert nose, pillowy lips, and a shapely body. She was a bit lighter skinned than Daniel preferred — evidence of her mixed racial heritage, which wasn't uncommon amongst the enslaved. Her general comeliness was all it took to distract a person, he supposed. He'd been more interested in her gaze than her body.

She'd clearly been nervous, but despite that her gaze had remained guarded and had revealed nothing. And she was observant. Keenly so. She'd been deferential to him until the moment she realized that he was operating as a lone wolf. She'd picked up on that quicker than most. Then she'd nipped at him — just a bit. Just enough to garner the respect of the other operatives. He'd seen the same technique in canny lawyers putting on performances for their juries that had nothing to do with their real goal, and everything.

He wondered what her goal was, exactly. Logan had laid out her background for him, along with whatever contrived reason Dyson had for forcing Daniel to take her on as a partner, but Daniel still wondered how she'd found herself mixed up in this detective business.

He heard a sound that didn't belong in the forest night, and though he remained seated, he unsheathed the knife that hung from his belt. It was a long, sharp blade that he'd taken from a Reb — the first member of the Sons of Confederacy that he'd squared off with and come away the victor. It was only afterward that Daniel had learned how other detectives avoided tangling with the members of that abhorrent organization. He'd been treated with a new respect, and an awe imbued by fear, when word had spread of his deed. The knife gave him a kind of comfort, like a talisman. He had taken it from a man using it for evil — a man who'd sown the land with hatred and bigotry and cultivated a crop that would be disastrous for Negroes — and turned it against that man. When Daniel held it, it reminded him that he might be able to turn the evil of the Confederacy against itself, too.

What does it mean that such a thing brings you joy?

Sometimes he had different, even darker, thoughts about his knife. He imagined the relief that would come from running it over his wrists and letting his own blood soak into the soil of this country that had already consumed every other part of him.

He pressed the blade into the sensitive skin just below the heel of his palm as he sat and listened in the darkness of the autumn wood, taking a morbid joy in the scrape of the knife's sharp edge against his pulse and the sense of control that flowed through him as it did. Everything would be so much simpler if he applied just a bit more pressure to the blade. He would no longer burden those around him — all those formerly enslaved who were somehow so much stronger than him, who survived instead of enduring — with his sulking presence and stormy moods.

Footsteps approached and Daniel lifted the knife away; no time for existential thoughts on the nature of inanimate objects, including himself. It might be someone dangerous approaching. He *hoped* it was someone dangerous approaching; his nerves were jangly with the excess energy that had driven him from the barn.

"Cumberland?" The voice was soft and accented — and there was the slightest tremor of fear.

Of course, the meddlesome woman had sought him out, even though he'd be stuck with her for who knew how long. He sheathed his knife, but didn't answer. Didn't move.

Let her find me if she's so determined.

"I know you're here. It's cold, and I have a flask if you need to warm up."

Attempting to ply him with alcohol? She really was new to this.

He breathed in slowly and then out. She was passing right in front of him now and for a moment he was struck by the utter loneliness of a life lived in the shadows. This was every day for him; having someone this close yet being utterly unable to reach out.

"I understand that you don't want to work with me. But acting like a child won—"

Her boot caught on his foot and though part of him was content to let her crash to the ground, he reached out instinctively to catch her. His hands gripped a soft, pliant waistline as her skirts crushed against his legs, and he heard her gasp and curse just before she realized he had her secured against his chest.

"Ay Dios," she exhaled on a ragged breath.

"Quite the detective," he said. "Literally tripping over your quarry."

The next few weeks really would be a waste of his time. Pairing him with an unskilled, annoying, and greener-than-collards detective was something Dyson would pay for later.

Anything for the Union.

She shifted in his hold as she got her bearings and his grip tightened on her hips, steadying her. He could smell her, sweat and sweet vanilla, and he could feel her warmth in the cool night. A sensation that he hadn't felt in a long while streaked down Daniel's spine and settled into a bittersweet ache in his groin. This was the danger of reaching out from the shadows — you might catch hold of something that felt this good, when goodness was far from what you needed and the last thing you deserved.

He released her as if she'd burnt him, and she stumbled and then righted herself. There was shuffling, then the scratch of a match and a burst of illumination revealing the pleasing planes of her face and the way her brows were drawn in annoyance.

"Well, I suppose that's why I've been assigned to work with *you,*" she said. "You must be their best operative for them to put up with such an endearing personality."

She closed the short distance between them and took a place on the log beside him, not waiting to be invited. Her match guttered out along the way, leaving them in darkness again as she settled herself.

"They paired me with a new detective with no training and no common sense because they know I won't show you any mercy — and to punish me for my contrariness," he said bluntly. "And they put up with me because the North needs all the help it can get, and because it's useful to have someone like me around."

"Someone rude and antagonistic?" she asked in a sweet tone that belied the insult.

Daniel felt another strange sensation burble up in him. Laughter. She hadn't appreciated his jab. Well, he didn't appreciate her presence.

"Someone who doesn't mind getting his hands dirty now and again."

Someone who perhaps enjoyed it. Who saw each life he'd taken as payment toward a debt that could never be cleared.

"I wouldn't think that would be too hard to find in this war," she said. "That's one thing men seem to have in common, no matter what side they're on."

She pulled at the lapel of her jacket, elbow pressing into him a bit as she rummaged around for something. Then there was a popping sound and the smell of sweet alcohol mixed with the tangy scent of her.

"You like rum?" she asked.

"Was it made by slaves?"

"Probably. Yes." She sighed. "There isn't much in this godforsaken world that isn't right now."

True. So true that it could have crushed him if he dwelled upon it for too long.

He heard a gulp and a harsh exhale; then the flask was being pressed against his arm, slipping a bit against the dirt-worn fabric of his jacket. He hesitated, then reached for it. There was a quick brush of fingertips as they made the exchange, and he expected her to lean away from him then, but she stayed where she was — improperly near. It was disconcerting, as his fellow detectives usually gave him a wide berth. Logan chanced the occasional touch, but understood that Daniel didn't like it, so those were often accidents that he apologized for. Janeta didn't know much about Daniel yet, and clearly didn't have the sense to leave a suitable space between them. He could have asked her to move, as he wasn't exactly afraid of hurting her feelings, but he stayed quiet. He told himself it was simply a human need for body heat; she served as a buffer from the brisk wind that had been pressing through his thin jacket. If he had to be saddled with her, she could at least serve some purpose.

"You said you'd met one of my countrymen before," she said eventually. *"Hablas español?"*

"He taught me a thing or two," Daniel said. He hadn't spoken of Pete, as the master had renamed him, to anyone before. Pete, who had told him of the horrors of cutting cane and shown him his arms scarred from stripping the abrasive leaves. "*Yo soy* Daniel."

She giggled, and instead of annoying him as it should have, he found that he wanted to hear it again. He would speak no more Spanish, though, as he only remembered one other phrase apart from some random cuss words and it was nothing to laugh at.

Un día seré libre.

"What's your last name?" he asked. Allowing her to sit beside him was intimate enough; he wouldn't call her Janeta, as if they were friends, or more. He took a pull of the rum, a sweet burn that left a pleasant warmth in his chest.

"Sanchez," she said, taking the flask back from him. Her cold fingers briefly wrapped around his as she got a grip on the metal this time, and the hairs on Daniel's arms raised.

"I don't want to work with you, Sanchez," he said bluntly, crossing his arms over his chest.

"You could have told me that before drinking my rum," she replied evenly.

Daniel smiled and was glad for the darkness that hid it. "See? You don't want to work with me, either. Rude, antagonistic, etcetera. Also, most definitely prone to getting in your way, as you demonstrated a moment ago. Tomorrow morning, ask Dyson to reassign you to someone who won't trip you up."

That might resolve this situation. It was worth a try if it meant not having to mind this woman for the foreseeable future. There were certainly others better suited for the task.

"And what if he says no?" she asked. Daniel knew that she really meant, What if I refuse to?

"Then we set off tomorrow. And you'll regret not taking this opportunity."

She stared at him for a long moment. "If

that's the way you want things to be, all right."

She stood and moved away without saying anything else. He doubted she was too put out. If she had any sense at all, she'd do as he suggested.

A gust of wind snaked through the meager protection of his jacket, and before he could stop himself he was thinking of Janeta's warmth. Funny how quickly the body adjusted to the presence of another. How it made you feel their loss. He rubbed his hands together and forced himself to endure the chill night air.

For both of their sakes, he hoped she was marching straight to Dyson for reassignment.

Chapter 4

Cool autumn air slipped through the cracks in the shabby room where Janeta was sleeping four to a bed with the other female detectives. The breeze was a crisp, unfamiliar caress over her face. As a child, she'd only ever experienced the tropical heat of Santiago. She remembered being read a story about a man who fell off a boat into the ocean and froze, and laughing at that impossibility. How could the ocean, warm and wonderful, cause someone to die from the cold? Her world had been so small then. Florida had been warm as well, though when the war started and the *Yanquis* arrived to "safeguard" the port town, they'd complained so much about the weather that Janeta had finally begun to understand that there were places where the sun didn't heat your skin every day and humidity didn't make your clothes stick to your skin.

She was frightened of what true winter

would be like in the North.

She was just plain frightened.

Come, you are a Sanchez. You are made of stronger stuff than this.

Lynne shifted and stretched beside her, easing herself from sleep, and Janeta slammed her eyes shut. She wished for her soft, comfortable bed, her private room, and a life where her every wish was attended to. Her toilette had been laid out each morning, her dresses were buttoned up for her, her hair had been brushed and oiled and pinned — all by someone else. The house had been cleaned, food had been cooked — all by someone else. In her worst moments of discomfort since she'd left Palatka, she'd thought perhaps the Southerners had the right of it, for a life without servants was a harsh one indeed. But *servants* was the gentle word for the people who toiled for her family. There were harsher, and more common, terms — slave. Darkie. And worse.

In those moments of weakness, when she longed for someone else to make her life easier, she remembered her mother and was ashamed. But Mami had been freed from enslavement, eventually. It was Mami who had taught Janeta that only the Lord could judge you for what you did to survive in this world. Benita Sanchez had risen from the ranks of slave girl to Don Sanchez's beautiful second wife, whom he'd loved to the point of obsession despite the gossip and judgment from the Santiago elite.

La gente me llama descarada y tienen razón, querida. Soy descarada y soy libre.

Janeta had been called *descarada,* shameless, too, without doing much at all besides being a girl with dark skin who would someday be a woman. That had been shameless in itself, it seemed, judging from how women had snubbed her and men had leered at her as soon as her figure had begun to shape the bodice of her dress.

Janeta had begun hiding herself away, then, but Mami had told her she was beautiful and that her beauty was a gift she must use as best she could — a currency that she couldn't afford to hoard. She'd stared at Janeta's face with such intensity at times that it had been frightening, stared and smiled as she told her that she would one day be lovely enough to bring any man to his knees.

Este es nuestro poder, she'd said the first time she'd applied rouge to Janeta's lips. *This is our power.*

Her mother had seemed formidable to Janeta — after all, hadn't the women who visited Villa Sanchez envied her beauty and the men who visited wanted to possess it for their own?

Her mother had been ignorant of neither thing and played both to her advantage. Sometimes it had embarrassed Janeta, but now she wondered if Mami hadn't simply been using the only tools she had: her body and her brown skin, and what value society placed on them.

"I knew when your father first looked at me that he would give me anything I asked for, except for my freedom outright," her mother had said one day, after she had become ill. "So I watched and I waited and I learned what he liked; I know what your father likes better than he does, can anticipate his every need, and because of this I was worth more in his parlor than in his fields."

Janeta had used her body the night before, "tripping" over Daniel as if she hadn't seen him. He'd caught her; his touch hadn't lingered, though a shock had gone through her at the strength of his hands around her waist. She'd wanted only Henry to touch her, had rebuffed the other men who'd tried to seduce her. But Daniel's grip had been firm — his hands had the strength of a man who would hold his woman and not let go. And with the way he'd released her, almost pushing her away, he was still holding on to *someone* tightly. She wondered about the woman who could be loved by a man like Cumberland.

These are not the things you need to be thinking about.

She'd known as soon as the warmth had rushed to her cheeks that playing the seductress wouldn't work well for her in this case, but she was still her mother's daughter.

"I know what your father likes better than he does, can anticipate his every need . . ."

Daniel needed an ally to make him feel strong more than he needed a woman to make him feel big. Everyone saw his anger and disdain, but they were simply the shiny, distracting clasps that held the cloak of loneliness he wore in place. He'd liked having her beside him, even as he'd told her to go away. She wouldn't. She would be his partner and make him pleased that she was. She much preferred that role, especially since she could still feel the press of his fingertips through the layers of fabric if she thought on it too long.

Friendship was better, even if desire was easier to secure; Mami hadn't told her about the double-edged blade of giving all of yourself to a man to ensure he loved you. Janeta had seen what came of that, though.

Mami's power had not been infinite, and

it had cost her everything.

The other female detectives began to talk more loudly as they prepared for their day, signaling their consideration for the exhausted recruit had reached its end and it was time for Janeta to get up. She tossed a bit and began to go through the motions of awakening.

"I'd be reluctant to get out of bed today if I was you, too," Abbie, a former cook from Maryland, said before gliding out of the room.

"I'm making a crossing into Louisiana today and that's more tolerable than the thought of being paired with Cumberland," Carla said. The short, plump woman pulled out her derringer and inspected it before tucking it back into the pocket of her jacket. She pulled out the matching gun from her other pocket and began inspecting it in the same way.

"Nice guns," Janeta said, and not just to fit in. She'd always appreciated a finely made weapon, to the exasperation of her family.

"The sisters do right by me," Carla replied with a broad smile. "What's your make?"

Janeta stretched, then reached under the rolled-up petticoat she had used for a pillow and produced the two beautiful guns that fit perfectly into the palms of her hands. Silver inlaid with ivory; artworks in miniature. Her father had gifted them to her at the party celebrating her fifteenth birthday and her passage into young womanhood, but Janeta had learned to use them long before, during afternoon walks with Mami. The guns had originally belonged to her mother, given as protection against the near-constant fear of a slave uprising amongst the plantation owners. Now they were hers, and these women thought they would be used to help stop slavery.

Janeta swallowed against the sourness rising in her throat. Lying had been much easier when she hadn't done it to purposely hurt others.

But you'll be helping Papi. Remember this!

Carla let out a whistle, and Janeta caught herself before she startled.

"My kind of woman," Carla said with a wink. "Hope you won't have to use them on your partner today. Though Cumberland's so hardheaded, a gun wouldn't be of much use."

Everyone in the room laughed, and Janeta felt the brief happiness brought by good fellow-feeling. She had so rarely shared the weapons, or the feeling of camaraderie, with other women. Her sisters loved her, but had been constantly after her to stand properly and sit properly — to stop being herself entirely. Janeta had become all too good at that.

"So I watched and I waited and I learned what he liked. . ."

Janeta had studied at her mother's knee, had perhaps surpassed her. She'd hidden *herself* under so many layers of pleasing aspects, with those aspects constantly shifting depending on whom she was speaking to, that she wasn't even sure that *herself* still existed.

Her sisters had hated her guns, and her knives even more, because they weren't feminine, and of course Janeta had to try harder to be feminine because she didn't share their pale skin. Janeta had hidden her weapons, told her sisters they had just been a phase, though she'd still secretly trained with her knives every once in a while. She could think of nothing more feminine than the way a blade curved down to a sharp tip or a trigger fit snug against the crook of your finger. She had been called *mi princesa hermosa,* but the tales her mother had told weren't only about the pale blond ones locked in towers waiting for a prince to come. Janeta had heard tales of African princesses, brave and strong, fighting to protect their people.

Shame edged up on her as she looked at Abbie and Lynne, but she shook it off. Protecting her own family was important, too, even if she had to lie. Even if she had to undermine everything the Loyal League was working toward.

Papi.

"This would be my weapon of choice, if I had to deal with Cumberland," Janeta said, forcing herself to be chipper. She pulled the slim throwing knife from the sheath in her sleeve, grinning when Carla's eyes went wide with admiration.

"Definitely my kind of woman! If I wasn't leaving today I'd ask you to show me a thing or two with those."

Janeta blushed at the insinuation in Carla's tone, and at the pleasure of sharing something she loved with someone who understood it. No one judged her or called her a wild girl. No one said she brought shame to herself and her family, or that she had to behave herself at all times because she didn't want to be confused with *them.*

"You must not play with Julio anymore, Janeta."

"Why, Mami? Julio is my friend."

"Julio is a slave. You are not. Everyone, especially you, must be very clear about that

difference."

If she were back home, she would have averted her gaze from Lynne and Carla, and never deigned to speak with them. She would have carefully erased them from her reality, as she had been taught to do. But no one had ever taught her what to do when she stared into her looking glass every morning — she couldn't erase that.

"I should warn you not to pull that weapon, or any weapon, on Cumberland, even in jest," Lynne cut in. "I'm not saying you need to walk on eggshells around him, but sometimes he get spooked by regular things, and act before he think."

Janeta had wondered when he'd stormed out of the barn; it was strange behavior. But he hadn't seemed too bothered by her toppling onto him in the woods.

"I'll be careful," Janeta said before splashing water over her face from a shared basin. The water contained no scented oil to mask the fact that it was far from fresh.

"He was born free, you know," Carla said, shaking her head. "Fine, upstanding family. Got snatched up by some men pretending to be abolitionists."

A sick, sharp shudder hit Janeta in the stomach like a fist. She had always been warned to be careful, of course, but her family had been rich. Powerful. She'd never truly seen slavery as a threat to herself. Her family owned slaves and she was not one. It was as simple as that. Or at least it had been before she'd left Palatka. Now, with the things she had seen along the way, she wasn't so sure.

No. Papi is the only thing that matters. The North did this to him. You *did.*

"We all been hurt," Lynne snapped. "The things my master did to me —" She shook her head, her mouth snapping into a grim line. "I won't let that man have power over me anymore. I got free, and soon we all gonna get free, and if I let Old Cheswick keep me from glory, he wins. I ain't gonna let him win."

Emotion was bright in Lynne's eyes, and Carla walked over and squeezed her arm. "Folks handle things different. You know that. And I hate to say it, but I was glad when I heard what he done to that man the other day. He said there was a little girl."

Lynne closed her eyes. "I'm glad, too. Lord forgive me, but I'm glad. And I hate that I can rejoice in a death, but I ain't gonna let these devils take my soul just as sure they took my body. Hope Cumberland don't learn that too late."

The women shuffled out of the room,

leaving Janeta alone. She placed a hand to her chest, squeezed her eyes against the burning warmth of gathering tears.

Janeta slipped out of the house, leaving her sisters crying in the parlor, and rushed through the woods toward where she and Henry had planned to meet.

"Henry! Henry!"

He stepped out into the moonlight, handsome as ever, and relief washed through her. Henry would help. He would make everything right.

"They've taken Papi," she cried, stumbling into his arms. He just barely caught her — he'd been scanning for Union pickets.

"I heard," he said, his expression grim. "These bastard Northmen have no level they won't sink to. They could have left the man his pride instead of parading him in front of his neighbors."

Janeta was confused. "Pride? They should have taken me instead. I am the one they were looking for."

"What?" Henry looked at her with brows raised, and Janeta shook her head from the frustration of having to explain to him.

"Don't you see? There's been some mistake! I am the one in the Sanchez household who has been aiding and abetting the Confederacy. I'm the one who gave the information about the regiment positions. I must go to the *Yanquis.* I have to tell them."

She started to pull away, but Henry gripped her by the arms hard. "No, Janeta. Do you know what they'll do to a woman like you? You belong to me."

She'd heard of the marauding *Yanquis,* ravaging women as they passed through Southern towns. She'd seen the way they looked at her and her sisters, overheard their remarks, slipped away from their groping hands.

"Yes," she said. "Yes, that's why I gave you so much information. I wanted them gone. I didn't want *this.* Papi is innocent."

She began to sob, and Henry pulled her close.

"You know, my commander mentioned something to me. There's a way in which you, and only you, could be helpful to the cause."

"What does this have to do with Papi, Henry?" Irritation sparked in her again. He was always pressing for something from her — her body, the information she provided. She gave him those things because she loved him and she knew what he needed. But in that moment, all she wanted was for him to hold her, for him to vow to make things right, and instead he was asking of her again.

"You can fix this dreadful mistake. You can

help your father, and me, and the Rebel Cause, if you are brave enough. Do you think you are?"

Janeta didn't feel brave, and she didn't care about the Rebel Cause. She thought of her father, though, of how frightened he had looked as the Yanquis pulled him out of the house. How hunched and small he had appeared. Her irritation with Henry faded; all she felt was a fury that wrapped her up so tight she could barely breathe.

"What can I do?" she asked.

"Remember that group I mentioned? The Sons of the Confederacy? We need someone to get to the source of all these darkies leaking info to the Yanks. Someone they won't suspect, like you. Will you do it? For me? For your father? For the Confederacy?"

"I will do anything to make the Union pay for this," she said, hands clenched around Henry's lapels. "Anything to free Papi."

Henry smiled and began lifting her skirts, marching her back until her shoulder blades pressed into the rough bark of a tree.

"I knew you would, sweetheart."

Janeta hadn't understood what was being asked of her, and now that she did, she saw that everything was upside down.

The men she'd been taught were hardworking and brave were fighting to maintain the right to own and control other humans they could force to work for them — force to do anything. And she would help them do this. The people who she'd been taught were enslaved for their own good were bravely fighting for their freedom. And she would betray them. She swallowed as the saliva pooled in her mouth, and shut her eyes. She refused to retch.

You can do this. You must. If not, Papi will die.

She inhaled deeply, opened her eyes, and stared at the warped wood floor.

She was no longer a spoiled child. She was a spy with a mission. She would complete it.

When she came upon Daniel that morning, he was seated on a stool out behind the barn where she'd first encountered him, his gaze focused on his hands. He gripped his large knife and was moving it slowly, gently almost, against something cradled in his palm. A piece of wood; he was carving something. His expression was almost serene. The heavy furrows were gone from his brow and there was the slightest smile on his face. It was likely a product of his concentration, not joy, but the fact that his expression didn't default into a frown was startling.

What happened when he was enslaved? What made him this way?

She could have turned those questions on herself, though they had different backgrounds; she wasn't sure her face could be so serene without being forced.

The smile faded abruptly as he raised his head and glanced in her direction.

"You decided to come," he said, shoving whatever he had been carving into his pocket and then sheathing his knife.

"You don't seem pleased by that fact," she said. She should have been afraid after what Lynne had told her of his unpredictable nature, but the early morning sunlight draped over him, softening his menacing air; he looked like a fairy king, burnished in gold, waiting for the adulation of his court, or like some bemused spirit of the woods. But then she remembered that in the tales of fairies and woodland spirits, their beauty did not negate their strength and they cared little for the lives of humans. That suited Daniel, and the dark gleam in his eye.

"I was hoping you'd used a lick or two of that common sense you supposedly have," he said.

"I did," she said, walking up to him. "Common sense tells me you need someone to watch your back."

She smiled.

He didn't.

"You know, that isn't a bad idea," he said as he stood, and for a moment Janeta thought that it really would be so easy. Then he shucked his jacket and began unbuttoning his shirt, his gaze locked with hers. The look in his eyes was not one of newfound camaraderie, but bitterness.

His fingers moved swiftly, revealing a glimpse of the broad expanse of his chest and the ridged muscles of his upper abdomen. Heat raced to Janeta's face.

"What are you —"

He turned and let his opened shirt fall away to reveal the upper half of his back to her.

"Dios mío," she gasped, raising a hand to her mouth.

"God has nothing to do with this," he said in a flat tone.

The surface of his back was a topographical map of pain, raised trails of scars as thick as two of her fingers crossing each other to form hideous junctions. He'd been whipped, more than once, his skin reflecting the evil one man could do unto another.

Janeta thought of the time her family had gone into the city center in Santiago. Her mother had clapped her hand over Janeta's eyes when they'd walked by a man tied to a post with his bloody back exposed.

"You don't need to see such things. You are a Sanchez. You don't have to endure such ugliness."

She couldn't look away now, though. Daniel had bared to her this proof of his ill treatment and all she could ask herself was, "Why?"

"That man tried to start an insurrection. They had to make an example of him."

That's what her father had told her later when she'd questioned him about what she had seen. He'd handed her a gift when she'd asked why insurrection was bad, a beautiful porcelain doll with creamy skin, rouged cheeks, and blue eyes, and she'd let the matter drop.

"What did you do?" she asked Daniel, and saw the muscles beneath the scars tense.

"You think I did something to bring this upon myself?" he asked, his voice taut, and Janeta's fear came to the surface then. Not that he would hurt her, but that she'd made yet another misstep.

"No! I-I meant, why did they do this to you?"

He shook his head and pulled his shirt back up over his shoulder, not turning to face her as he did up his buttons.

"I was born Negro in a country where that is a crime, and I was ignorant enough not to know that I had already been convicted." He grabbed his coat and shoved his arms into the sleeves, adjusting his collar as he turned to face her. "Since you already asked two questions any Loyal League detective should know the answer to, I was right to guess that you're greener than new corn."

She couldn't argue with that. It was true, if not in the way he intended, and it was better he thought her ignorant than that he suspected the truth: she'd been taught that if a Negro was beaten like an animal, it was because they deserved it. That had been repeated to her time and time again, but she could think of few things that would merit the mess of scar tissue Daniel carried with him.

"Why did you show me this?" she asked.

"Because you seem like the questioning type," he said. "And I hate questions. If you ever see fit to ask why I do something, or why I don't, when it comes to the Confederacy? Know that you already have your answer."

She had been thinking in terms of Cuba, and her childhood, but people *here* had done this to Daniel. The Confederacy. The very system she was currently assisting.

Carla and Lynne came around the side of the barn, and Lynne's eyes narrowed as she took in the scene.

"Showed him your toys yet?" Carla asked.

"Not yet," Janeta said, trying to sound as if she hadn't just forgotten to breathe for a moment. "I haven't ruled it out, though."

Lynne snorted. "Well, we're heading off. I know we say 'Anything for the Union,' but if this man get funny with you . . ." She looked at Daniel, tilting her head sideways.

"I won't hurt your precious Cuban," Daniel said, his voice dripping with condescension. "You may not think much of me, but you know hurting innocents isn't in my repertoire."

Carla twisted her mouth. "Yeah, well, keep it that way, Cumberland."

The women waved goodbye, and Daniel heaved a deep breath as he looked after them. It seemed that it wasn't lost on him that they liked her more than him. She was elated at that small victory, but she couldn't help but pity him. He certainly wasn't trying to endear himself, but anyone who paid him the slightest bit of attention could see that he was a man who didn't enjoy his solitude.

"I guess we'd best get down to business,"

he said, adjusting his jacket.

He stalked off and Janeta followed.

Lynne and Carla thought to protect her, but little did they know she was far from innocent. Hopefully Daniel wouldn't figure that out, either.

CHAPTER 5

Daniel hadn't slept during the night, as usual, and the only purpose the scrap of sleep he'd grabbed hold of had served was allowing him to awaken with a headache; the beginnings of one at least.

He'd simply endured the blinding pain that was a keepsake of his imprisonment until he'd met a woman a few months back who knew how to take nature's bounty and heal with it. Marlie Lynch. He didn't like to think of her because thinking of her invariably led him to think of Elle, Marlie's future sister-in-law.

Damned lucky McCalls.

He strode into the cooking room, Janeta's light steps behind him. He'd have to get used to that. He still didn't know whether Dyson thought this assignment was a good idea or whether he'd doled it out as punishment — his head throbbed as annoyance surged through him anew.

There was already water put to boil for the chicory coffee everyone had to make due with. He poured himself a cup of the hot liquid, took out a few dried leaves from a sachet in his pocket, and dropped them into the water. The brew was one of the few things that helped with the headaches. It also calmed his frantic thoughts and, if brewed to full potency, made him drift away from the constant turmoil in his mind. Marlie had warned him not to overindulge and Daniel hadn't. Yet. Horrible memories haunted him, but they were a keen reminder of the truth of the world; a truth he sometimes felt he alone was privy to.

This world is a cruel and unbearable place. This country isn't worth fighting for.

But someone had to, and sometimes doing that meant dealing with unexpected annoyances, such as Sanchez.

"Would you like coffee?" he asked her, his manners kicking in.

"I would. Are you offering?" He could hear the confusion in her voice. The hesitation.

"Yes, I know I'm the frightening monster of the League, but never let it be said that I denied a fellow detective their coffee, if you can call this swill coffee. Besides, we need to talk and it's quiet here."

He tried not to grimace as pain began to unfurl in his skull. He'd have to wait a few moments for the tea to steep, though. He turned and pressed a finger against his brow.

"Did you eat?" she asked, gaze keen. "There's bread. I can toast it."

Ah, of course. Daniel couldn't remember the last time he'd eaten. Not for lack of food, but lack of appetite; sometimes he forgot and didn't remember until the edges of his vision started to go dark. That might account for his headache. He wasn't hungry, but he'd eat because he needed to. He remembered a time when food had given him such pleasure. Now it was just fuel to keep him on his feet. To keep him marching toward vengeance.

"Toasted bread would be appreciated, thank you." He brewed her coffee as she plated up their breakfast, and Daniel was not amused by the way they seemed to work well together. They didn't even bump into each other in the small space as they navigated the preparation of the meager repast. Daniel knew from humiliating experience that domestic work was a dance of its own; he'd thrown off the work of his fellow slaves often enough. So it wasn't the worst thing, this compatibility, but he had a feeling it wasn't the best, either, given how much he wanted to be rid of her.

She walked over to a table and placed their plates side by side before sitting and looking at him. Her expression was neutral, but those eyes of hers were large and expectant. She didn't have the best poker face he'd ever encountered, but he suspected she'd win more hands than someone able to dim the playful curiosity in their gaze.

She was taking his measure.

She seemed to be a woman who was constantly watching and evaluating and responding as required. She would be a bigger pain in the ass than he'd anticipated, green or no.

"What do you know about Europe?" he asked as he sat down beside her and handed her the coffee. He sipped at his tea, inhaling the scent and enjoying the light touch of languor that began to seep through him. He'd steeped it a bit too strongly, distracted by Janeta's presence, but he couldn't regret it. His mind began to clear, if not sharpen. The knots of anger and pain loosened along with the grip of his headache. His respite would be brief, but it was a peace he didn't get even in sleep. He understood the soldiers who demanded more laudanum, more morphine, from their field hospital beds. It was jarring to leave the sweet embrace of peace and return to brutal reality.

"Europeans? Can you be a bit more specific?" Janeta asked, a small grin tugging at her lips. "Druids? The Roman Empire? Russians?"

He regarded her for a long moment, turned over the information that a few sentences had revealed about her. She was an educated woman — a highly educated one. He remembered those times when Elle had told him some random bit of information she'd retained as he struggled over his law books — the envy he'd felt for her along with the love. He'd snapped at her once, told her it was unbecoming to flaunt her strange gift. The shocked hurt on her face was yet another shameful memory, especially because he hadn't truly meant it.

Had he?

It didn't matter anymore, and was beside the point. Elle had educated herself using that stupendous memory of hers. He wondered how Janeta could casually toss about such knowledge. He'd find out in due time, he supposed.

"I mean the impact of Europe on the war here, and vice versa," he said. "Do you know anything about the mission we're undertaking? The information we seek?"

"Well, no, how could I when you have me

playing guessing games instead of just telling me what it is you want to know?"

There was some bite underlying her tone. Nerves. It seemed Sanchez didn't like speaking when she wasn't sure what was wanted from her. Daniel took a sip of his tea.

She made an annoyed sound around her bite of toast.

"Well, I know that the Confederates hope to win England or France to their cause," she said. "They point out that the loss of cotton will leave countless British without manufacturing jobs."

"They point out many things, and somehow those things all seem to be to their benefit," Daniel mused. "They have some very talented agents on the ground in London, whispering into the ears of men in power. One of their spies apparently garnered herself an invitation to meet with Napoleon in France."

"Truly?" Janeta asked, whipping her head toward Daniel.

He nodded grimly. "There is a war of words playing out away from these blood-soaked battles and it's just as important. Which side can gain the most sympathy from the European public, or inspire the most fear? Which side can make themselves seem like the best dog to pick in the fight?

"Words have meaning, Janeta. They are perhaps the most valuable weapon in our society. Have you never wondered why slaves are denied access to education, why it is illegal for them to be taught to read and write?"

"Because it gives them ideas they shouldn't have," she said automatically, then shot him a wary look. "That's what they say, at least."

"Words provide knowledge, and knowledge provides power," Daniel said. He remembered one of the very few enjoyable memories from during his enslavement — him crouched in the middle of one of the wooden shacks, tracing letters into the dust on the ground as a group of children stood around him. The joy of the children as he spelled out each of their names and they realized that their name was a word, with substance and heft. That they were something substantial.

Liz. Thomas. Carl. Winnie.

His good memory crumbled away at that last name, and nausea roiled his belly and crept up his throat.

Winnie stood humming in the shade, a stick in her hand as she traced something into the packed clay. Daniel saw this from the corner of his eye but was too focused on the pain in his back and the work he was forced to do despite it. His brain was a haze of anger and despair. It was why he didn't give a second thought to the scratching motion of Winnie's stick until Finnegan the overseer rode up on his horse and grabbed the girl's thin wrist.

She looked up at Finnegan in shocked fear, her pleasant hum catching in her throat.

"Who taught you them letters, girl?"

Winnie frantically scrubbed at the dirt with her bare foot. "Ain't no letters, Mr. Finnegan!"

"You think a little pickaninny gonna know how to read and write when I can't?" Finnegan lifted her into the air, shaking her small, thin body back and forth. "That ain't for you. You gonna learn that ain't for you."

He whirled on his horse and headed toward the whipping post as Winne's mother pushed past Daniel screaming. "No! She don't know no letters, sah! Who would teach her that? Who?"

"What does this have to do with the Europeans?" Janeta asked, pulling Daniel's thoughts back from the awful, dark place they'd returned to. The path to that memory was worn deep in his mind, and the wheels of his thoughts slipped into the groove of it with the slightest urging. It was much more difficult to pull himself free from that rut.

"This country has always used words as weapons that only certain of its citizens could wield," he said eventually. He was glad Janeta hadn't pressed as he composed himself. " 'We hold these truths to be self-evident.' 'Liberty and justice for all.' 'All men are created equal.' These phrases were all forged in the fires of tyranny, honed into blades by the lies of the Founding Fathers. These words have all been used to perpetuate evil."

He relished the way she startled as she bit into her toast, dropping crumbs down the front of her dress. Her brows were drawn as she chewed and regarded him, and finally she swallowed. "Evil? Are these not the foundation of America, of the Union we are sworn to protect?"

He rolled his eyes at her.

"I didn't swear the Four L's," he said. "Loyalty, Legacy, Life, and Lincoln. More words that mean nothing in the end."

"Then what *do* you believe in?" she asked. There was no judgment in her tone; she seemed truly curious.

Nothing.

"What is there to believe in?" He'd had enough of people trying to persuade him that there was good in the world; there was only what could and could not be tolerated, and what must be done to stop the latter.

"There are thousands of men fighting and dying to defend those words you think so little of," she pointed out.

"Exactly!" Daniel paused, just long enough to collect himself. "Such is the power of words used with malicious, manipulative intent. They are the cause of our present turmoil. When the Founding Fathers put quill to parchment and scrawled 'all men are created equal' they codified this country as a shining beacon of hope in the world. On paper. In reality, the same men who signed that document went back to their homes and were greeted by their slaves. Slaves to cook for them. Slaves to clean for them. Slaves to fuck."

She jumped again at the curse and Daniel felt a bit of shame, but not much. It was the truth — he would not be abashed by it. He would not soften that reality, either. Not after what he had seen. Not with so much at stake in the journey before them.

"But they'd written those words, shared them with the world like a new religion," he continued. "They'd fooled everyone, including themselves. Their words held more weight than their actions, and provided them sanctuary from the truth of themselves."

She was no longer eating. Simply staring at him. It bothered him, that earnest confusion.

"Take *you,* for example. Mulatto is the word they'd use to describe you. Why do you suppose that is?"

Her cheeks went dusky pink, as if he'd slapped her.

"It's a means of classification," she said sharply.

"It's a means of *control,*" he corrected. "We all know what it means. Because these aren't categories, they are hierarchies, and while none of us Negroes have it good, they damn sure try to make us think some of us deserve better. Which means some of us deserve worse. Above all, it means they get to decide and we get to suffer those decisions. So. Now you see the power of one little word?"

Her mouth was thin from her lips being pressed together. She nodded.

"Now imagine columns and columns of words in the British press about the insufferable North, forcing their will on the poor, proud Southerners. All the South wants is its freedom. Isn't that *noble*?"

He could hear the anger in his voice, feel it calcifying in his veins as if he were turning to stone and could smash the world to bits just to be done with this farce.

"And the gall of it? The gall? Is that what the British, so proud of their abolition, say, 'Oh, but of course they will free the slaves once the war is over.' "

Janeta was quiet. "Maybe they really believe this. It's possible, is it not?"

Daniel resisted the urge to knock her plate from the table in frustration. He wouldn't, ever, but the dark thoughts came unbidden as they always did.

"If such a thing were possible, why did this war start? Why was Lincoln's Proclamation such an affront to Southern sensibilities? And if they were to win, how would they manage having to pay the slaves they now count as property?" He shook his head at her ridiculous question. "It's like a farmer saying he'll begin to pay his sheep for the wool they produce — there is no profit in it. Slavery has made many a white man rich and has made existence easier for many a poor one. Such benefits will not be laid down willingly."

"Perhaps this is true," she said. She squinted, as if turning a thought over in her mind. "The idea of freedom from tyranny is a strong one, in this country and back home in Cuba, where they seek freedom from Spain while using slaves in every aspect of life. It seems that it's quite easy for a man to justify why his particular circumstances require freedom while others require shackles — either real or those in the form of laws of subjugation."

Daniel had been ready to continue arguing his views — he had examples lined up, ready to use as sharp points to push her away from him. He didn't know how to respond to her agreement and expansion of his ideas without seeming unnecessarily friendly, so he simply grunted.

She downed the rest of her coffee, her gaze dropping away from his. "What is our mission?" she asked.

"I was told you speak Russian." Dyson had marveled over the fact. Daniel had wondered why Sanchez hadn't been interrogated as to why and how.

Her gaze did turn to his then, sparking with interest. *"Ya nemnogo govoryu po russki."* She preened a little before continuing. "I had a Russian tutor as a child. She was supposed to be teaching me French, but I convinced her to teach me her language, too. I think she only agreed because she was so hungry for someone to speak to, which is why I understand more than I can speak."

She'd been rich enough to have people

brought into her home expressly to educate her. Interesting.

"Excellent. Then you're well prepared for our task, and that's all you need to know. We'll gather provisions and head out soon."

He expected her to demand more information as he downed the last of his tea and stood, but instead she nodded. When she looked up at him, determination shone in her eyes.

"I know you aren't happy about working with me, but you seem to be a brave and honorable detective, and I am glad to have been paired with you. I hope that we can do our part, together, to end this war."

Daniel would not be swayed. He would not acknowledge the warm sensation in his chest, though his tea had long since gone cold. She was a nuisance to be tolerated, and he wouldn't allow himself to see her as anything else.

"We'll see if you even make it to this evening, Sanchez," he said. "Then we can talk about ending wars."

CHAPTER 6

Janeta was starting to regret not having asked Dyson to be paired with someone else, as Daniel had suggested. Anyone else.

It was their second day of travel and Daniel was not an ideal companion, to say the least. When she'd finally asked where they were going, he'd responded "south" and stalked ahead of her. He hadn't spoken much besides that, apart from pressing her to keep up with his pace and muttering under his breath when she wanted to stop and rest.

She'd been taken aback; he had no problem talking to her at the camp, even if he hadn't been exactly friendly. Despite his brusqueness, he'd spoken to her as his equal, something she'd rarely experienced. It wasn't that people usually spoke down to her, but there was always a sense of underlying amusement. As if she were being tolerated. Daniel had indulged no such pretense, but even in his rudeness he had treated her as if he thought her wise enough to consider and act on the information he was sharing with her. He'd warned her off from working with him, but within that warning had been a *choice.* Janeta had been spoiled, spoiled beyond the wildest dreams of most of the people she'd met on the trek from Palatka to Illinois, but choice? That had never really factored into her life. She did what she knew others wanted of her, and while there were a million small *decisions* in those actions, the choice had never felt like hers.

She'd thought something exceedingly silly as they'd set off on their journey — she'd thought they might become friends. She was intrigued by him, and not just because he held information she'd need to pass on. She wanted to discuss his ideas about his country, which had made her think about the condition of her own. She wanted to see if perhaps she might make him smile, which had nothing to do with why she had joined the Loyal League.

Have you forgotten your mission already? Have you forgotten Papi?

Papi.

When Daniel had asked her what she knew of the Europeans, she'd tried to think of the discussions she'd overheard between her father and his friends before the Northerners had arrived. They'd spoken of losing income, and the news from Spain. They'd argued whether independence, after the insurrection in Haiti that rid it of France, might come to Cuba, too, and if so, by whose hands and at what cost.

"And what will these darkies do once they are free?" Papi had asked loudly, his voice echoing in the parlor. Mrs. Perez, seated beside Janeta on the couches where the women were gathered, had stiffened awkwardly and looked away from her. Janeta had turned to Mrs. Rodriguez on her other side and struck up a conversation about gloves, having noticed the young woman glancing admiringly at hers.

And now here she was with Daniel, who refused to speak of gloves or any other topic with her apart from the occasional command to hurry. Janeta had begun talking aloud to herself after what felt like hours of walking in tense silence, repeating phrases in Spanish in the hopes that that would spark Daniel's interest since he seemed like a man who liked to know things. She'd also vented her annoyance at him.

"*Yo soy* Daniel. I want to talk to Janeta, but a devil has cursed me. I've been forced to pretend to be stubborn and rude until the curse is broken."

Daniel had finally turned an angry glare at her and shushed her, and she'd quieted with a scowl.

"Are we almost *south,* Cumberland?" she finally asked in English, when his silent, brooding tension and long stride had pushed her to her very limits. She knew she shouldn't show her pique, or risk having him question her commitment, but she thought even the staunchest Unionist might be aggravated in her shoes. She stopped and refused to take another step forward.

"Too tired to go on?" He didn't slow his pace. "We've barely begun this journey. I told you —"

"I've been keeping up quite well, even though you've made no allowance for my skirts," Janeta bit out. "Perhaps we can switch clothing if you find my speed unsatisfactory."

Daniel stopped with a huff of frustration and looked down at her, and for a moment she thought he might very well make the trade. He seemed to be piecing something together in his mind; his gaze was active, searching.

"Why didn't you mention this the several times I've admonished you for your slow pace?" he asked.

"Would it have made a difference?" Janeta scoffed. She didn't suppress the shake in her voice that revealed her anger, as she usually would have. She didn't make her tone sweet and cajoling. She had been traveling for weeks now, even if she'd only been with Daniel for a couple of days, and she was exhausted. "In my experience, men don't particularly care if a woman gives them reason why she can or cannot do something. Truly, I should be the one asking why you didn't question how I was faring. Aren't you the master detective?"

"I should have asked," he said, his gaze darting past her and to the side. He wouldn't even give her his full attention.

Janeta wasn't used to declaring her dismay like this, without artifice. It felt wrong, but being relentlessly ignored had left her nerves jangling. "Oh, we both know why you didn't ask. You were setting me up for failure because you don't want me around."

He made a harrumphing sound and wiped the sweat from his face. "You're half right. I don't want you here, and with good reason — I've made no show of hiding that. But that's not why I've been pushing you." He seemed to fold in on himself a bit somehow, even though he still towered over her. "Traversing these woods isn't safe. Illinois is a Union state, but cruelty to people of our race doesn't acknowledge the Mason–Dixon."

It was strange for Janeta to be included in that *our.* Yes, it was the basis of her entry into the Loyal League, allowing her to spy for Henry, but she still thought of her fellow detectives as *them.* She had always been a Sanchez, first and foremost. She was lighter than her mother, though still very much *morenita,* but few people had ever equated her with the slaves. Not to her face at least. She'd been admonished for noticing their similarity herself as a child. She'd been told she was *different.*

She remembered the first time Henry had kissed her; he'd pulled back, stroking her face and staring at her as if she were a treasure he'd discovered.

"You're so different from all these silly girls chasing after me with their parasols and pale skin," he'd drawled, running his fingertips over the brown skin of her knuckles. *"You're special. And now you're mine."*

In the moment, it had felt wonderful to be claimed by someone, to be told she was *special* for the very thing she'd always been instructed to ignore and dismiss. Henry's attentions had made her feel superior in a way "you're not like the slaves" never had.

He touched her like she was sacred, rhapsodized about her curls and her coloring — he reveled in everything that embarrassed her older sisters about her, the things her mother had tried to teach her to downplay. Because of that Janeta had overlooked things about Henry that were obvious to her now — had ignored the natural instincts that had helped her win the confidence of Rebel and detective alike.

She'd believed his honeyed words — believed them because she had wanted Henry's affection so desperately — but she was beginning to see they had coated an ugly truth.

She'd traveled enough now to know that she was not special — despite the supposed stricter rules against whites and Negroes interacting in the States, she'd seen men and women who looked to be of the same mixed racial background as her. Women like her were no rarity. She'd seen people who were as light as Papi working the fields in rags. She'd also learned enough of the US to begin to understand why Henry had claimed her body but had given her no ring or token of his supposed love.

"We have our forged passes," Janeta said to Daniel. This was no time to think of Henry, beyond the fact that she needed him to free her father. "If anyone stops us, there should not be a problem." She pulled her canteen from her sack, taking advantage of their pause to refresh herself. Her feet ached, her legs shook, and she was ready to keel over from fatigue, but she wouldn't have him know that.

"I had my free papers when I was taken," he said grimly, "and they were real. In a country where you need papers to show you're free, where you need some white man's signature to walk the land of a nation that the sweat and blood of your people has pushed into prosperity, your life rests on the balance of whether the person who sees those papers decides to imbue them with any power. America is a nation without honor, that it would allow its people to be treated in this way."

There was something in his words, and in his behavior now that she was paying attention and not sulking over being ill-treated, that made her throat go rough.

His body was tense, and it had been since they'd left the Loyal League camp. She'd attributed it to his annoyance with her, but she now realized she'd made the same mistake she had with Henry — she was fitting Daniel's behavior to the frame she'd made for it. She'd wanted to believe Henry had loved her, so she'd stretched his behavior to that particular frame like canvas for needlepoint. She'd decided Daniel's behavior could only be motivated by his distaste for her, but there was something more.

His hand rested on the hilt of his knife; she'd seen him search it out reflexively many times as he strode ahead of her. He looked to and fro, vigilant as he had been since they'd started out. It struck her then, the reality of the situation — he hadn't been ignoring her all this time, or punishing her — he'd been on alert. He'd been *afraid.*

After the *Yanquis* had taken her father, they hadn't stopped visiting his daughters. They'd come more often, free to use Villa Sanchez as a base now that the Rebels had been driven to the next town and the head of house was gone. Every time she'd heard the hooves of their horses approaching, Janeta would be seized by panic. Her sisters' fears were more corporeal, as the soldiers in blue made more pressing and overt romantic overtures, but Janeta was also constantly aware that at any moment they might discover that it was *her* who passed their information to the Rebels. At any moment, her family and friends might discover that her father had paid for her crimes — that she'd let him — and her family would expel her as she'd always known they would after Mami had died.

Had Daniel been trapped in that awful mist of fear for their entire journey? She remembered the scars on his back. Was he ever free of it?

"Here." She handed him the canteen.

"Is it rum or water?" he asked apprehensively. He looked around as if each shadow thrown by the half-bare trees might hide some threat, and Janeta's heart squeezed painfully in her chest. He was looking in all the wrong places; the actual danger stood just a foot away from him, offering him a drink and wishing this damned war had never drawn either of them into its gears.

"I think you could use some liquor, to be honest, but it's just water." He nodded, and she watched as his lips parted and he tipped the water into his mouth, how his throat worked and droplets spilled down his beard. Warmth flowered in her, despite the cold breeze rushing through the forest as if pushing them to continue their journey. She pulled her gaze away from him.

"I will try to walk faster," she said as he handed her back the canteen. "I hadn't considered the danger we'd face before even reaching our assignment."

He grunted in acknowledgment, and they

set off again.

"We're headed to Cairo," he said eventually. She glanced at him, catching sight of how his full lips thinned as he frowned. "There's a large contraband camp there, where they hold folks who've escaped into Illinois."

"Contraband? Slaves?"

"Not anymore," he said, either not understanding her slipup or correcting it. "They're free people, coming here with the idea that people up North might treat them better."

Janeta was caught in the whiplash of her own belief and Daniel's cynical worldview. "Of course, their lives will be better. They can no longer be enslaved. They are *free.*"

Daniel glanced at her, his expression making what he thought of her words clear.

"Not being enslaved is the very least thing these people are owed, and even that is not guaranteed," Daniel said. "The whites here aren't exactly welcoming them with open arms. The newly freed leave the camp on trains and are deposited in towns with hostile people who don't want freed Negroes living among them. Some Negro men recently settled in a town they weren't supposed to because of some law they knew nothing about."

"What happened?" Janeta asked. The bitterness in his tone had already given her an answer, but it made no sense. Back home, the Rebels had talked of all the darkie lovers up North, how they were weak and pathetic because they let Negroes do as they wished. Janeta had always wanted to disappear during those conversations. Instead, she had lifted her chin haughtily and laughed more loudly than was necessary with the men during those conversations. Afterward, she'd stare into her mirror wondering what they saw when they looked at her.

Daniel took her arm and guided her around a hole she would have tripped into, as her eyes were on his face and not the ground. He dropped it immediately. "What happened? The same thing that happens to our people everywhere in this godforsaken country. They were arrested, tried, and convicted of breaking the Black Laws. As punishment, they were sold back into slavery, auctioned off to the highest bidder."

Janeta's throat went tight. "No."

Her mother had been free. She was free. Those men had thought they were free, and they'd had their hopes for the future ripped away from them. Their own government, supposedly fighting on their behalf, had sent them back into slavery. After Mami had died, Janeta started having nightmares in which Papi took her down to the cane field and told her she must earn her keep. She'd awakened sick with betrayal and fear every time. That nightmare was a reality in this strange country.

"Yes," Daniel said. "For a while before the Proclamation, Union soldiers would even return runaways to their masters. If there is one hard truth every Negro in this land must face, it's that many of our countrymen would rather see us dead than free."

"That can't be true. Don't you think most of the Southerners fight not for slavery, but for freedom from taxes and the like? Like George Washington and those men."

That was another favorite topic of the plantation owners who'd gathered in her family's parlor. They'd said over and over again that the South only wanted freedom from tyranny, and they were adamant that it was nothing more than that, no matter what slanderous, yellow-bellied Northmen said.

Daniel gave her a narrow look. "They fight to keep slaves and the profit they make from slaves. Like George Washington and those men."

His tone showed that he thought her a fool, and Janeta felt like one. She was ashamed and confused. Because what Daniel said made sense, but Papi had said the war wasn't about slavery. Not really. That the North just wanted to take control of the South and its wealth. And the *Yanquis* who had shown up had done just that in Palatka, taking over homes and demanding food and drink and all manner of things. Papi had told her that the Confederates were just trying to protect what was theirs, as they tried to protect their assets in Cuba from Spain. He'd made it sound so reasonable, though she had seen many an unreasonable thing since her departure.

"You are from the North and were born free, yes?" she asked

"I was," he said flatly.

"And you feel you were treated no better than a slave?"

He stopped and looked at her not with anger or disgust, but with sadness. "Should that be our standard of a good life? Being treated better than a slave?"

Janeta's body was taut with fear not because she was afraid of him, but because she didn't know how to answer. She shook her head slowly.

"I lived a much better life than any slave, I imagine. I was a law clerk, a respected man from a respected family. I might have lived a long and happy life never knowing that I was in chains, too."

"I'm sure a person working in the cane field might take offense at your comparison," she said, and was pleased to elicit surprise from him. She was tired of feeling foolish, tired of the way everything Daniel said was in direct opposition to what she had been taught. He couldn't be right about everything, could he?

She remembered the road through the field on the plantation in Santiago. So many dark bodies, sweating and chopping in the hot sun as Janeta and her family passed by in their covered coach. She'd once seen a girl who looked so much like her, but slightly older, carrying a parcel of cut cane down the road.

"She looks like me, Mami!"

Her mother hadn't looked out to where Janeta pointed with a pudgy finger. "No, she doesn't."

"Will I have to work like her one day?" she'd asked. Her mother, sitting with her chin up and her eyes locked ahead as she always did when they passed through the cane fields, had turned and grabbed Janeta by the jaw. The touch was so unlike Mami's usual loving caresses that tears of shock had sprung immediately to Janeta's eyes.

Her mother's dark skin was usually unlined, but her brow had been furrowed and lines had bracketed her frown as she stared into Janeta's eyes. "Never. *Nunca en la vida, comprende?* You aren't like them. I made sure of that. Never compare yourself to a slave again."

Janeta had started to cry, not understanding what she had done wrong. She still didn't understand. She didn't understand Daniel, either. She'd been free, and had never suffered because of the color of her skin. Not much, anyway . . . had she?

Daniel scoffed. "My privilege isn't lost on me, but neither is this fact: a life that can be disrupted, ruptured, and ruined for the sole offense of the color of your skin is not freedom by any definition. But that is the lot of every Negro in the United States. It's the lot of every Native who's had their land snatched and their tribe decimated. We can be intelligent, we can accrue wealth, we can strive to make this country better, and lose everything at the whim of some pale sir or madam. It doesn't even require much effort on their part. That's the worst of it. They don't even have to try hard to ruin us." He turned from her then and started walking. "I knew you were the questioning sort, but it seems I overestimated your intelligence."

Janeta stood where she was, still caught in the riptide of his words. She wanted to follow him, but the tug of his ideas had dragged her deep into uncharted territory.

"No, you don't get to just dismiss me like that." Her legs were carrying her toward him now, her frustration propelling her. She grabbed his arm and he whirled quickly, shaking her off.

"You studied law. You learned about the laws behind slavery, and government. I have some education, but not — not in that area. If I ask you a question and I'm wrong, that's fine. If you don't want to answer, that is fine, too. But I'm not a bad person for not knowing all of these things. I am not American."

"You are a Negro," he said.

"I am Cubana, descended of slaves and conquistadores," she retorted. "And I am not the only one ignorant of how things work in other countries. What is truth here is not truth everywhere."

Daniel sighed heavily. He looked tired — so tired that she knew the next words out of his mouth would be an apology.

"I'm sorry," he said. She was ready to accept his apology, but then he continued. "Sorry that you think language and culture create deeper ties than the common journeys our ancestors made across the Atlantic, crammed into the filthy holds of ships. That's a language, too. If you can't speak it yet, then you are lucky. If you refuse to learn it, then you have no business with the Loyal League."

Outrage and shame coated her like the grime that had built up over her long journey, and a familiar frustration filled her. Her family had told her who and what she was so many times it had become reflex. *"You are a Sanchez. That's all that matters."* When she'd left Palatka, following Henry's instructions and searching out Loyal League members, she'd been told, *"You're Negro, and that's all that matters,"* and that was if people bothered to say it nicely. Why did it have to matter at all? Why couldn't she just be Janeta Sanchez?

Still, she couldn't help but think on his earlier words.

"Slaves to cook for them. Slaves to clean for them. Slaves to fuck."

Her mother had been a slave. Her father had owned her mother. Yes, he had married her after his first wife died, but what had she been to him before that? Her parents had spoken little of the time before their marriage, though her mother had not shied away from boasting of how she'd won over

Don Sanchez. The *how* of the courtship hadn't been elaborated on, and Janeta had embellished things in her imagination. Her mother had been beautiful, and her father had been enchanted by that beauty.

But now Janeta thought about how it had been impressed on her that she was *not* like those people who toiled for them day in and day out. That her mother was not like them. That she must never confuse herself with them because they were lower than her. How had a courtship commenced when her mother had been bound to her father's household, when slaves could not leave or protest their treatment without punishment? How had her mother been different, and how had her father known?

Slaves to fuck.

Janeta didn't want to think of it. She had never wanted to. Her father had loved her mother, and her mother had loved him. *Eso fue todo.* She couldn't imagine anything as unseemly as what Cumberland had insinuated. But she hadn't been able to imagine a great many things until she'd left Palatka.

They walked on in silence, and soon they began to encounter more people in the road. Slaves. Slaves who had escaped.

The family slaves had never spoken about their feelings with her, obviously, and she hadn't ever asked. When her mother had been alive, she'd told Janeta that she made sure they were treated well because she had been one of them, though if she'd had any friends amongst them she never acknowledged it. Janeta had always been told that the slaves on the Santiago plantation and in their household were happy. But if they had been happy, why had there been guns to prevent rebellion? Why had there been a whipping post? Janeta had once been curious about such things, but eventually had just accepted it as the way things were.

"It seems I overestimated your intelligence."

Her thoughts were a jumble as an area crowded with tents and people came into view.

"Welcome to Cairo," Daniel said, finally speaking after ignoring her for miles. "If you want to educate yourself, you could find no better place for instruction."

She looked away from Daniel and took in the people they passed: two men talking jovially; a father throwing his child up into the air and catching him. A little girl who sat on the ground, sucking her thumb as tears streamed down her face.

She tore her gaze away. She needed to focus. She didn't need an education; she needed information, and hopefully a telegraph line.

"Why are we here?" she asked.

"The question every modern man asks himself," Daniel said, gaze fixed ahead of him. He was a big man, and people moved out of his way, as if they could sense the pent-up rage inside of him. Or perhaps they felt the same since they'd all been recently enslaved, too — why wouldn't they be angry? Why hadn't she thought they *should* be?

"Cumberland."

He didn't answer. Could he suspect? Could this be a trap?

Janeta's gaze darted about. People watched them as they walked, obviously eyeing their clothing and shoes and demeanor. Fear shivered up her spine. She'd been told for years that she was different from slaves because she was civilized, and they couldn't be trusted not to act like savages. Would one of them hurt her? Like Papi always warned?

She felt suddenly ill, not from fear, but from the thoughts filling her head — thoughts that had been purposely forced into her mind by family and friends who said they were trying to keep her safe. To do so, they'd pointed out repeatedly how the people who looked like her were less than, childlike, unable to control their impulses or take care of themselves.

She looked at the people around her. A woman smiled in her direction. A little girl hid behind the woman's skirt and peeked around it cautiously before being swung up into an embrace by a man who was likely her father, given their matching smiles. Janeta didn't *really* think these people would hurt her, did she? Her mother had once worked out in the fields, like many of the people before her. Janeta could have been the child of any of these people, could have been —

She walked directly into Daniel's back, and he turned and looked down at her. She expected annoyance, but his expression was flat. She could feel how tense his body was in the moment before he stepped away.

"Sorry," she said.

She was overwhelmed, but he looked ready to crack like a coconut under a machete.

She reached out and touched his arm. He bristled but didn't pull away.

"Is it hard for you? Being here?"

"You and your damned questions," he growled.

"This is what detectives do," she said gently. "They ask questions, and they try to help if they can."

"You really are terrible at this if these are the questions you choose to ask," he muttered.

He was right — she wasn't asking the questions that she should be. Not at all. She had nothing to give Henry yet, even if she did find a means to convey information. Worse, she didn't feel bad about it. She should have been racing to get him something, anything to help her father, but she found that the thought of telling him about Daniel or the other detectives she had met gave her vertigo.

Papi, I'm sorry.

"Yes, it's hard," Daniel huffed out. "Because most of these people have suffered far, far worse than I ever have, and for far longer. And yet they still laugh and smile. They still have hope. It's a reminder of my own weakness."

Weak? Is that how Cumberland saw himself? His hand moved to rest over hers on his arm, and for a moment she thought he would take her comfort and was strangely glad of it. Then he firmly pulled her grip away from him and dropped her hand.

"It's also a reminder of my resolve," he said. "The fate of all these people rests in the hands of the Union. We must help the

Northern forces win, Sanchez, because our loss is greater than the loss of a nation. It's a condemnation for our people."

Janeta's throat constricted. He was staring at her, his brown eyes reflecting his intense conviction. For a moment, she was sure he knew, sure he was simply toying with her. If he wasn't, how could he so easily undermine her resolve?

"Yes," she said. "We must free those we hold dear from unjust imprisonment. That is my sole purpose."

He held his gaze on her, and Janeta found that she could not look away, though she wanted to. There was turmoil in his eyes, and something that held her fast and made it hard to breathe. Daniel had said he believed in nothing, but there was a purpose in him that belied that claim. A drive that couldn't be fueled only by empty rage. He was a detective because he wanted to do good for his people. Their people? And she had been sent to stop him from doing that good.

"Hey, Cumberland!"

Janeta and Daniel both swung their gaze toward the tall, slim, dark-skinned man approaching them.

"A friend of yours?" she asked lightly, trying to dispel the intensity of his gaze that lingered in her mind, and the sickness in her heart about her own path.

"No, that's Lake, one of Furney Bryant's men. Before you ask, Bryant is someone who has a lot of ears on the ground. Those ears collect information and pass it on to our detectives and those of other networks. Lake sent word that he had some visitors I might be interested in."

Janeta held that bit of info dear. It was something solid she could pass on, even if doing so would feel like another kind of betrayal. She was confused, but she could not let her purpose be lost in that confusion. Helping to destroy the Loyal League was her mission, and her burden, and it would be done. She would not betray her father a second time for the regard of a man.

She was a Sanchez.

CHAPTER 7

Daniel followed Lake to the tent, forcing himself to not look at the people around him. He certainly had no aversion to the sight of his people: they were the most beautiful in the world in his mind. But, sometimes, looking upon the decrepit conditions America had forced on them awoke in him a fury that could barely be contained. In that particular moment, he took some comfort in moving among them — the only ones who could understand what he had gone through, if not his personal torment.

Negroes of every shade, from as light as Lincoln to dark as Daniel's own father, bustled about the makeshift camp. Tents had been raised, and laundry had been washed and hung on makeshift lines. Food cooked on fires. It was as normal as could be possible for a people displaced in a land that cared nothing for their welfare when it didn't line the pockets of the rich.

Some of these people had made daring escapes, sneaking from plantations under cover of night and guided only by the North Star and the inscrutable hope that it sparked in them. Others had been working the fields when Union forces arrived in their towns; they had dropped their plows, gathered what they could, and followed the Blue-clad soldiers toward the unknown. Daniel's throat went raw just thinking of it. What trust. What *bravery.* To leave everything they'd known to seek out a better life than had been given to them; to take those first steps into an abyss of change.

He watched a couple laugh out loud, the man throwing his head back, and he felt the laughter like a brand, marking Daniel as forever broken. He wondered what it was like to live through the deprivations these people had experienced and still be able to laugh with your whole body, including your soul. He wondered why they were capable and he still wasn't, and might never be. He didn't begrudge them their resilience; he berated himself for not possessing it.

Pathetic. Weak. Why were you given freedom when so many better people still toil in chains?

His breathing shallowed and he curled his left hand into a fist, digging his unkempt nails into his palm to summon a pain that would distract him from his own traitorous mind — a pain that he had some control over.

The sharp pressure drew his attention, but it took all of his focus not to slide into the sudden panic that tried to overtake him. Daniel was so tired.

He wished everything would stop. The talking, the laughter, the pounding in his chest, and the low, ugly voice in his head. While there were many possible paths to peace for the Union, and for the people around him, there was only one for him. He would not hold hands with a wife in front of a fire or watch his children grow. Daniel was not long for this world, that he was sure of. Whenever his time arrived, whether by chance or appointment, he hoped he could say that he'd done his utmost to better the world for those who lived on after him.

"In here, Cumberland," Lake said. He pushed aside the tent flap and ushered Daniel and Janeta inside the large space. Daniel froze when he spotted the two large white men sitting at the table in the center of the tent. His first instinct was to size them up, form a plan of attack and defense. There were a few rifles atop a trunk on the other side of the men. He could flip their table back and —

"These are allies of ours," Lake said quickly, and Daniel nodded, lowering their threat level in his mind. He didn't lower his guard, though. Just because they were allies didn't mean they weren't dangerous.

He took in the cut of their jackets and shirts, which were different than the typical American man would wear. Hell, even the style of their hair wasn't quite what he was used to.

Both men stood. *"Zdravstvuyte,"* one of the men said, and the other man followed suit, and Daniel understood that these were Russians. Bryant's message had said they'd happened upon Russian intel, but Daniel hadn't known that they'd made contact with actual agents.

"Cumberland and Sanchez, meet Sokolov and Vasiliev. They are delegates touring the States."

The way Lake said *touring,* with just a bit of emphasis, grabbed Daniel's attention.

"You've chosen a dangerous time to visit," Daniel said, drawing a chuckle from one of the men.

"Yes, we wanted to see for ourselves what was happening. We are to report back to our compatriots who are curious about this country built on the premise of freedom but so invested in slavery."

"It's a pleasure tour, then? Gawk at the remains of American democracy, then run home and tell your friends?" Daniel couldn't soften the bite in his tone. He didn't like these men, and he was sure the Polish would find their supposed support of freedom amusing.

"Is this your first time visiting the country?" Janeta asked, voice sweet as honey. "It can be quite overwhelming, understanding these Americans."

The men laughed, relaxing a bit, and Daniel glanced at her. Her expression was bright and open, her smile attractive. She rolled the *r* in Americans hard, making clear that she, too, was in foreign territory. She'd honed right in on the best way to put the men at ease. Just as she had with the other detectives. She'd had two staunch protectors leveling not quite joking threats at him before they'd left her with him.

She would have made a fine lawyer. Instead, they were in a cold tent dealing with possibly hostile strangers, all for a country that laughed at the idea of either of them making arguments in a courtroom.

Vasiliev settled more firmly in his seat to look up at her, interest glinting in his eyes.

"And where are you from, lovely Miss Sanchez?"

"Cuba," she said proudly. Her mouth wrapped around that *u* in a distinct way, and Vasiliev seemed to appreciate it judging by how his gaze lingered on her lips. She licked them, just the quickest dart of pink tongue, and Daniel looked away before she continued speaking. "My family came to the US years ago, but it's still a land of discovery for me. And what about you?"

"Oh, we came on a ship to see the sights last month and accidentally caused some trouble," Sokolov said.

"Yes," Vasiliev said. "When our ship lingered off of New York Harbor, many saw it as a threat to the British and the French, who are always sticking their long noses into situations that don't concern them. Much like rats."

Sokolov shrugged. "Russia, of course, has declared no such support, but if that is how people wish to interpret it, then I suppose there is not much we can do."

Both men smiled slyly. Janeta smiled as well, following their lead, but Daniel found nothing amusing about the situation. Russia's not so subtle show of interest had been a boon to the North, to be certain, but it was galling enough having the future of his country dependent on politicians above and below the Mason–Dixon. Seeing agents of foreign powers treat this as a game wasn't funny at all.

"And if people made suppositions like that, they may have wished to share information with you?" Daniel asked, getting to the point. Either they could be useful to him or they were wasting his time, and he had enough to deal with watching over Janeta.

"They may have," Vasiliev said with an enigmatic grin. The two men turned toward each other and began speaking in Russian, not bothering to lower their voices.

Anger flared in Daniel and he opened his mouth to speak, but Janeta crossed in front of him, hands clasped together.

"Would you be willing to share such information?" she asked sweetly, interrupting them and preventing Daniel from undertaking his own method of questioning. "I am *so* interested in how the European powers have positioned themselves, like cats watching two mice fight and deciding whether to pounce."

"And sometimes the cat does not know, but it is watched by a bear," Vasiliev said, taking a sip from his canteen.

"Bears have good sight," Sokolov said.

"They are very patient, too."

Daniel rolled his eyes. This nonsense bantering was why he preferred the rough task of tracking the Sons of the Confederacy. Daniel had gotten to skulk in the darkness while hunting them, and there hadn't been a need for pleasantries with men who thought him subhuman. He'd often been able to dispense with words and speak with his fists. Punching Rebels wasn't exactly Loyal League protocol, but someone had to show these men what fear felt like, and Daniel would volunteer for that position every time.

"Are you willing to share what you've seen or heard?" He tried to sound undemanding as he brought them back to the task at hand. "I started following this lead because a member of a Rebel spy group was found with correspondence with a British agent on his person."

Interest sparked in the Russians' eyes. "Was he questioned?" Sokolov asked.

"Dead men don't answer questions," Daniel said bluntly. Janeta glanced at him. Was that fear in her eyes? No matter. He'd told her who he was and what he was capable of. She of all people should hold no illusions about him, given their mission and proximity for the foreseeable future. "But they do sometimes leave valuable information behind. The message discussed a movement to press the Southern cause with European diplomats on the ground in the States, while their compatriots exerted pressure abroad."

Sokolov nodded. "That matches with rumors we have heard. We are willing to share what we know. In fact, we specifically sought out the Negro detectives to do so."

Daniel's expression must have betrayed something because the man held up his hands as if warding off doubt.

"We sought out the Blacks for two reasons. Because every operative knows that if you want good information in this war, you get it from the Blacks. And if you have sensitive information, you give it to the Blacks, too."

Vasiliev shifted in his seat. "No other people have more at stake in this war. The Loyal League, Furney Bryant, a slave on the side of the road — they all have an interest in not allowing information to get into the wrong hands, no? If the North loses, all these people will go back into chains."

The man said it with a bizarre smile, holding out his hands as if they were manacled. Daniel very much wanted to get a feel for Vasiliev's jaw with the knuckle of his left hand.

"I don't see what's so amusing about that," Daniel said calmly.

"There is nothing amusing," Sokolov said, dark brows bunching. "We are still recovering from a war that claimed the lives of too many of our people, and our country is not eager to enter another because someone's big mouth paints us as more involved than we are. We are neutral observers who happen to know a thing or two, and maybe are not so neutral about France or Britain gaining power through any alliances. If you happen to hear anything from us, it is intended for you and you alone."

There was no mistaking the threat in his tone.

Daniel gave a short nod. "As you said, we have a very strong incentive to prevent any information obtained from getting into the wrong hands."

He glanced at Janeta, who looked on with a tight expression. Her gaze jumped to his in awareness; then her features relaxed.

"Yes, you can trust us, and we can judge if this information is really as valuable as you seem to think," she said. He had to admire how she gently pushed the men with her dismissiveness.

The men glanced at each other.

"Well, then," Sokolov said. "We have

heard here and there that there is a British consul in Mississippi with strong ties to the Sons of the Confederacy. I assume you know this group."

Daniel fought against the shudder that trembled at the base of his neck, ready to rush down his spine. It lay there, an awful sick vibration that he was all too familiar with.

"Sons of the Confederacy," Janeta said slowly. The confusion in her eyes didn't seem forced, though any detective should have heard of them.

The Russians glanced at her and Sokolov grimaced. "Very bad men. Be glad if you have not crossed them."

The two men began to converse in Russian again, ignoring them. Daniel tried to meet Janeta's eye, but she was patting at her hair, seemingly more interested in her appearance than whatever the men were saying.

He heaved a sigh.

Vasiliev took a swig from his canteen and smacked his lips. "This consul has made it very clear that he has sway with Parliament, since he is part of the aristocracy, a lord or viscount or something of the sort."

The British were already set against Secretary Seward and thus not very amenable to the North, even though they supposedly fought to end slavery everywhere — after they'd filled their coffers from it, of course. Daniel didn't like the Rebels having a direct line to Parliament from the States, on top of the disinformation they fed to the British press on English soil and the incidents that had threatened the Union's standing. The Trent situation, in which two British agents were arrested onboard a Confederate ship, had nearly pushed the North into war with England, and the two countries were still ill at ease. Daniel had thought that the message he'd found was wishful thinking on the behalf of the Sons, but now he wasn't so sure.

"Before I found that message, I'd heard that Chattanooga and Vicksburg had put an end to rumors of the Europeans intervening," Daniel said carefully. He knew that to be false, but wondered at what these men had heard. "The idea of a meeting, to take place here in America, shows a boldness I hadn't expected, even if those rumors were false."

"Well, one must always wonder what purpose a rumor has. Occasionally, it is diverting attention from the truth." Vasiliev shrugged. "The South will inevitably lose because they lack munitions and manpower, it is said. But if they were to be provided these things they lack? Well. Perhaps they wouldn't lose."

"And," Sokolov cut in, giving the word weight, "I'm sure you know of President Davis's tour. He is currently on his way South from Atlanta, if his itinerary is correct."

Daniel's stomach clenched.

"Davis has left Richmond? Why?" Janeta asked, clearly surprised. Daniel was, too. The president had been holed up in Richmond for some time, both for his safety and, according to Daniel's sources, due to chronic ill health.

"Morale in the Confederate States of America is low, my sweet. People have lost their confidence, and not without good reason! If you knew the things we knew." Vasiliev chuckled and tugged at the collar of his shirt. "All I will say is that he is trying to rally the troops before they mutiny. Or mutiny any more, since Bragg's men out in Tennessee have already been calling for his replacement."

"And elections are coming up," Daniel added, trying to reposition himself in the conversation. Right now, the Russians had the upper hand, but he wanted to at least show them that he knew what was what.

Vasiliev nodded. "When you've stocked your cabinet with men ill-fitted for the job apart from their friendship and supposed loyalty, even your staunchest supporter might need some prodding to vote for you again. So, the President of the South is on tour."

Daniel's body felt suddenly heavy, but his mind was quick. Davis would be away from his normal retinue of security in Richmond. Elle had been stationed in Richmond — it was where she'd met her husband. Other Loyal League detectives had been there, too. So close to Davis's home. They'd probably passed him by during their exploits. Daniel had always wondered why they hadn't just —

"Ah, these Americans and their politics," Sokolov said. "The growing pains of youth."

"Davis is going to meet with this consul?" Daniel's palms felt clammy. He curled his hands into fists as a memory assailed him.

"You in Davis's country now, boy. Down here, we don't coddle our darkies. You gonna work and if you don't like it, well? You best get used to it, that's all I'll say."

Daniel's overseer, Finnegan, had been poor and uneducated. But with that whip in his hand, he'd had just as much power over Daniel as any white man in Congress. And even if Finnegan hadn't known that, he'd felt it. That was why he'd kicked and beaten the Negroes on the plantation without provocation or reason. That was why he'd manufactured offense where there was none and demanded that black men, women, and children bow down to him — and worse. It was why he'd lashed out at Daniel's attempts to talk to him man-to-man. Because he'd been born no richer than a poor Negro, but with the power he'd been given over the slaves on that plantation, he'd become a god. That people assumed a Rebel nation full of men like Finnegan would give up such power showed the naïveté that had led America to its present predicament.

Vasiliev shifted in his chair. "It might be that Davis and some important men from the Sons of the Confederacy are planning to meet. That would be quite an interesting gathering, yes?"

Daniel's heart began to beat faster. The inner circle of the Sons of the Confederacy was just as guarded as that of the Loyal League. If he could get this information, it would be a boon to the 4L. If he could get *close enough* to get such information, that was another matter entirely.

"Where exactly in Mississippi might we find this consul?" Janeta was ever prepared with her questions.

The two men spoke to each other in Russian again and laughed, low and insinuating.

"Hm. What are you willing to give me for such valuable information?" Vasiliev held Janeta's gaze and smiled lecherously.

Daniel stepped closer to her. His instinct was to block her from the view of the men, but he pulled himself up short. He wouldn't do the same for a male detective. Besides, he needed to see how she handled this.

She batted her lashes at the men, and Daniel frowned. If she wanted to flirt in addition to being a burden, they were going to have to part ways sooner rather than later, Dyson be damned. He didn't want to have to watch over her more than he already was.

"It depends, Mr. Vasiliev," Janeta said, her smile wide. Her teeth pressed into her bottom lip for a moment and Daniel was physically jolted by it, though he wouldn't examine why. "I suppose I can give you many things, but if you keep looking at me like that the only thing you'll receive is the sharp end of my blade."

The Russian sputtered out a laugh. Janeta did not. Instead, she reached into her pocket and pulled out a thin, flat blade, suitable for throwing. She held it with a delicate control, paired with an air of bored expectation, as if it didn't matter to her either way whether she had to draw blood.

The jolt of annoyance that had gone through Daniel resolved itself into amusement and something that warmed his neck a bit. There was more to Sanchez than he'd given her credit for; perhaps he would have known that if he hadn't spent most of their time together focusing on the aggravation it caused him. He'd planned on ignoring her because she seemed unequal to her task, but he was going to have to reevaluate. She was still green, but some people had innate talent, and if it was the latter he'd be in for an entirely different journey.

Sokolov nodded and raised his hands, as if acknowledging that she had been justified in her threat. "I like that. Yes, I like it a lot. But I do not like blood, so I will apologize."

"Accepted," Janeta said graciously, though her mouth remained an impassive line and her gaze was serious. She slipped the knife away.

Sokolov spoke. "A town called Enterprise. His name is Roberts. Brendan Roberts. We cannot go ourselves after the incident with our ships. Russians would raise suspicion and, well, we are what we are."

"I suppose we *could* try passing ourselves

off as aristocracy, like that Pole did for the Union," Vasiliev said, chortling. "Can you believe these Southerners? So hungry for legitimacy that they treated a Pole like a king because he said he was a duke."

Sokolov laughed disdainfully, before turning back to Daniel and Janeta. "We will not do that, though it might be amusing. But perhaps you will find some useful information and, if it is relevant to our mutual interests, make sure that the Russian consul at the capital is informed of it."

"I can do that," Daniel said absently. His head was already spinning: they'd have to get to Mississippi without being captured, find this Roberts, and figure out how to insinuate themselves into his life.

"We'll come up with something. Thank you for trusting us with such valuable information," Janeta said.

Things would be different from when he traveled alone. He'd have to take Janeta into account. He'd have to think for two, and wouldn't be able to just sleep rough, or deal with more unseemly elements. Or maybe he would. If he could get rid of her before he got to Enterprise, he wouldn't have to worry about her getting into trouble.

"Thank you for your help, gentlemen," Daniel said.

He and Janeta walked in silence after leaving the tent. Her expression was now contemplative.

"The group they mentioned," she said quietly. "The Sons of the Confederacy. They really are bad men?"

"You know nothing of them?" he asked irritably. He was tired but also anxious for the journey ahead, and this was beyond ignorance. It was negligent for a detective, recruit or no, to be this ill-informed.

"No," she said, then heaved a sigh. "Well, I've heard their name mentioned. But I don't know who they are or what they do." She looked up at him, and he could see her humiliation in having to ask what she did. "Please. I know I should be more aware, but you are training me. Tell me who they are."

How she had gotten this far without knowing who they were was a mystery, but she seemed sincere enough that Daniel actually felt a pang of something like pity that he'd be the one to tell her of such evil. It was possible that she was simply trying to force conversation; he'd seen plainly enough that she excelled at winning people over to her side. He'd tell her; if she truly didn't know, she was about to learn exactly what they were dealing with.

" 'Bad men' was an understatement," Daniel said. "Just as there are forces like the Loyal League that conspire to push the country toward reunification and freedom, there are those that push toward chaos and slavery for their own selfish aims.

"The Sons show how a passionate belief can be twisted: while the Confederacy at least pretends that their true aim is financial freedom, the Sons push for the idea at the core of that desire for freedom — that the white race is superior. Any person or institution that challenges that idea is a traitor or threat that needs to be crushed. They glory in causing pain and chaos, and their sworn enemies are the North and the Negro. I've been tracking them and had a few run-ins, but most people run the other way if they hear that group is around."

"But . . ." Janeta shook her head. "I don't understand."

"Look, why did you join the Loyal League?" he asked tersely, and her head whipped in his direction. For a second, she looked afraid, and her fear worked his nerves, which were already taut. He wouldn't pity her; she'd signed up for this job just as he had, and she had to know what it entailed.

"You told me you joined because of abolition and justice or some similar tripe. The Sons? They don't give a damn about justice. They want this country to be a place where men like them will always have absolute power. They are driven by hatred and contempt for anyone who is not one of them."

"I see," she said quietly, looking at the ground.

"Do you?" He felt an incomprehensible annoyance at her presence, at the way she walked so close to him, like he was a friend, and asked him questions she damn well should have known the answer to, given their situation.

He was suddenly tired and frustrated thinking of days and maybe weeks more of this nonsense; when he'd spoken to Logan he'd agreed to stay with her for as long as it took for the mission to prove fruitful. With their newfound information, it seemed he'd be stuck with her for longer than anticipated, and in more dangerous territory than he'd imagined.

"Your Russian, your one supposed skill, was a great help," he spit out, knowing the words were harsh and unnecessary and only served to vent his anger. That didn't stop him from going on. "Slow, ignorant, and not even able to garner anything useful to us. You've been a boon to this investigation."

Janeta didn't look at him, but he wished she would so he could will her to acknowledge what he'd told her from the beginning. *Now do you see?* This *is why no one wants to be partnered with Cumberland.*

"The information they gave us is unverified. They're using us as canaries in the coal mine because they have no idea what this fellow in Enterprise is up to," she said calmly. "They have conflicting reports and want us to see if he's really for the Confederacy, and if he is, they want to know what he's been up to and what it means for Europe. They want to know why a member of the British aristocracy would take a station in a small Mississippi town, and whether his promises are being made to those who would harm their interests."

She looked up at him.

"They also wanted to know whether you were fucking me, and whether you would be willing to share." Perhaps she had expected the curse to shock him, but it was her eyes that did. They were dark with anger and a frustration that resonated deep within him.

"Why didn't you —"

"Why didn't I what? Reveal the one advantage I had over them by letting them know

I understood? I thought you were supposed to be training me, Detective Cumberland. Perhaps you aren't as wise as you imagine."

With that she strode ahead of him, walking up to Lake, a smile on her face as if the conversation between her and Daniel had never occurred. Daniel had underestimated both her and the Russians, distracted by the news they had given him. He'd need to be more careful. If not, the plan brewing in his mind would be over before he could think it through. And though he was quite willing to die, he now had a definitive purpose. It awaited him in Enterprise.

CHAPTER 8

Janeta wished for privacy, but that wasn't something available at the contraband camp. Many things were not available, things that she'd thought were a given in life until she'd set off on her mission full of guilt and absent foresight.

The words of the Russians kept replaying in her memory. Not the leering — that was common enough — but the assumption they'd made that their information would be safe because it benefited Janeta and Daniel to keep it so, simply because of the color of their skin. Little did they know that it benefited her more to tell.

"It would be a pity if him and your sisters found out that he'd been imprisoned because of you . . ."

Henry had been right, of course. Her family would have been devastated that her lack of caution had led to their father's imprisonment, and she had always known that her place with them was tenuous after Mami's death. She couldn't risk it. But when she had gone to Henry for help, she'd expected support, not to be sent out into the thick of the war to get information he needed. She knew penance was necessary for atonement, though, and she would do anything for that.

"Don't you want to make the Yanks pay for what they've done to your father?"

She'd wanted that, too, in the immediate aftermath. Revenge. To make the Union soldiers who occupied her town and her home suffer for their actions against Papi. She had been righteous in her fury, but now she looked around her and her surety faded. If she were honest, it had begun to fade very soon after she'd set out on her journey.

In Palatka, at Villa Sanchez, the war had been very clear-cut — the Yankees were villainous, trying to bend the noble South to their will. Any doubts had been drowned out by the constant tales of evil Northerners, the talk of how secession was what was good and right, and how once the South was free, men like Papi would be able to grow their fortunes without interference. But once she'd left, she'd been able to think of *how* those fortunes would grow unfettered.

How many times since she'd set out had

she been ready to stop? At first it had been because she was tired and afraid, but as she'd traveled, she'd seen and heard things that had shaken her resolve. Only knowing that her father's freedom and perhaps his life was on the line pushed her forward.

Before, she hadn't known better. And she hadn't known about the Sons of the Confederacy. Henry had only mentioned them a handful of times, this group he wanted to join. The men whom he would be passing Janeta's information on to. She'd thought it was just a silly name they'd given to themselves to feel important, as men were wont to do.

Daniel's description of them had made her blood run cold; there was nothing silly about their intentions. If she gave Henry any information, these men would benefit. She would be aiding evil. Could she do this? She hated to ask herself, because she'd said she would do anything for love of her father, but did love have its limits?

She took a tiny bite of the succulent roast pork she'd been given without question, then forced herself to raise her eyes and look at the people it'd been so easy to forget about when she had desperately agreed to Henry's plan.

"It's good, huh?" the man who had called

her over to join them for dinner asked. He was lean, but she could see his strength in the forearms revealed by the rolled-up sleeves of his shabby shirt. The firelight danced over his dark skin, showing the gray creeping through his short hair.

"*Sí.* Yes. Thank you."

It was delicious, considering the food she'd been subjected to since she'd left Palatka. She almost told him about the tangy *mojo* sauce that she ate with pork at home, but then she remembered that sauce was made by their cook, Roberto. Roberto was enslaved, as this man had been. Roberto had always been nice to her, sneaking her sweet bread and not telling her sisters when he caught her sharpening her knives. He'd even been kind to her after the day she'd found him weeping in the kitchen, when his own son had been sold away to another plantation.

Why? Why didn't Roberto hate me?

She forced herself to take another bite of her food.

The man smiled. "When them Yanks showed up and drove off ol' massa, we didn't rightly know what to do. We was scared. Then we realized we was *free.* I spent most of my life raising these swine and got nothing but chitlins and pig feet and tails. So I rounded up a bunch of the hogs and put them on the wagon with us. Wasn't exactly a comfortable journey, but now we get to eat that which we put our sweat into. All of it, not just the scraps. Now we get to share it. And that's how it should be."

He smiled, but there was deep emotion in his eyes as he took another bite. Janeta swallowed, her throat dry. She didn't deserve to share this meal.

She glanced over at Daniel, who was flanked by two small children. He had out a little notebook and some charcoal, and the children looked on in excitement at what he was writing.

"S-I-M-O-N-E," he said. "Simone."

"S-I-M-O-N-E," the little girl beside him parroted, then burst into laughter. "That's me!"

"Yes, it is," he said, and for the first time since she'd met him, his features were relaxed. Calm. "Those six letters make up your name."

"Mama say I gonna get to go to school now, just like massa's son."

"I wanna go to school, too," the boy on Daniel's other side said anxiously, like if he didn't say it, he might get left behind.

"You can do anything you want now, boy,"

the man beside Janeta said. "We free people now. We done reached the promised land. Once you learn them letters, ain't nothing can stop you."

Daniel sighed and closed his notebook, slipping it back into his pocket. "Lake said we can sleep in his tent, Janeta. I'm going to go to bed. We have a long journey ahead of us."

He didn't say anything to the children as he stood heavily, but he did briefly rest a hand on each of their heads before walking off. He moved slowly, as if he dragged a weight behind him. Janeta was used to thinking of how to give people what they wanted, what they needed, but she didn't know what to give to a man like Daniel. She didn't know *why* she wanted to give him something.

"That fella of yours. He got it bad, huh?"

Janeta whipped her head to the man beside her. She thought about correcting him — Daniel wasn't hers — but that wasn't necessary. They were leaving in the morning.

"Got what?" she asked, her mind flipping through English words trying to figure out his meaning.

"There's some folk who survive in body, but they souls got all crushed, understand?

My brother was like that. Massa sold his wife and baby boy, and after that, he just started . . . wilting, like a plant baking in the heat with no rain for weeks. One day he walked off into the woods and they found him floating in the lake." The man shook his head. "Massa said he was trying to run off, but Deke ain't know how to swim; he wouldn't try to cross no lake. I think he walked in and didn't want to walk back out."

"I'm sorry," she said. A memory that she'd avoided for years swam to the forefront of her mind. Mami — who had prided herself on her beauty and stylishness — thin and weak and unkempt in her bed, tears slipping down her cheeks.

"You must be perfect. I tried. I tried so hard. The minute you are not perfect they will remind you that you're just another morena *who should be cutting cane. That they can send you to the field and nothing will save you." Janeta tried to give her mother some of the cane juice Roberto had pressed for her, and Mami knocked the glass to the floor, shattering it. She grabbed Janeta by the wrist, hard, and rubbed at the skin of her face with her bony hand. "I wish you hadn't been born so dark,* princesa. *What will they do to you? What will they do?"*

Janeta's chest went tight. She wasn't supposed to think of this. She tried to remember only the good times with Mami, of her beauty and flirtatiousness and how she was the queen of any parlor she entered, not her sobs that echoed in the halls until one morning there had been silence. But she wondered about this soul crushing. Maybe Mami had walked into the lake of her own pain and not wanted to walk back out.

The man sighed. "Watch out for him, all right?"

Back home, big, strong men like Daniel were valued for how much cane they could cut and how much value they brought a plantation. The idea that they, too, had inner lives — emotions, hopes, and dreams — was not a consideration for those who owned them. If a master was kind, he thought of the strain on a slave's body. She'd never heard of one who thought of the strain on their slaves' hearts and souls.

"They don't feel the same way that we do. They are happier with this life, because they need guidance. They cannot think for themselves. We are helping them."

This didn't make sense to Janeta. She knew Papi was the smartest man in the world, but it seemed to her that the slaves were the ones helping him. After all, he couldn't work the land himself, could he? Or clean the house or maintain the sugar mill?

"But, Papi, if they're happy, why do they try to escape? And how do they come up with a plan if they cannot think for themselves?"

"Because some of them are wicked, and they are punished for this wickedness."

"But if Mami was happy being a slave, why did you free her? Mami is sad and can't get out of bed. Is it because she misses being a slave?"

"Dios, *Janeta! Enough of the questions. Finish your dinner."*

Janeta looked at the man beside her, who was sopping the grease from his plate with a hunk of bread.

"What is your name?"

He paused. "Hudson."

"Hudson, did you ever think that your master was kind?"

Hudson's eyes narrowed.

"That man always went on about how *kind* he was to us. For giving us these clothes that scratched our skin all day long even though the cotton we picked was softer than you could imagine. For only selling one child away, instead of all of them. For only doling out ten lashes instead of fifty, when truth is he was just too lazy to do more than that. Wasn't a kind bone anywhere in that man's body, 'cept for in his imagination."

He took a disgruntled bite of the bread and his features, which had just been bright with celebration, darkened with anger.

Shame washed over Janeta, for she had made another misstep.

"I apologize," she said smoothly. "I just hear people say that, about the kindness of masters in the States, and wondered why they did."

"To make themselves feel better," Hudson said. "Same way massa said my wife wanted to give what he took from her. They tell those lies so much, they start to believe 'em. But God ain't ever lied, and when they meet they Maker — whoo boy! — they gonna be in for a surprise."

He grinned viciously and Janeta's stomach turned.

Papi must have been confused. He just didn't understand. God forgives mistakes, doesn't he?

Her heart squeezed in her chest because she had always thought her father a good man, but in that moment, she wasn't sure what would happen were he to be judged. She had an awful, awful thought.

Perhaps he wouldn't be forgiven. And perhaps I won't be either.

"Was your massa kind to you?" Hudson asked suddenly, looking at her from the corner of his eye.

She stood abruptly. “I must go to bed, Hudson. Thank you for sharing your food.”

“Night,” he said, then scrubbed roughly at the back of his neck with one hand. “Don’t go asking nobody else around here them kind of questions. I know you mean well, but some people not gonna take it as kindly as I did.”

“*Sí.* I apologize.”

He nodded, and she moved off toward the tent. The murmurs and conversations all around mixed with the sound of autumn night birds, creating a buzz in her head that almost drowned out her own frantic thoughts. Flashes of her father the last time she’d seen him, manacled and humiliated. Henry, telling her there was only one way to help Papi. Hudson. Daniel. Mami.

Before leaving Palatka, she’d never imagined that she could doubt anything her father said, or the things Mami had shared with her before she’d gone to bed and hadn’t left it. She’d been told time and time again of her place in the world, of everything she was *despite* her brown skin. Now she was learning what she was *because of it.*

She was someone who shouldn’t be spying for the Confederates.

She clenched her fist and shuddered as a

cool breeze gusted against her, the slap of cold a reminder that she didn't have the option of *should.* It didn't matter who anyone thought she should be. The only thing of importance was ensuring that her father made it out of prison alive, and soon, and there was only one way to do that.

When she ducked into the tent, a low candle burned in the darkness, just faintly illuminating Daniel stretched out on the bare ground. He'd left a bedroll for her.

She settled down onto the ground, hard even through the bedroll, and bit back her annoyance. There would be no soft mattresses for her now.

She moved to roll back an edge of the bedroll to place one of her knives under it, just in case, and for a moment was confused when instead of the ground she saw more fabric.

Daniel hadn't left her the single bedroll. He'd given her his, too. Despite his threats of driving her away, he'd done her this small kindness.

Tears welled up in her eyes and she leaned over and blew out the candle, a sob catching in her throat as she exhaled.

Daniel was right. She was a fool.

She sniffled.

"Everything all right, Sanchez?"

"You're awake?" she asked, silently wiping at her eyes and nose in the darkness. She'd lost her handkerchief several states back.

"I don't sleep much," he replied. There was no trace of slumber in his deep voice.

"Thank you. For giving me your bedroll."

He grunted in response.

"Cumberland . . ." She took a deep breath and tried to swallow the tremble in her voice. "This evening I asked a man whether he thought slave masters could be kind."

"Why would you do a fool thing like that?"

"Because sometimes you want to believe in a thing even if you know it to be false." She closed her eyes and let the warm tears stream, catching in the hair at her temple and cooling in the night air. "If they're all bad, and they are the people held up as the pillars of our societies, then what kind of world is this?"

If my spying keeps people like Hudson in chains, what kind of person am I?

"Sanchez, instead of asking others such questions, you might puzzle out if you don't know the answer already."

He was silent after that, and so was she. She closed her eyes and wished that this war had never started, that her family had never left Cuba, and maybe even that she had never been born. Whatever it would take so that this awful knowledge had never been set before her. More than that, she wished she really was a Loyal League agent, brave and good. She wasn't either of those things.

Different memories came to her in the darkness: Papi and Mami holding hands when they didn't know she was watching, her father letting her sit on his knee as he spoke with his friends. How he always, always told her that he loved her and wanted the best for her. She was confused about many things, but not about how much her father loved her. And not about the fact that her foolishness had led him to be arrested.

She wasn't a Loyal League agent, she was a Sanchez, and at the next opportunity she would pass on the information she had gathered from the Russians. Her newfound worldliness didn't change the fact that she had to save her father; it just meant that she'd pay an even greater price. But Papi was her world, and she wouldn't abandon him, even if the cost was her soul.

Chapter 9

Daniel was wide awake when Lake entered the tent with his lantern and took a seat on the ground between him and Janeta.

His body was exhausted from their travels, but his mind had refused to allow him even a moment of rest. He longed for sleep, but it eluded him like so many of the things he'd previously taken for granted. It rarely came to him, and when it did there was no guarantee it would be peaceful. It was another bit of comfort just out of his reach.

"Cumberland? Sanchez?" Lake's voice was gravelly; Daniel wasn't the only one who hadn't slept.

Always thinking of your own struggles. Selfish. Weak.

"*Estoy despierto.* Oh! I am awake." Sanchez's voice was husky with sleep and Daniel didn't like the way it vibrated through his whole body, despite his fatigue.

He'd spent some of the night as he usually did — curled in on himself as memories from his time on the plantation assailed him. His anger, how he had assumed he knew more than the enslaved people who seemed to work willingly, and the repercussions of his stubborn resistance to his new reality. His insistence on trying to reason with evil, to circumvent it, had brought the lash down on his own back and worse, onto others.

He'd also turned the words of the Russians over in his head. Jefferson Davis was on the move, away from the heavily fortified Richmond, where he'd been untouchable as he led this war to uphold evil. The figurehead of the Confederacy would be vulnerable, as would the men who controlled the Sons of the Confederacy. Daniel had been taught by the institution of slavery itself just how to break a people down using their vulnerabilities. Take away their hopes and dreams, rend the bonds that provide them with the illusion of security.

Could he do this? He of all people? He was weak, but perhaps he had enough strength in him for this one act. Perhaps his life would have meaning if he could accomplish this one thing.

Other, less noble thoughts had plagued him, distressing in a vastly different way.

His mind had meandered down a road lined with musings on Sanchez. The way she'd batted her lashes at the Russians before doling out threats. How she took a moment to evaluate each situation before speaking, and managed to say the right thing at the right time. The devastation in her voice at her belated realization that the world operated on explicit unkindness.

He'd brushed aside her attempt to talk, but it had reminded him of his debates with Elle, where she'd informed him in that superior tone of hers that morality and justice had nothing to do with freedom, that he could study himself sick and not find a cure for the evil of slavery.

Daniel had once been the one asking questions he now had the answers to inscribed on his back with the lash.

"Do not doubt my belief in the rule of law, Daniel, but understand that laws are put in place by men. They do not spring from the ether. Until I can trust that those men care about people like us — or that we can force them to care — laws alone will not suffice."

Her constant corrections had driven him mad — just once he'd wanted to show her that he could be right. He'd wanted her to feel the same awe and reverence he experienced when she shared her formidable intellect, and the jealousy and frustration he felt when his argumentation withered before hers. He'd learned too late that you could no more compel the type of admiration you wanted from a person than you could the type of love.

It didn't matter anymore — Daniel had thought that eventually he would change Elle's mind, but, by all accounts, the man she'd chosen instead of him followed her around like a lovesick Scottish puppy. He'd been wrong about her, as he had been about everything in his pathetic life.

"Cumberland? You all right?"

Daniel rolled over and took in Lake, the man's stark features barely visible in the early morning darkness.

"Close enough," he answered. He was still alive and still able to fight. That would do.

"I met with some Union men from Camp Defiance," Lake said. The nearby fortification was at the apex of the Ohio and Mississippi rivers, a strategically advantageous position for the North.

Daniel pulled himself to a sitting position, his longing for sleep pushing down on him like the bales of cotton he'd been forced to haul.

"Any news?" Daniel asked. Obviously, there was; otherwise Lake would still be out searching for it.

"They have a transport carrying troops and supplies heading South tonight. There's room for you two. Not planning on making another trip for a few days, so if you want to get, you got to get now."

South.

Daniel's stomach flipped and he tried not to show the brief panic that gripped him. The boundary between North and South was intangible, but the fear that slithered over him and squeezed the breath from him felt more real than anything. Fear that he would be taken back into slavery, be forced into perhaps even worse circumstances than he'd faced before, always rose within him before he had to undertake these dangerous missions. People thought him brave to the point of recklessness, but he was a coward, trying to still the sudden trembling of his hands.

Run. Enough of this. You are too weak, unfit to bear the title of detective.

Daniel ran a hand over his face, as if he could wipe off the residue of the dark thoughts lashing at him. He hummed tonelessly to drown them out in his head before answering. "We shall go."

Sanchez began gathering her things, and he did the same. He pressed his hand against the letters from Ellen after he tucked them into the pack. He couldn't read them, but the crinkle of them against the palm of his hand calmed him a bit.

"Is it possible? Traveling by boat?" Janeta asked doubtfully.

"How did you get here from Florida?" Daniel asked in an aggravated tone.

"I flew," she responded with a grin as she stretched and flapped her arms.

Daniel rolled his eyes. She was here, and he was stuck with her, no matter how she'd arrived.

"The North has had control of the Mississippi since Vicksburg fell," Lake responded helpfully. "There're still attacks from the shores, but I imagine you'll be in a pook turtle, so you'll be safe."

"Pook?" Janeta's head tilted to the side, her gaze drifting to a corner of the tent. It was then that Daniel remembered English wasn't her first language, and the reference to the City-class ship had thrown her off.

"It's an ironclad," he said. "The navy has outfitted steamboats with sheets of metal to protect those onboard from attack."

"Oh. Thank you," she said, looking sheepish. "Pook turtle. What a strange name."

Lake chuckled, pulled back the tent flap, and waited for Janeta to pass through it.

Daniel tucked his knife into the sheath at his belt and rubbed at his weary eyes before following them out into the chill autumn morning.

The camp was quiet and dark; most people still slept, though there were murmurs of conversation here and there. They passed a man sitting before a low-burning fire, wrapped in a blanket, rocking on his heels and glancing about. His gaze locked with Daniel's, and Daniel felt a jolt of kinship at the fear in the man's eyes. In those dark depths, he found a shared knowledge: that the people in this camp were free, but they were not safe. That they might never be safe.

Emotion lodged in Daniel's throat, and he swallowed against it, nodding at the man, who gave Daniel a nod in return before turning his gaze toward the flames.

While Daniel often thought of the reasons he *should* leave the Loyal League, he generally kept a safe distance from pondering his motivations for staying. The reason was in that man's eyes, and it couldn't be escaped. He did the work for people like that man. Perhaps because he wished someone had done the work for him. If the government had abolished the barbarous trade, or if the fugitive slave laws hadn't allowed free

Negroes to be kidnapped so easily, or if instead of compromise, the slavery question had been met with a definitive and resounding rejection . . . but none of those things had come to pass. Now Daniel had to work with the materials he'd been given. His anger and his pain, his body and his blood.

The North prevailing might not be the salvation so many thought it would be, but it was a damn sight better than the situation that produced men who couldn't sleep for fear they might lose their family, life, or liberty if they blinked too long.

He considered what could give a man like the one before the fire a good night's sleep, even just one, and his thoughts strayed to Enterprise. To Jefferson Davis traveling freely and in style, unafraid.

Daniel's hand went to the hilt of his knife; he would see what he could do to give the man rocking before the flames succor.

"Is it true that Davis's wife is a *mulata*?" Janeta asked, as if they had been in the midst of lively conversation and not walking in silence.

Daniel wondered at what her thoughts must be like. She was full of questions, but never asked the ones he expected from a detective.

She looked about suddenly, as if realizing

it was a strange thing to inquire about. "I heard someone say it last night and I wondered."

"Wondered why one of us would be married to the president of the Rebels?" Lake asked with a harsh laugh. "I think that rumor is hogwash. No one would sink so low."

"I can certainly imagine why one of us who could pass as one of them might do it," Daniel said. Lake scoffed and began to talk, but Daniel cut him off. "Marry Jefferson Davis, that is, not the President of the Confederacy. He was just a man like any other when they married."

"Well, he ain't a man no more," Lake said. "These fool Rebs treat him like a god."

"Maybe she feels she can't leave," Janeta said.

"Lots of folk feel they can't leave their husband or wife, but they don't got a choice in the matter, because of men like Davis. Instead they watch their love get sold away," Lake replied, then shook his head. "I think it's just a rumor, but if she is one of us, well, she's made her decision about where she stands."

"Sí," Janeta said quietly.

"She might think about sharing some information for the Cause, though." Lake added with a low laugh, dissipating the tension left behind by Janeta's question. "Help us out, Varina. Come on now."

Daniel chuckled.

They walked out of the contraband camp, with Lake stopping to chat with Union pickets posted along the path. Daniel couldn't help but notice how all the men they passed eyed Janeta, some blushing, some leering. She walked with her chin high, responding politely to salutations, but there was something different in her demeanor. Her gait was stiff, her hands clenched. He couldn't quite get a grasp on Janeta — her behavior changed like the waves breaking along Massachusetts's rocky shores — but if she was showing that she was ill at ease, he'd do something about that.

Daniel sighed in annoyance, then quickened his pace until he was walking beside her. She glanced up at him, but turned her gaze back to the trail before them. Still, her body leaned toward his as they walked, her arm brushing his every now and again because she was so near. If they hadn't been heading deep into enemy territory, and she hadn't been an unwanted burden who might get him killed, they could have been mistaken for a couple on a pleasant stroll.

He supposed it was as good a time as any to find out more about her.

He tried to remember what he'd talked about with Elle on their walks — abolition, his future as a lawyer, their country. Topics that were unsavory to him now, but it occurred to him he'd never asked Elle much about her own future, because he'd assumed it would be by his side.

"What did you plan to do with your life before this war began?" he asked Janeta, surprising himself as much as he had her, judging from the way her eyebrows flew up and she had to wrestle her expression into composure. He should have been asking about the here and now, but he told himself that he was using one of the more practical tools in any detective's tool kit: banal conversation.

"I . . . well, there is a man who said he wanted to ask to marry me," she said. There was a hesitant embarrassment in her tone that Daniel was familiar with.

"He wanted to?" he pressed. "Wanted to in the past or intends to in the future?"

"Intends to, I suppose."

"What stopped him from doing it when he made this declaration of want?" It seemed odd to make your intentions known for the hell of it. He'd told Elle he'd marry her when they were children, but when he'd gone down on one knee as an adult he'd wanted her as his wife with no delay.

Janeta sighed. "Well, things were complicated. There's his family to think of, and their status. He wanted to wait until the war was over and our situations were settled. It wouldn't be fair to leave me a widow, he said."

She said the words with a decisiveness that told Daniel everything he needed to know. Such resolve was only necessary when trying to convince yourself; he'd used the same tone when he'd told everyone Ellen would change her mind once she returned from Liberia. He could have told Janeta that the situation was already settled, but he let her keep her fantasy. "Right."

"And you?" she asked. "Who is she?"

Daniel whipped his head in her direction. "She?"

"The woman who has your heart," Janeta said.

"No woman," he said gruffly. "No heart, either."

"I see."

He wasn't the only one feeling pity for a misguided partner, it seemed.

They walked on in silence and soon arrived at Camp Defiance, where even more men bustled about. White Union soldiers readying provisions; freed Negroes working as labor loading the provisions onto boats.

"These are the detectives I told you about, Captain Hooper," Lake said, walking up to an officer with a thick blond mustache and graying sideburns.

Hooper turned his attention to them, eyes narrowing as they settled on Janeta. "A woman?"

Lake was obviously confused at the annoyance in his tone, too. "Sir?"

Hooper closed his eyes and exhaled. "They can ride up front, in the pilot house. I can't have a woman like her in the middle of men heading to battle."

"A woman like me?" Janeta looked into the face of each man, brows raised, before returning her gaze to Hooper.

"Women are bad luck. And I must question the morality of a woman who would want to ride with a pack of stinking soldiers," Hooper said, lip curled.

Daniel had encountered reticence and outright hostility when working with Union officers before, but it had been directed at him. It was strange to see prejudice directed elsewhere, and to hear thoughts that were shockingly similar to his remonstrances of Elle when she'd first set her mind to the

Loyal League. His frustration with himself and the look of embarrassed shock on Janeta's face acted as a bellows to the flame beneath the anger that was always simmering in him.

He took a step toward Hooper, ready to give the man a piece of his mind, but Janeta raised a hand to her mouth demurely and made a sound of pity. "Oh, I see. I am accustomed to officers whose men respect them enough not to behave dishonorably toward any woman in their presence. Since you lack control over your men, *sir,* I am quite happy to pass the voyage in the pilot house."

With a sweep of her skirts, she walked past Hooper to the man who appeared to be his second in command. "If this gentleman would be willing to lead the way?"

The burly man glanced uneasily at Hooper, who gave a stilted nod of the head despite his flushed face. Janeta waved her goodbye to Lake and followed the man toward the bizarre looking ship.

"Well, she seems able to take care of herself," Lake said, grinning as he took in Daniel's stiff stance — he hadn't yet had time to relax, she'd turned that situation around so quickly.

"We'll be off soon," Hooper said, turning

and following Janeta.

Daniel and Lake clasped hands, and Daniel nodded. "Thank you for the information, and for arranging our passage."

Lake shook his head. "You're heading into the danger to try to help end this war; I'm the one who should be giving thanks. You two stay safe, hear?"

"That's my plan," Daniel said, trying to inject some enthusiasm into his voice as he'd once been able to.

Lake headed back toward the camp and Daniel walked toward the ship, where he found Janeta conversing with the man whom she'd asked to take her over.

The pook turtle was a marvel of ridiculous design. It was a broad-bottomed thing, with two huge paddles at midship and two chimneys jutting out from the steam engines. The pilot house where they would spend the journey was on the hurricane deck of the ship, an octagonal iron shield surrounding it, and bulwarks ran along the ship's upper decks shoulder high. The protective iron plates and the fact that much of the ship couldn't be seen beneath the surface truly made it look like some ancient turtle risen from the muddy depths of the Mississippi — a turtle prepared for battle.

"There are three guns in the bow, eight in

the broadside battery, and two in the stern battery, ranging from a sixty-four pounder to a thirty-two pounder." Janeta's guide was pointing out the guns to her as he talked.

"My so many big guns!" she exclaimed with a laugh of delight, and the man's cheeks went pink. "And the Confederate weapons are useless against this type of ship?"

"Oh, not useless, but less effective, unless they hit us with something big or we run into one of the floating torpedoes."

"I see." Janeta shot him a worried glance. "Does that happen often?"

"Oh no, we have a scuttle to detonate anything in our path, after losing one of these in '62."

"Are you done with the Inquisition?" Daniel asked.

"I was just curious," Janeta said, rolling her eyes.

"Curiosity is your resting state," he muttered.

"If you don't ask questions, how do you learn things?" she replied with a smile. Some very small and inconsequential part of him took note of the smile and how effective a tool it was, rendering its recipient incapable of a comeback. Her arsenal was perhaps more formidable than he'd given her credit for.

A group of soldiers near the ship had turned to stare at her and their grins had a lascivious tilt to them. They'd noticed the smile, too.

"We can head aboard now," Daniel said, stepping closer to her. He tried to tamp down the protective urge, but Janeta had already shown that unwanted male attention unsettled her, and he was her partner, as much as he resented that fact.

She nodded and slid her arm into his, the brush of her coat sleeve against his waist sending a frisson of unexpected sensation through his body. Good sensation. He stiffened and almost pulled away from her.

"I'm sorry," she said quietly as they followed the man up through the gangplank. "In my experience, men only respect that which they believe to be claimed. It's a bit frightening walking onto this ship full of soldiers after being told that my safety is an inconvenience."

"An unfortunate truth," he replied with a sigh. He couldn't tell her otherwise. She faced different dangers, the very same that he had pointed out to Elle to try to dissuade her from leaving for Liberia.

Daniel steeled himself a moment before they entered the pilot house: it wasn't a very small space, but it wasn't a large one either. Sweat sprung out on his brow as they entered. He could often avoid the memory of waking up in that coffin, but his body and mind seemed unable to forget the sensation. Now every place that might hold him captive triggered not a fear of being trapped, but the fear of how his body would react if he thought he was.

He walked through the door, saw that it had a latch on the inside to hold it fast, but no keyhole. The door pulled inward, and no one could bar them in from the outside. His tension dropped as he wiped his palms on his pants and shook hands with the taciturn Captain Kendall, who seemed no more interested in him and Janeta than a pair of flies that had buzzed into the enclosed space and rested on the wall.

Kendall was busy prepping for the voyage.

"How can we help?" Janeta asked.

"You can go sit over there," Kendall said without looking at them, but his tone was more focused than derisive.

The coal engines roared to life, and the boat juddered around them. Janeta gasped and placed her hand against the iron wall, slipping her finger through one of several bullet holes that mottled the metal.

"Should we be worried about this noise?

And swaying?" she asked the captain, raising her voice in order to be heard.

"No point worrying over that which God has planned for us," was all Kendall said before turning to the wheel. "But a prayer won't hurt none."

Janeta made the sign of the cross and began whispering to herself. Daniel did nothing — there were worse things than dying. He settled onto the sacks of grain against the iron wall behind the wheel. Janeta stood beside him, peering through the slit window above him.

"When we sailed to the US from Cuba, there was just blue ocean and blue sky," Janeta said amiably. She spun and sank down beside him. "I was terrified the entire trip, but I forced myself to stand at the railing with Papi. He wanted me to see the view."

The boat rocked from side to side as it was buffeted by the river's current, and her fingers dug into the sack beneath her.

"You're afraid of water," Daniel noted, taking in her ramrod-straight back and the way her teeth seemed to be set hard against one another.

"Don't be silly. I'm not afraid of anything." She said it so confidently he was confused, thinking he'd misunderstood her story about her trip from Cuba; then the boat lurched, and she sucked in a breath and glanced up at him with wide eyes. "Can you swim?"

Daniel sighed. He might have been annoyed at her nerviness, but he wasn't exactly some bastion of unflinching bravery. If the door had been hung on its hinges in the opposite direction he might have been in the throes of panic. It helped him, having to put someone else's fear before his own.

"Can't swim, but I suppose I could float if it came down to it," he replied, settling into the grain as it shifted under his thighs. "I used to manage it as a boy."

"Did you grow up near the water?" She didn't pull her gaze away from his; she *was* curious. And frightened. They had hours ahead of them, and if he could distract her with a bit of small talk, perhaps he could have peace for the rest of the voyage.

"There was a lake, but we didn't do much swimming," he said. "We weren't allowed to because the white families did their swimming there. Sometimes we would sneak in a soak on days when it was too damned hot to stand it. In the winter, the lake would freeze over and we would go out on ice skates my father had made."

Janeta squealed with delight. "Ice skating? I've read about that in books, though I admit I find it hard to imagine. What does it feel like?"

Daniel opened his mouth to answer, then realized he had never given it much thought. It had been a treat, something he'd looked forward to, but he'd never much thought about why. He remembered Elle stepping out onto the ice, her first wobbling steps forward. He thought about gliding along, carefree, with her and the other colored children of their church during the time allotted to them.

"Well, it's cold, of course," he said.

"Colder than it is here?" She shuddered dramatically, and he frowned to avoid the smile that almost pulled his mouth up.

"This is nothing. It's autumn yet and not even as cold as autumn gets." He tried to recall what it felt like, all those winters on the ice. "When we would skate, it would be so cold that your fingers went numb after a few moments of exposure and tears sprang to your eyes, and each breath felt like swallowing a lungful of frost needles."

"That sounds awful," Janeta said, raising a hand to her chest.

"No, it was good. There was something about being out in the winter air that made you feel . . . alive, I suppose." He leaned back into the iron wall a little harder. "Like each pinprick of icy air was a reminder that warm blood was pumping in your veins. And the skating? It's like — have you ever seen a bird fly? How it just kind of catches a breeze and glides?"

He made a long, sweeping motion with his hand, and she nodded.

"If you caught a good patch of ice, you could get a bit of that feeling, with the cold wind buffeting your face and your heart beating hard in your chest."

Daniel had forgotten about simple pleasures like strapping blades to the bottom of your shoes and feeling for a moment like nothing in this life could catch you. Joy had once been such a simple thing that he could chase it with a good push across the ice. He couldn't imagine having such trivial fun now.

"That actually sounds wonderful," she said. "I'd like to try it."

Daniel shrugged. His family had tried to take him skating after he'd returned home, but he hadn't been able to muster the energy to even step outside the house.

"I've never felt true cold," Janeta said. "When we left for Florida, I was so scared that I might freeze to death there. I told that to one of the men on our ship and he laughed at me."

"Why did your family leave Cuba?" Daniel asked as casually as he could muster.

Her head tilted a bit and she looked at the wooden planks of the floor before her. "My mother died," she said. "She felt bad, and started moving more slowly, and then started getting out of bed less and less. My father tried to save her, but after she died he wanted to leave. A business opportunity arose in Florida, and me, him, and my sisters packed up and followed it."

She didn't look sad exactly — wistful was perhaps a better word for it. But her story raised more questions for him. One didn't die from not leaving a bed, though Daniel had wished that was possible when he'd returned home, and moving from one country to another wasn't something just anyone could do, especially anyone like them.

"Were your parents both mulatto?"

She glanced up at him, holding his gaze. Her face was slightly taut with indignation. "My mother was born a slave. And my father was not."

That didn't quite answer his question either, but he didn't press. Not yet. If someone asked him something he didn't want to answer and wouldn't let it drop, he'd lie. Daniel wanted the truth, and the fact that she hadn't given it freely meant it was likely worth looking into. His fellow detectives took him for a mad brute, but he did have a good nose for sniffing out a lead, and it was twitching just then.

"My parents were born free," he said. He'd circle back to her own lineage at some other time. "My grandparents were freed people, manumitted after their master's death."

"I see. I heard you say that you joined the Loyal League for vengeance. How did you come to be . . . not free?"

Daniel's neck tensed. The engines growled somewhere behind them, and the waters of the Mississippi slapped against the sides of the boat. The conversation of soldiers drifted into the air. He focused on those sounds as he talked instead of his heart beating in his ears.

"I was kidnapped by slavers. They told me they were recruiting for abolitionist work. I thought I was joining some fine cause, only to be manacled and shoved into a coffin. I was sold onto a plantation, where I was forced to work from dawn until past dark."

She shifted beside him. He expected her to offer him her false sympathy while secretly pitying him for the pathetic man he was. Perhaps she would finally consider switching partners now.

"Surviving that must have required an enormous strength of will," she said quietly.

"No more than any of my brethren who were born into it," he said.

She shook her head. "Sometimes I'm so homesick I just want to lie down and weep. Sometimes I feel so changed that I don't know how I will ever return home. But I left by choice and haven't been forced to labor. To have your life change so suddenly, and to now be here fighting is admirable."

She was looking at him strangely, with something like respect.

"Forced labor is just one part of the horrors of slavery," he said tightly. He was angry for some reason, angry at how she had called him strong, and how she had so neatly described how he felt.

Things weren't supposed to be like this between them. He wanted to shock her, to push her away from him in the small pilot house. "I would have rather plucked tobacco under the hot sun until I died than know of the other things they see fit to force us Negroes to do."

His mind started to slip into the past, but then she was speaking again, pulling him back into the conversation.

"How were you freed?"

I was saved by the white man who won the

love of my life.

No. Elle wasn't an object to be won.

"Happenstance. A childhood friend learned of my impending sale and her husband helped secure my freedom."

That was close enough to the truth, though he'd glossed over some details.

"She learned of your sale by chance, and you are free because of this?"

He nodded.

Janeta's eyes went wide. "That's a miracle! You are a miracle, Cumberland."

She looked at him like he was Christ emerging from his tomb, and it made his skin prickle with shame — he always turned a jaundiced eye toward his rescue. Elle's pity; McCall's quick thinking; their union. God had turned his back on Daniel Cumberland, he was certain. He didn't like the way the word *miracle* falling from Janeta's lips challenged his view of the situation, one that he'd thought was set in stone.

"That's one way of looking at it," he said.

She scoffed, her fear of the ship seemingly forgotten. "What other way is there?"

That it would have been better to die than live with what happened.

He could feel a headache beginning to build and didn't want to discuss himself any longer. "How did you come to join the

Loyal League?" he asked. If she was so fond of questions, she could answer some of his.

The expression of awe on her face slipped away by degrees.

"My father. He is imprisoned because the army occupying our town thought he was committing treason. He wasn't." She pressed her lips together and looked away from him. "Joining the Loyal League means I can help end this war and free him."

Her fingers were clenching at the grain sack again, but this time not out of fear. When she looked up at him, her gaze was fierce. "I will stop at nothing to do that."

When she had scurried into the Loyal League meetinghouse, wide-eyed and talking of abolition, Daniel had been annoyed. After he had been assigned as her partner, he'd been angry. But there was feeling in her eyes now, determination overlaid with pain, and it sparked the briefest sense of kinship in him. This was something he could understand better than pithy remarks designed to impress him.

"Do you see your own goal as admirable? Freeing your father?" he asked, and she frowned.

"No, not admirable. But it's what I must do all the same."

Her expression was serious, and she didn't

say anything for a long while. Daniel watched her from the corner of his eye. Eventually she murmured something in Spanish and chuckled quietly.

"What is it?" Daniel asked, stiffening. Was she laughing at him?

"I was just thinking that this was perhaps the most pleasant conversation I've ever had with a man. On a boat outfitted for war, cruising into enemy territory."

Daniel was oddly moved. People avoided him now, thought him mad. No one had talked to him like he was a man whose opinion mattered in some time, let alone implied that he was enjoyable to talk to. He'd made sure of that. He didn't want the bother of interacting with others. And yet . . .

"I used to be known for my charming nature," he said, and it was a reminder to himself, too. Friends had sought him out after church; peers had listened to him speak. He'd often found himself at the center of social circles at gatherings in any sphere of his life. Perhaps that was why home had been so torturous when he'd returned. He'd been relegated to the outskirts of every group, pushed away by probing questions or pitying stares or uncomfortable silences.

"Your charming nature?" Janeta smiled up at him, and it was warm, much too warm to be calculated.

Daniel had also once known when a woman found him pleasing, though he'd only ever wanted to please but the one. Janeta's eyes were clear brown, like maple syrup spooling into a pail, and there was something alluring in their disconcerting depths. His gaze slipped away from her eyes, tracing over the curve of her button nose and the shape of her full lower lip as he shifted to look at the floor of the pilot house.

"You might be known for it yet if you aren't careful," she said.

"Let's not put the horse before the cart. I wasn't entirely annoyed by our discussion, and that's all," he added, and was rewarded with a laugh.

"That is high praise from Detective Cumberland. Don't worry, I won't tell anyone that you can be quite the conversationalist if you're trapped on a boat."

She stood again to gaze through the slit in the metal wall, and Daniel turned his head away from the curve of her hip that was now in his line of sight.

He forced his thoughts away from their conversation to Enterprise, and what would await them there. His new objective was to find a way into this meeting. Conversation was well and good, but Janeta was not the only one with a goal that must be met.

Daniel's eyes flew open — had he fallen asleep? One moment everything was shrouded in darkness, the next he was wide awake, his gaze scanning the pilot house. His head rested on something firm; fabric rubbed against his cheek and the slightest hint of vanilla tickled his nose. When he shifted away he realized he'd been resting on Janeta's shoulder.

Heat rushed to his face — the job required some intimacies with fellow detectives, but usually not this. He'd never allowed himself the liberty of using one of them as a pillow. When he glanced at her face, her expression was tight.

"We're —"

The sound of pellet shot hitting the metal walls enclosing them, followed by shouted orders from the deck of the ship, cut her off, and he understood why he'd awoken.

He grabbed Janeta by the lapels of her coat and shoved her to the floor, laying his body over hers as the hail of bullets assailed the ship. Soldiers shouted as they took their positions; Hooper's voice rose above the fracas, calling the men into order. Daniel hoped he had more control over his men than Janeta had conjectured.

The fusillade lasted what seemed like forever, and then finally there was the sound of return fire from their boat, the boom of the heavy guns firing out toward the banks of the river along with the soldiers' rifles.

Beneath him, Janeta's heart thudded under her rib cage, and he could feel it in his own chest. Her face was pressed into his collarbone, then he had the top of her head cradled in his hands.

He remembered his own first engagement with the enemy. He wasn't some natural-born warrior, for God's sake. He was large, and years of helping his father at his smithing had made him strong. But even after all he'd been through — even with his burning desire for vengeance — he'd nearly pissed himself the first time a bullet had whizzed past him. He didn't value his life dearly, but something inside of him had cried out in fear and displeasure that such a small, inconsequential glob of metal might end it. After the fear had come the rage. He hadn't survived so much to be killed so easily.

But Sanchez was new to this, and soft for all her bravado and her supposed purpose — she hadn't had time to harden, and seemed to be just beginning to understand the gravity of what she'd undertaken. He felt the slightest twinge of pity for her, though he shouldn't have. She was a detective, like any other, and had chosen to be one.

She shivered with fear beneath him and he began to push himself up and away from her.

"I'm going to return fire," he said calmly, raising his head to locate each of the slits that would allow for offensive action. Somewhere in his mind he understood that if anyone should have been receiving his protection it was the Captain Kendall, but that was no matter now.

"There's a rifle just here," the captain said. "I imagine it's a sight more useful than whatever you're carrying."

Daniel grabbed the weapon and munitions and loaded the shot, ignoring the pellets that slammed into the iron encasing the pilot house at regular intervals. He was sliding the muzzle of the rifle through the slot allotted for just that when he heard clambering behind him. When he glanced over his shoulder, Janeta had stumbled up to her feet and was loading her small revolver with shaking hands.

"Stay low, near the grain," he ground out, and turned back to take his shot.

"I am your partner," she said. Her voice was farther from him — she had moved to the slot on the other side of the cabin. "I will not leave the defense of my life or your own solely on your shoulders."

Her voice shook, but there was a resolve there that surprised him. She had no questions, had simply overcome her shock and begun to do what was needed of her.

Daniel didn't argue, and he didn't pay attention to the admiration that slammed into him harder than anything he'd felt in months. Anything more than wary resignation was dangerous when it came to this woman. Instead, he peered through the slot, watching for tell-tale flashes in the shadowy forest along the riverbank, took aim, and fired.

Chapter 10

Janeta thought she'd known darkness, but the inky black of a Mississippi woods on a moonless night was something else entirely. It was full of unfamiliar sounds and strange rustlings, and she was frightened. The darkness reminded her of tales her serving girl — her slave — would tell her, of *El Cuco, El Viejo del Saco,* the monster wandering the night with his giant sack looking for misbehaving children to snatch up and carry away.

She was no longer a child, but she would deserve any punishment meted out to her if *El Cuco* came upon their camp.

She had plaited her hair into a single braid after they'd made camp, and tucked the folded notes she'd taken at the Loyal League camp and on the boat as Daniel slept into her hair. She had calmly prepared herself to betray him, and the Loyal League, and the North.

She wasn't sure what to do next.

Henry and his superiors had explained that she was to find Confederate forces and pass on information, to find telegraph stations if she could. All she had managed since her first and only letter to Henry letting him know she'd made contact and was being taken to a Loyal League meeting was this clumsy, misshapen braid with a note tucked inside. She couldn't bring herself to think of the reality of handing off her information to Confederate forces now, after everything she'd seen since leaving Palatka. After the last few days with Daniel and the other detectives.

She hadn't thought this through at all. She'd agreed to do it because she hadn't wanted to disappoint Papi or Henry, but now she didn't want to disappoint Daniel, either. More surprisingly, she didn't want to disappoint herself.

She was hopelessly lost, stumbling deeper into her own emotional labyrinth the more she tried to understand just how she'd ended up in this situation. Her efforts to win Henry over had cost her father his freedom, and her efforts to free her father could cost people like Daniel his life — and people like her, too. She was coming to understand both her place in this country and her own inner geography better; she was recharting the map of herself now that she could go out and explore its surrounding terrain. But her new knowledge didn't change much in the end. If she didn't send any dispatches, she would lose her father and Henry both. She could deal with the latter, though that had once been unthinkable, but the former . . . she couldn't lose Papi.

She'd been so silly, thinking that love was some pure thing. Doing what was right by her heart could rip her to pieces and cost her her very soul.

There was a brief spark; then the tinder caught light. Daniel leaned over the flame of their camp fire to stoke it, the dim orange glow capturing the curve of his cheekbone and the breadth of his nose.

She had seen that face up close, had felt the weight of him when he'd thrown himself over her, protecting her with his own body when the pook turtle had come under fire. She'd known the weight of Henry's body on hers as he'd taken his pleasure — Daniel had been trying to give her his life. It didn't help that after they'd come through the attack alive, after her jangled nerves had settled, she'd been unable to stop her mind from wandering back to that moment beneath him on the floor of the pilot house. It had changed something for her.

When she'd gone to Henry for assistance, his first response had been to convince her to put herself in harm's way. His second had been to caress her face, her neck — she'd thought he was offering comfort, until one hand had moved to her shoulder and pressed her back toward the tree while his other hand moved to his belt. He'd said he wanted to make love to her one more time, and he hadn't cared that she'd been too overcome with grief to want the same. She'd held on to the tree as he rutted on her and muttered how much he loved her into her nape. She'd always assumed that's what love was, when you got down to it — giving yourself over to someone's desires in the hopes they would perhaps care about yours.

Daniel had looked into her eyes when he'd lain on top of her, bullets peppering the iron walls, and in his gaze she'd found what she'd been searching for when she'd run to Henry that night that had changed her life.

Strength. Worry for her well-being. Determination to protect her.

It wasn't love, but it had pinned her as much as his body had, with the added weight of the knowledge that she was in the midst of betraying him.

She was a fool.

"Thank you. Again." Her words were so low that they were almost eaten by the crackling of the fire, but he seemed to hear her.

He sat back on his heels beside the fire. "No need for it. Again."

"Were you telling the truth earlier?" she asked suddenly. "About having no woman?"

"I don't see what that has to do with anything," he replied tersely.

"Sorry for prodding." She felt odd, like a leaf picked up by the wind and buffeted about. She wasn't used to talking about what she was truly thinking. But something about the dark Mississippi night, and about Daniel, allowed her to. "I was just thinking about love. How I was always told that it was the only thing that could protect me." She sucked in a breath as she realized that awful truth. That was what Mami had taught her, with her lessons in how to make herself pleasing. That if you got the right man to love you, you wouldn't have to worry about anything else. Love hadn't saved Mami, though, and now Janeta was beginning to think of her mother's raving and wonder if perhaps love was what had pushed her to her doom.

She sighed. "Does anyone really love? Is everyone just acting out what society wants of them, or using it to get what they want from society?"

Daniel glanced at her. His mouth was pulled into a frown.

"I can't answer that. No heart, remember? Those seem like questions better suited for your intended, anyhow." He poked at the fire. "Don't worry, I haven't gotten any ideas about you. You don't have to warn me away with discussions on the nature of love."

Heat flushed to her cheeks — embarrassment and anger. "That's not why I asked." She thought of Daniel's cynicism about Henry's intentions to marry her. She thought of Henry being part of the Sons of the Confederacy, and how he had sent her out into the world to please a group that would apparently sooner kill someone like her than see her stay free. "And he's not my intended."

"How fickle of you."

"I'm not the fickle one," she said. "Foolish, perhaps, for believing his talk of our future but ignoring his present actions."

Her sinuses burned as they always did when she held back her tears. All the little worries about Henry that she'd pushed to the back of her mind now seemed to press at her eyes, and she blinked away tears.

"Ah, that's right. 'Wanted to marry.' "

Daniel threw his twig into the fire. "Could his reticence on marriage have been because he didn't want you to join the 4L?"

She laughed, not bothering to smooth the edge of resentment in her tone. "No, he was all too happy for me to serve. My success would be a success for him after all."

"Hm. So he pushed you to become a detective?"

She nodded, feeling ashamed. "He told me it was how I could help my father. But I'm starting to think that it's not a coincidence that it benefits him, too."

"That's the way of it, then. Love will make you do outrageous things." Daniel's expression didn't change, but his voice was a little softer when he spoke again. "Do you wish that he'd asked you to stay instead?"

The pain in her sinuses was joined by a roughening of her throat. She wouldn't cry.

"I wish many things, Cumberland. But mostly I wish I had considered why he could so easily pack me off. Being away from him has helped me to start seeing some things more clearly, though, and the view is not lovely." She shook her head. "I believe that sometimes a man sees something he wants and covets it, whether it be property or a woman or prestige. Some men don't see a difference among the three. They do anything they can to get them. A means to an end — is that the saying? For something that helps you get what you want?"

She glanced at him and he nodded.

"I think maybe I was the means and had confused myself for the end. And maybe I had done the same with him. Women want things, too, you know." She sighed and laughed again, trying to lighten the mood. "I am sorry. I should keep these thoughts to myself and not bother you with them."

She'd always known, on some level, that Henry had whispered exactly what she wanted to hear. She'd told herself that he did it for the same reason she did — to please her so that she would like him. She hadn't considered more nefarious reasons for his manipulation.

Daniel sighed. "I had a woman I loved my whole life. My best friend since I was a child." He found another twig, picked it up, and snapped it. "She wanted to help the Union and I told her it wasn't her place."

Janeta wrinkled her nose. "Did you say those words to her? 'Not your place'? *Dios mío.* And now you have no woman."

"And no heart." He grimaced. "She's the most decorated detective the Loyal League has, though. And she's married to another man."

Janeta thought of things she'd overheard. Burns, was the name that had been whispered. Something about setting fire to a house and a stolen Confederate warship. A heroine whose story would be told long after the war, if the world was just — of course Daniel had loved someone like that. Someone who could do such things wouldn't worry about pleasing others.

"You must hate this man," she whispered.

"Wrong to hate the man who helped free you," he said. "But I managed. I managed for a good long while because it doesn't take much work to hate. But I've been thinking, despite trying not to think." He sighed. "I loved Ellen, but perhaps she was my means to an end, as you put it. A shortcut to the comfort and happiness I felt I deserved — that I coveted. I'd built a future for us in my head, when she'd already told me she had her own plans and they didn't include me. You've given me something to think on, Sanchez."

Something clicked for Janeta then.

"You didn't want her to join, but you are here. Why?"

"Well, when I was rescued I was offered a way to get vengeance. And I think part of me wanted to show her that I could do this, too. That I could make a difference, too."

"So you know what it feels like, doing this thing because it was the desire of the one you thought you loved."

"In a way, I guess. But now I do it for me and my own reasons. And you should only stay if you really believe in why you're doing it, too." He stretched and then looked at her across the fire. "We should try to sleep."

She didn't want him to go to sleep; if he slept, then she would have to try to pass her information. Not for Henry. But for Papi, whom she'd gotten into this mess because of her infatuation with Henry. Henry had manipulated her for her body, but right now he was the only hope she had of freeing her father, however tenuous. Papi shouldn't have to pay for her mistakes.

She dug into her pack. "I have some bread and beef. Captain Hooper gave it to me while you were helping to clear the deck. I believe he felt a bit of guilt over placing us in harm's way."

"I'll have it for breakfast," he said as he settled onto his bedroll. "Now sleep. We'll have to be up at first light and may have to travel well into the night."

"All right." She broke off a bit for herself and ate it quickly as Daniel stretched out beside the fire with his back to her. When she'd finished eating she stretched out onto the thin fabric over the hard, cold ground, too, using her sack as a pillow.

The sharp end of the note she had folded and braided into her hair pressed into her scalp, a reminder of what needed to be done. She had to find someone she could safely pass the information off to, her soul be damned. It was a small bit of information really, just enough to show Henry and his superiors that she was trying — enough to persuade them to help Papi as much as they could.

She lay staring at clouds scudding below the starry sky for what could have been hours. She stared so long that she began to see that there were more than she had ever thought possible, small clusters that appeared after her eyes adjusted, adding new depth to what she'd thought she'd known of the constellations. How had anyone ever used such a confusing morass of bright, blinking beauty as a guide? Maybe in truth, everyone was just as lost as she was, arriving at their destinations by confidence-driven chance, like Columbus bumbling onto the shores of the Caribbean.

She listened as she stared, and eventually Daniel's breath came even and slow — he slept. He'd suspected a Confederate picket was in the area a few miles back. Could she make the journey to pass off the letter and return before he awoke?

She could try. As much as she hated it, she would have to.

She stood silently, holding up her skirts so that she wouldn't rustle the leaves around her, and began making her way toward the path they had followed. *Por suerte,* she wouldn't have to rely on the stars.

"Where are you going?"

She stopped, one foot raised and her heart pounding out of her chest.

"To relieve myself," she lied.

"Don't go too far. If a Rebel were to come across you, or a slave patrol . . ." He let the sentence trail off. She understood what he did not say aloud.

The truth of his implication was like another cluster of stars that had been just outside her field of vision but now came into focus and was now blinding in its obviousness.

She sucked in a sharp breath.

Daniel had been telling her since he'd met her — in the States she was a Negro and in the South she was any number of coarser words for the same. Henry had set her up with an escort toward the Northern line, where she had been able to insinuate herself into a Loyal League recruitment. As for passing along intelligence, she was lacking the only thing that would unequivocally show her allegiance to the Confederacy and protect her: white skin.

How perfectly ironic.

She walked back to her bedroll and threw herself on the ground with some force, ignoring the pain that jolted through her bones. She'd set out with the intention to spy for people who would do her harm in the blink of an eye without some visible sign that she was "one of the good ones," and somehow she had still rationalized the decision. It had made so much sense in Palatka, with Henry feeding her sweet nothings.

You're not like the others.

Something inside of her was rent in two at the memory of Henry's words — she burned with shame that her ego had been so easily wielded against her. She thought of every morning when Lucia, her serving girl, had dressed her and brushed sweet-smelling oil through her hair. How Janeta had traipsed around in her fancy dress and ate fine food, keeping her gaze carefully averted from the slaves toiling everywhere around her. How she'd stopped asking those questions that had enraged her father and annoyed her mother once some part of her had begun to understand that she would not like their answers. She'd suppressed her curiosity and swallowed the lies, sweet and easy to eat, like flan.

She pressed her face into her rucksack and let the tears come. She had been silly to think she could free Papi this way and now she was trapped, unless she ran off in the night. If she did, she'd be alone and with no idea where she was going or how to get home without being captured, or worse. Henry had made it all seem so straightforward, but she now edged along a winding, rocky path through her very soul.

Who was Janeta Sanchez? What could she do in this world? To her father, she had been a princess; to her mother, evidence of her triumph over the manacles that had once bound her. To her sisters, she was the little girl who needed to be more feminine, more demure, less the *morenita*.

To Henry she had been an exotic delicacy to be consumed in the dark of night, when no one else could see. He'd always had some reason why he couldn't tell his parents or friends, or make his intentions known to her father. She'd always made herself swallow his sweet lies, but distance from him had given the truths she'd once ignored with all of her might room to gallop — they'd been on her trail from Palatka to

Atlanta to Illinois, and they'd finally caught up and trampled the fantasy world she'd built with Henry beneath their feet.

Janeta had always been the questioning kind, as Daniel had called her, but she'd stopped questioning Henry, just as she had stopped questioning her parents, and there could be only one reason for that. She hadn't wanted to know what he would say if she'd pushed him hard enough. She'd placed her life and her soul into the hands of a man she couldn't even trust to be honest with her.

Oh, you fool. You ridiculous fool.

She knew Daniel was awake, listening, as she should have known he was awake when she tried to creep away. He slept little, haunted by the hurt inflicted by the very system that she was supposed to be aiding.

For the first time, she didn't fear what would happen if she were caught by the authorities. She feared the expression on Daniel's face when he realized her betrayal. She feared that he would look at her with disgust and hatred and, worse, that it would be deserved. She lay in the darkness, wallowing in the knowledge of her own wretchedness, until sleep took her.

A howl so pained as to be inhuman woke

her. A growl cut through whatever vestige of sleep clung to her, and she grasped for her knives, ready to take on whatever beast had happened upon them. As she fought through the clinging haze of sleep, she wondered if perhaps it wasn't *El Cuco,* come for her at last.

She stumbled to her feet and searched for Daniel, and fear iced her heart when her gaze landed on him. His face was a rictus of pain in the light thrown off by the low-burning fire, mouth agape and eyes squeezed shut. No, not pain — fear unlike any she'd ever known. His hands went to his neck and scratched at his skin, and his feet kicked at the ground.

She rushed over to him, unsure of what to do. Lucia had told her tales of men who'd died when awoken from the throes of a nightmare, and she'd never seen a man so deep in the dream world as Daniel was now.

She sheathed her knife and scrambled the dew-frosted leaves beside the smoking embers of their fire. She couldn't wake him, but seeing him in such agony was too much to bear. More pragmatically, they also couldn't afford to attract attention with his cries. She knelt beside him and took hold of his hands, gently trying to stop their grating. He resisted at first, but then gave in and began thrashing his head about instead. She moved her knees closer so that when his head lifted it landed on her lap instead of banging against the hard ground.

After dropping hard into her bunched skirt a few times, his head slowly nestled into her lap with his eyes squeezed shut. He shifted and drew his body up, the heavy bulk of him shifting so that his face pressed into her thighs. The warmth of his exhalations passed through the layers of fabric, just barely, warming her skin, but there was nothing untoward in the motion. Instead, it evoked a cloying tenderness, the same her sisters had probably experienced when trying to figure out just what to do with her torn dresses and frizzy hair after Mami had died and before Lucia had taken on that role.

Mami.

Janeta dropped his hands and did what her mother had always done when Janeta had been frightened by bad dreams. She ran a hand over his soft, tight curls, humming along to a lullaby her mother had sung only when they were alone.

Drume negrita,
Que yo voy a comprar nueva cunita . . .

Strange how her mother had insisted she was not like the slaves during the daylight hours, but sang the same songs of comfort one could hear in the slave quarters in the dark of night.

Janeta sang quietly, caressing Daniel gently and hoping he'd awaken soon. The woods around them were quiet, but she kept her ears open for the sound of breaking twigs. His cry had been so loud; anyone could be heading toward them.

A la negrita se le salen
Los pies de la cunita
Y la negra Merce
Ya no sabe que hace

His head was warm and damp with sweat, and his eyelashes fluttered. His gaze met hers for a moment, wide and filled with fear, and then a second later he was up and on his feet faster than a startled cat.

"What happened?" He was still breathing heavily, but he was breaking down camp, listing to the side as he kicked dirt over the remains of their fire.

"You had a nightmare —"

"God*dammit.*"

Janeta startled, but he wasn't cursing at her. He leaned over the flames, fists balled and resting on his thighs. "My throat is hoarse. I screamed, didn't I?"

"Yes," she said.

"I'm sorry," he said, fists tightening. He breathed heavily, then shook his head.

"I do not think you could control it, Cumberland. There is no need for an apology."

"I apologize for that very reason. I *should* be able to control it, and because I can't, the enemy may be heading in our direction as we speak."

His movements were still slowed by sleep, but he began rolling up their sleeping blankets and grabbing up their rucksacks. She suddenly felt keenly aware of the dark woods around them, and the lightening sky, and the very real threat of the Confederate pickets that she had just a few hours ago thought to seek out.

"All right. We need to orient ourselves," she said. "We are supposed to be heading east, yes?"

"Yes." Daniel looked this way and that, his expression grim; then he reached into his pocket for a compass. Before he could open it, a voice sounded from behind them in the trees.

"You all runaways?" It was a man's voice, and the sound of it sent a chill down Janeta's spine. They'd heard nothing, no footsteps approaching or breaking twigs or shuffling leaves.

Daniel dropped the compass back into his pocket and reached for his gun. "No, we're not runaways. We're free people and have the papers to prove it."

"I can't read none. Don't need to see no papers."

No. Oh God, Janeta hadn't thought of that either — many of the very men sent out to catch slaves were illiterate.

"We'll just be on our way, if you don't mind," Daniel said in a voice that made it quite clear that they'd be off if their questioner minded, too.

"Y'all all right? We heard hollerin' and we thought it was a haint."

"We're fine," Daniel responded. His breath was still coming fast; for him this may have been his nightmare becoming reality.

"All right, then. You hungry?"

The voice was closer now, and Janeta could hear the leaves moving nearby.

"It's a trap," Daniel muttered. "Don't fall for any false kindness."

She remembered how he had come to be sold into slavery.

"Well, we set up not too far from here," the man said. " 'Bout to have breakfast before heading out if you want some company on the road. Heading toward Meridian."

Lake had mentioned that Meridian was near their destination. Something stirred in Janeta. Could this truly be chance? Or was it a trap? Had the Russians set them up?

"Why would you offer us food and ask us along?" Daniel had his revolver in his hand now. Janeta's pulse had quickened, her heart hammering loudly in her ears.

A white man stepped out from behind a tree. His hair hung straight under the brim of his hat, fine enough to get caught up in a gust of wind, but when he stepped close, it was clear he wasn't just white. The planes and angles of his face weren't so very different from Daniel's, even though his complexion was.

One of the sleeves of his coat caught in the wind, flapping against his chest. The sleeve was tied off toward the middle, showing that his left arm came to an end near his elbow.

"We getting refugeed," the man said. His eyes were clear and blue. "Massa done sent us along to his people in Meridian 'cause he was scared the Yanks would come set us free. We on our way, and if you on your way . . ." He shrugged. "Just seemed like it wouldn't hurt none to ask."

"Refugeed? Does that mean that there are soldiers or an overseer with you?" Daniel's grip on his gun tightened. He glanced briefly at Janeta, who was tilting her head as she did when she tried to understand a word. "Some masters send their slaves to areas where they think they'll be safe from Union soldiers, often with an armed detail to prevent them getting stolen or running off themselves. They call it refugeeing."

The man shook his head. "No, nothing like that. Massa ain't that rich, and we ain't got no need for an overseer. The old man know we gonna go where he told us to go." His brow furrowed a bit.

Janeta stared at the man. His expression was too earnest to hide malice, unless he was very, very good at pretending. She had been fooled before, but mostly because she'd wanted to be. That was not the case here, and she studied him intently. There was concern in his eyes, and a hesitation that someone pressing a lie wouldn't have left room for. He wanted them to come along, certainly, but mostly because he seemed to be worried about their welfare.

Janeta approached Daniel and spoke in a low voice. "It would seem to me that if we wish to avoid being discovered for who we are, it might not hurt to surround ourselves with those who we aren't."

"What do you mean?" Daniel kept his eye on the man but leaned his ear toward Janeta.

"I mean that when we were on the pook turtle we came under attack just as if we were soldiers. If we are with a band of refugeeing slaves, people will not think to check to see if we are detectives. We can part ways when we get to Meridian, and we have our papers to prove we're free." He didn't say anything, and she wondered if perhaps she wasn't being naïve again.

"I'm not sure it's that simple," Daniel said. "But let's see what there is to see."

She was surprised he capitulated so easily.

"Perhaps it will be safer for you to be with others. I put you in danger with my wailing," he added grimly before turning to the man. "We will come visit your camp and then decide whether to head out with you, if that's all right."

"I'm Augustus," the man said, holding out his right hand. Daniel shook it reluctantly and Janeta inclined her head in his direction.

Augustus smiled, revealing two large front teeth that were so immediately endearing that Janeta was even more sure he wasn't leading them into harm's way. She hoped she was right.

"Let's head back."

Chapter 11

Daniel wasn't sure what he'd expected to find — he'd been tensed and prepared for a trap, which wasn't much different from how he navigated most every situation these days — but instead they found a small group of Negro men, women, and children engaged with preparing breakfast or breaking up their camp.

It unsettled him, how near they had been in the great stretch of woodland. If Daniel's pathetic cries had attracted unwanted attention, these people could suffer for it as well. And if they were this close, that meant others might be as well.

Daniel followed Augustus over to where a man who resembled an older, more haggard version of Augustus was loading up the wagon. His hair was curly instead of pin straight and his skin a shade darker, though still light enough to unsettle Daniel at first glance.

"Jim, this here is Cumberland," Augustus said. Daniel could hear something underlying his tone — deference? Apology? Or perhaps something more sinister? "I found him and his lady out in the woods, and thought it would be nice for them to travel with us. They headin' toward Meridian, too, so it just makes sense."

Jim heaved a sigh, and Augustus shifted from foot to foot and frowned.

"If it's a problem, we can leave," Daniel said. He didn't know what the tension between the two men was, but he had troubles of his own and didn't need to get drawn into anyone else's.

"Ain't no problem with you. It's him that's workin' my last nerve. You got any siblings, Cumberland?" Jim asked, his gaze on Augustus.

"No." He glanced to his side and found Janeta had wandered off. He tracked movement in his peripheral vision and saw she'd made her way toward the women and children as if they weren't among possibly dangerous strangers. He would have thought she'd know to stick close to him, but if there was anything he'd learned about his partner it was that she was too trusting.

He looked back to Jim, who snatched off his hat and scrubbed at his curls.

"Then you might not understand how aggravatin' it is when you tell your fool-head little brother not to go chasing into the dark woods for sounds that might be slavers baitin' him, and he does it anyway."

Daniel felt something move through his body in a wave — the slightest unclenching of clenched muscles. There was no faking that type of anger for the well-being of another. That didn't mean Jim's care extended to Daniel and Janeta, but it did mean that they likely weren't a threat. At the very least, not the kind of threat Daniel had anticipated.

"Well, as luck would have it, I'm not a slaver, and if I happened upon any they'd sorely regret that our paths had crossed." He fixed Jim with a stare, but the man was too busy looking at his brother in consternation to pick up on Daniel's subtle threat.

Augustus huffed. "I'm sorry, Jim. I couldn't ignore someone hollerin' like that. No way. Mama raised us better than that."

Jim sighed again, bent and hauled a stack of blankets onto the back of the wagon. "You right. Long as these two ain't trouble they welcome. We could use the help." A peal of high laughter erupted and Jim's gaze jerked toward the source. "Go help Shelley gather the children so we can load 'em up."

After Augustus walked away, Jim turned to Daniel, rubbing his hands together to ward off the morning cold.

"You're in charge here?" Daniel wasn't quite rid of his suspicions.

"Yup. Though when we get stopped it's Augustus who does the talking. Got our daddy's colorin'."

Augustus could pass anytime, depending on who he encountered, and Jim by dark of night or by firelight. Sending an Augustus out with your refugeeing slaves — or even a Jim — with no overseer was risky at the least, and more like flat out foolish for a slave owner who really wanted to keep his property. But here they were, heading toward their assigned destination with no overseer in sight.

It didn't make sense, and Daniel couldn't put his trust in things that didn't add up. He could barely manage for things that did.

"Your master trusts you to travel without a chaperone? What's to stop you from running off?"

Jim spat, then ran the back of his hand over his mouth. "This ain't all of us." He hefted a barrel into the wagon, and Daniel heard the cluck of a disgruntled chicken somewhere behind the stacked belongings. "He got mine and Augustus's mama, Augustus's wife, my sons, Shelley's husband."

The sick vouchsafe that had been put in place by Jim and Augustus's master clicked into place for Daniel with a surge of anger. "He's making you choose between freedom and family?"

"I suppose that's always the choice for us, but yep." Jim pulled his hat down on his brow. "My old man ain't ever showed us a feeling besides anger, but he sure know how to use them soft ones against us when he need to. Some folk might run off, but all of us here got something to lose that we can't imagine living without. Like he stacked the checkerboard and gave hisself a bunch of kings to start with." Jim shook his head. "It is what it is. You welcome to join us long as you don't start no trouble, like I said."

Jim walked off, leaving Daniel beside the wagon. Daniel couldn't think too long on the awful cunning, of their father's plan. If they were heading the same way anyhow, perhaps they could be of use to one another.

He began loading children up onto the wagon as Augustus and the slight woman called Shelley brought them over. He realized this was another play by their master — escaping the South with this many young children would be near impossible.

Augustus made the introductions. "This

here is Mr. Cumberland. He gonna travel with us for a ways with his woman."

Shelley's features opened a bit once she understood that Janeta and Daniel were an item. "Welcome. Janeta is very kind. Already helping us with the children."

Daniel again almost disabused the strangers of the false notion about him and Janeta, and again failed to do so. It made no difference what strangers thought of them, and if his supposed attachment to her could make others comfortable, then he would let people presume. And if it kept her safe, well, that wouldn't be too bad, either.

He rolled his shoulders in annoyance with himself. This was the part of having a partner he hadn't wanted — caring about whether she was safe.

He could throw himself into dubious frays without a thought. It didn't matter whether he lived or died, and a great many things would be better if he happened upon the latter. But having a partner, even one as annoying as Sanchez, created a link similar to the one that had these slaves escorting themselves over dangerous territory because they'd not let their families come to harm if they ran.

The image of her pinned beneath him on the wooden planks of the boat came back to him suddenly. The fear in the wide eyes of a woman who'd gotten herself mixed up in a war she seemed to know nothing about really. The softness of her.

He rolled his shoulders again.

"She is very easy to get along with," he lied. He could be cordial when he wanted to. He'd once done it without even thinking. And though it strained him now, he allowed himself to savor the small mercies of this encounter. To these people, he was just a fellow traveler, who loved and was loved by a woman — the normalcy of that, in the middle of the awfulness of the truths that constantly cropped up in his mind unbidden, warmed him.

Of course, he could never love or be loved again, but he would take this brief oasis in the desert of his torment and continue the farce.

Janeta walked up, carrying a little boy on her hip who could be her own. A trail of children followed behind her, and a woman called Mavis, but the boy stared at Daniel wide-eyed.

"I found us a friend, Daniel," she said, using his first name. She'd already picked up on the roles they would be playing. "Moses said that he couldn't sleep because he was afraid of monsters attacking during the night. I told him that I knew a monster slayer."

She winked at him and Daniel felt the oddest twinge in his chest. He remembered a conversation he'd had with Elle, when he'd assumed that their future paths were one and the same. He'd been talking about how he wanted children, and she'd shaken her head and told him she didn't know how he could consider it in a world such as theirs.

"You can't keep them safe, Daniel. You don't know just how bad it can be."

He'd hated how he could never talk her around to his point of view, never be right. But she had been correct about this thing, too. He'd learned that the moment he'd been unloaded on the plantation and saw the children crouched in the field at their mothers' knees. He'd learned it when he'd thought he would use his education to help them, and had ended up providing nothing but sorrow.

Winnie's father barged out of the shack, moving through the crowd of his friends and arrowing straight for Daniel. His face was a mask of fury and though he was smaller, he shoved Daniel hard enough to knock him back onto the hard clay ground. Daniel probably could have been knocked over by a feather, after the punishment he'd endured — noose around his neck just enough to hold him upright and just enough to kill him if his legs gave out. He'd spent hours on his tiptoes, muscles burning and bloody back wracked with pain, unable to relax an inch without his airway being cut off.

"Is Winnie all right?" he rasped. He wasn't even sure the words made their way out. "I tried to stop him."

"No, she's not all right! Her hands —" Her father's face contorted with grief, but then his anger pulled him back from the precipice of tears. "We was fine 'til you came here thinking you was so smart. Ain't even smart enough to hide what you learned those children. Ain't even smart enough to make the overseer think you stupid. That big brain of yours gonna fix Winnie's hands? You know what use they find for a Black girl whose hands ain't good for pickin'?"

Her father's frustrated tears finally streaked down his cheeks, and bile rose in Daniel's raw throat.

He'd only wanted to help.

Her father kicked at Daniel in frustration, but without much force. "You always talking about how you don't belong here and you right. You don't. Been nothing but trouble for us."

He turned and walked back into the cabin,

the other enslaved people following him, leaving Daniel alone on the ground, gasping for air.

Worthless. He was worthless.

Daniel shut his mind against the bad memories. He'd already relived them in his dreams, and he needed to pull himself together. Besides, seeing Janeta holding the boy and hearing her tell him that Daniel could protect him made him feel good, even if it was a lie. He could pretend this thing for a little bit, too, just until they got to Meridian.

The boy looked up at him with open awe and Daniel sucked a breath in through his nose. It *wasn't* a lie. He would slay anyone who tried to harm this child, or any of the children they were traveling with. He would never let such a thing happen again.

He walked up to the boy, mustering up a conspiratorial smile and stroking his beard. "Morning, Moses. You've been informed correctly. I *am* in fact a monster hunter, and a monster slayer when the situation calls for it. I have a special knife that I use for the task." He lifted his wicked blade by its handle, revealing a flash of sharp metal before letting it drop snugly back into the sheath. The boy's eyes widened and Daniel continued with faux bravado. "The monsters are the ones who should be afraid now. Not you."

"Really? That knife kills monsters?" Moses glanced up at Janeta for verification and she nodded.

"*Sí.* But it's not his knife that makes the monsters afraid." She took Moses's hand in her own and stepped forward, closing the gap between them until she could press the boy's palm against Daniel's chest.

The warm pressure of the small hand filled Daniel with wonder and joy, erasing the last vestiges of the nightmare he'd had earlier.

"You feel that heartbeat?" she asked.

Moses nodded.

"*That* is what the monsters fear. A knife is sharp and deadly, but there is nothing more frightening to evil than a kind heart and a strong soul, and Daniel has both of those."

Anger slapped at the edges of Daniel's enjoyment in their game. He'd put up with Sanchez for these past few days, but this was a lie too far. His body was strong, but the heart and soul within were weak. She'd witnessed him yelling pathetically into the night. She'd held him while he wailed like a child. She must be making fun of him, pointing out his weaknesses for all to see and laugh at.

His anger rose sharp and fast; then Janeta spread her hand out on top of Moses's, the two warm palms pressing through the fabric of his coat as she turned that honey gaze up to his.

She didn't speak, simply looked at him in defiance, as if challenging him to object to her words.

She wasn't teasing, it seemed. Simply mistaken. Simply unaware that she was talking to a shell of a man whose only value was that the blood in his veins could be spilled in the service of his people, and even that wouldn't be enough to save them. But Moses didn't need to know those things. He'd learn one day, but Daniel would not be the one to teach him.

Daniel nodded, and stepped out of reach of their dual touch, the cold morning air rushing in to suck away the heat where their hands had been.

"Moses, you've got strength in you, too," he said. "And goodness. Never let anyone tell you otherwise."

With that he turned away from the pair and continued helping with the loading of the wagon. It was absurd how, despite the chill, it seemed like there was an ember glowing right in his middle, where he thought his fire had long since gone cold.

Daniel ignored it. He couldn't afford to warm himself at the fires of anything other than his own burning need for revenge.

This situation was pretend, but he *was* a monster slayer; they were working their way through a Southern labyrinth, and Daniel intended on killing the man, mythical as a minotaur, that supposedly awaited him if they reached their destination.

Chapter 12

"A lawyer, huh?" Augustus asked again, lips pressed together and brows drawn as they had been since Daniel had revealed the profession he'd once pursued. They were paused alongside the rutted country road after stopping to let the children stretch their legs.

Daniel had been unprepared when Augustus asked for his profession while peppering him with questions about life outside of slavery, and talking about the Loyal League didn't seem like the best move to make just yet, no matter how friendly these people were. All it would take was for one child to overhear and pass the information on to the wrong person. And perhaps it wasn't fair, but Augustus and Jim were as close to white as any mixed-race Negro Daniel had ever met. It would be so easy for them to use their privilege against him if the situation arose, and he couldn't risk his fellow detectives or the secrecy of the Loyal League. He'd already risked them enough with his laxness since being assigned a partner. Instead, he'd reached into the scar tissue of his own past and painfully pulled out the truth.

"Yes. A lawyer." He glanced over to where Janeta was conversing with Shelley and Jim, and a woman named Mavis. She was better at making conversation than he was, but he had once been a social young man and would do his part. "You changing your mind about asking me along?"

Augustus laughed and tugged at the brim of his hat. "No! It's just I never thought I'd meet a Negro lawyer. I guess it's true that anything is possible up North."

"You still haven't met one. I never achieved that dream," Daniel pointed out. He wouldn't share how his own naïveté had stopped him. "But I suppose that freedom, even the limited freedom we have there, makes many more things possible. I was lucky enough to be born in a place where there was a lawyer willing to take me on."

And his own weakness had lost him that chance.

"It seem unfair, don't it? How where you born can change everything? Jim always say that we was born cursed. Daddy said it say so in the Bible. Mama don't like that, but what can she do?" Augustus turned his baleful eyes on Daniel. "You think we cursed?"

"I think it's convenient to a great many people for us to think that we are," Daniel said, affronted. It was one thing for him to believe himself cursed, and his country cursed. He would never go so far to say his people were, especially in support of a man who used that idea to justify evil.

"Daddy like to talk about the glory of the South, too. Say we cursed, but men like him were blessed with the land and the slaves, and a leader like Davis to guide them toward victory." Augustus's blue gaze was no longer kind and jovial. "Davis. Some days I wish I never had to hear that man's name again."

Daniel nodded. This was something else he wouldn't share. He didn't want Davis's name wiped from memory. He wanted it to be a name remembered always — to be the name that struck fear into the hearts of those who had assumed the Confederacy could rise from the sweat of Negroes and not pay for its hubris in blood. He rested his hand on the hilt of his knife, wondering if the idea that had swirled in his mind since the Russians had told them of Davis's voyage was going too far — or not nearly far enough.

Janeta came over to them then, her teeth chattering a bit as she smiled at them both. She still found this cold unbearable and she hadn't even experienced her first snow. Her discomfort annoyed him, and he hated that part of that annoyance was the fact that he could do nothing about it. He shouldn't care about her comfort. Shouldn't amounted to a whole lot of nothing when he *did.*

No heart, he reminded himself. *This is just pretend.*

"Your man was telling me about his lawyering," Augustus said. "But you know all about that, I imagine."

Janeta shook her head. "No, I don't know very much. He doesn't know much about my life before we met, either. It can be hard sometimes, when you meet in the midst of war, to explain who you were before. Or sometimes you simply want to forget, so you make no explanations. And we are all of us changing, no? I am a different person than I was even a few days ago."

She said the words so casually that all he could do was look at her. What was she about? He'd thought he'd known, but she kept turning out to be different. Better. He reminded himself that she was nothing but a burden that Dyson had tied him with. She was someone who knew what to say to get on a person's good side.

He remembered the warmth of her hand over his heart.

"I guess I never thought about that. Just meeting someone," Augustus said sheepishly. He shoved his hand into his pocket. "My wife, Clea, grew up on the plantation, too, and Jim's wife was from the neighboring plantation. Most of us here grew up with each other, so we always knew what we was like."

"I'm sure you've still changed, though," Janeta said. "I grew up around the same people and I don't think they knew what I was like any more than Daniel does. But tell me more about where you lived, if you don't want to forget."

Daniel watched her as she spoke to this man she'd met only a day ago, how he blushed and started telling her what she'd asked of him. Daniel *had* underestimated her. Jim came over, more sober than Augustus, but he smiled a bit at the fact that his brother seemed to be enjoying himself.

If her conversation had seemed effortless, Daniel might have been jealous of Janeta's talent. But though her lips curved up, her eyes showed tension as her gaze darted from person to person, as she paused to think of questions or responses. Maybe being surrounded by strangers didn't set her on edge the way it did for him, but this was work for her, too, even if she did it without complaint or acting out.

He could manage until they parted ways with these people. It would, in fact, be good practice for whatever awaited them. Daniel preferred quick and dirty work, but if the Sons of the Confederacy really were meeting with European agents, it would take something more than brute force or even a well thought out attack.

"How did you two meet? If you didn't grow up together?" Shelley had joined the conversation, and it was only then that Daniel remembered Elle, whom he *had* grown up with. He expected to feel the same anger or sadness, but before he could Janeta began to speak.

"Well, some friends of ours introduced us and told Daniel they thought we'd work well together. Daniel, of course, hated me."

Everyone broke up into laughter — except him and Janeta.

"I wouldn't say it was so strong as hate," Daniel cut in. "It was distrust."

"That's just as bad!" Shelley rolled her eyes.

"Oh, I can hardly blame him. I think I earned his distrust. But then something happened. In a moment where he could have thought only of himself, he thought of me first. He protected me. And he probably would have done the same for anyone, because that's the kind of man he is, but no one had ever done that for me."

She was taking their brief shared past and bending it just enough so it wasn't exactly a lie. Daniel knew this, knew what had really happened, so why did it feel like the truth? They were two Loyal League detectives playing the roles of traveling lovers, but she wouldn't look him in the eye any longer.

"Don't get me wrong, he's still a pain when he wants to be." Janeta tugged at the hem of her glove. "But I admire him very much. And I want to be worthy of his admiration, too."

Daniel didn't find the weather cold, like Janeta did, but the contrast between the autumn air and the sudden heat suffusing his body was stark. He wanted her to be lying, because if she wasn't, that meant the truth was that she admired him. *Him.* She had told him so with compliments that he'd brushed aside like pesky gnats, but here it was, said out loud in front of all these people. Now they would all think him admirable, too.

She was wrong. They were wrong. But it ached like an abscess how much he wanted them to be right.

"Oh, you can tell how sweet he is on her, just look at his face," Shelley said, then sighed wistfully. "All right, we should probably get a move on."

Daniel took up the rear, and Augustus joined him.

"Shelley probably embarrassed you, but that Miss Sanchez is real sweet on you, too, if that eases the pain at all."

Daniel nodded, then busied himself listening for anyone who might be following them with ill intent. That was much more practical than listening to the thump of his own heart in his ears, racing along with anticipation instead of panic. It was better than recalling Janeta's words and being warmed by them.

His mother had once told him a story about haint fires that would lure travelers off roads in the dead of night. They burned bright and hot, but they sucked the heat from you while you gloried in the illusion. He couldn't trust the delicious warmth spreading through his body. He couldn't afford to.

He walked, alone, and he listened, and he

reminded himself that it wasn't admiration he wanted, but revenge.

After they ate a dinner of grits and salt pork, everyone retired to sleep and Daniel took up first watch. The occasional cooing of the chickens, who had lived to see yet another dawn, could be heard during the lull of the wind rushing through the leaves overhead.

Over dinner, the adults had shared their stories of meeting their husbands and wives as the children had interrupted with questions and charming demands for attention. Janeta had sat beside Daniel, but not too closely, her low laughter confusing him with the thrill it sent through him. Everyone was speaking of their first loves, and he should have been thinking of Elle with the same anger and regret he usually did, but instead he'd fondly shared peering over the fence as a boy and seeing her after her family had moved in.

"So you were always one to make quick decisions?" Janeta had teased.

"Decisions that perhaps weren't always correct," he'd bantered back, not feeling the usual shame at his rejection.

"I think we all make bad decisions when it comes to love," Janeta had said, hugging her arms around her knees. "But we learn from them, and maybe we can make better ones in the future. We learn what we want, and how to ask for it. That way we don't imagine someone can give us things they cannot."

Something seemed to stretch between them in the flickering firelight, like a thin, nearly invisible strand of a spider's web. He didn't feel caught by that web; it was a silent telegraph line between them through which unspoken feelings were being transmitted.

It was a connection. And as the evening passed and Daniel listened and then laughed and then joined in the conversation, he felt the connections between him and each of the others fall into place. Moses came over and settled against his knee, leaving a smudge of pork grease on Daniel's already filthy trousers. Shelley asked him about being born free, and he'd asked her about her life as well.

When he'd been kidnapped and enslaved, he hadn't known how to communicate with the others on the plantation. He'd never been farther South than New York City, and it had been like waking up in a strange land, where he wasn't sure how to speak the language. He'd been unable to process his new life — he'd been bitter and resistant. He hadn't cared about making friends. He'd been angry at the way people just carried on, how no one fought back.

And then he'd fought back and learned why no one else did; not because he was more intelligent than them, but because they knew that the consequences were worse than Daniel had been able to imagine. There was a time and a place for rebellion; he'd chosen incorrectly and had acted without thinking of others. Everyone had suffered because of that.

By the time he'd tried to reach out, after he'd been broken by rope and by lash, many had written him off as a nuisance who brought them nothing but trouble.

Listening to his traveling companions speak of their lives — the good, joyful parts of their lives — struck him deeply. Instead of feeling his usual guilt and recrimination, he forced himself to focus outward, on others. To focus on the good memories they shared, and the full lives they'd lived in a society designed to squeeze the very joy out of them. The world wasn't suddenly a better place, but perhaps it wasn't so hopeless as he'd imagined.

Now Daniel sat as everyone slept, his head so full that it may as well have been empty. He'd allowed himself feeling and memories, and now his thoughts turned to Elle. He didn't feel pain or shame or anger; those things had nothing to do with her anyhow. All he knew was that he missed his friend, the person who had always pushed him forward and never let him off easily. He missed Elle, and she clearly missed him if she insisted on continuing to write. Now that he wasn't so focused on his own misery he realized that his effort to spare her from his weakness had likely felt no different from hurting her. And, despite what he'd told himself, perhaps he had *wanted* her to hurt as he had.

He didn't flagellate himself. Instead, he took a deep breath and reached into his pocket for Elle's latest letter.

Maybe it was the alignment of the stars above. Maybe he'd simply grown tired of hating everything and feeling nothing. He didn't know how long his bravery would last; he ripped open the envelope.

Daniel,

I've been made aware that you haven't been reading my letters, so I shall start this one the same way I have started the previous ones: I miss you dearly and if I ever have the good fortune of meeting you again in this lifetime, I will kick you soundly in the left kneecap before hugging the life out of you.

I hope you are well. I hear things because, well, you know why. It's what I'm good at. And because when it comes to you, I want to hear it all.

I won't ask why you are angry with me, though I'm sure we could have a lively debate over your reasoning, but I must ask why you seem to be angry with yourself? I don't care if you've truly become mean-spirited and dangerous, as some are saying. I don't care if you've done some of the more outrageous things being gossiped about. I do care why you are behaving this way because I'm not sure you know the answer to that yourself. I say that not to judge you, but to let you know that I am here, I am listening, and I care. If you take anything from this letter, then please let it be that. I CARE.

If you'd rather not discuss anything serious, then I shall take it upon myself to reminisce about something you may have long forgotten — that summer when Caroline Dunst felt fond of you and began baking you blackberry pies, not knowing you hated blackberries. Luckily for us both, I had no such character flaw. I haven't had a good blackberry in some time, and never a pie so delicious as poor Caroline's. I hear she's a baker now, and perhaps if this war turns out as we wish, we might stop by her establishment when next we visit home.

Things are going well with me. I have quite taken to marriage now that I've learned that it doesn't mean sitting around the house mending socks (Malcolm is very good at mending, so I need never worry about that). So much has happened that I want to share with you. I will still write from time to time, and I hope that one day you see fit to do the same, my friend.

Yours with love and consternation,
Elle

P.S. All right, I am going to admit that pretending to be patient is not my strong suit. Write to me at your earliest convenience or I will tell everyone that your favorite pastime was whittling kitten figurines. Let's see how your "monster of the 4L" reputation survives that. Is this a threat? Yes.

Daniel read the letter once more, a smile in his heart if not on his lips, then folded it and put it away. He wasn't sure what he'd expected — recriminations? Taunts and jests? Why had he ever worried that Elle would try to do him harm? There was a difference between not loving him as he'd wanted her to and purposefully hurting him.

She was happy, it seemed. And she cared for him, even after all this.

He'd worried that she would pity him, or treat him like a broken man, as his parents and friends had, but she hadn't tiptoed around his feelings. He couldn't say he enjoyed reading about her marriage, but Elle wasn't one to hide the truth to make him feel better. That did him better than knowing she cared. She didn't know the man he had become, but she wouldn't be deterred from making his acquaintance. Perhaps it was time he did the same with himself.

He stared into the fire for some time after that, his sleeping blanket wrapped around his shoulders and his ears strained for sounds that would indicate danger. After some time passed, he heard Janeta's light steps approaching him, and the fact that he wasn't sure if they meant danger meant she probably was.

Daniel remembered that he threw himself headlong into danger these days.

"Couldn't sleep," she said as she approached. "I will be quiet if you don't want to talk, but I wanted to sit by the fire. This cold is unbearable."

She dropped down to the ground with clear fatigue and tucked her skirts tightly about her legs.

"You look like you'll drop off at any second," he noted.

"I didn't say I wasn't tired, I said I couldn't sleep." There was a bit of an edge to her voice, but he knew how irritable lack of sleep could make a person.

"Did the conversation over dinner rouse some unwanted memories?" He told himself he was poking at her, not that he actually cared to know her answer. She'd mentioned a man back home who had sent her off. Maybe she was thinking of him while stuck with a damaged imposter.

She didn't seem to feel stuck while describing how we met earlier.

Daniel tried to evade that thought. They were lying about their relationship to further their work. That was it.

"It did," she responded. When he glanced at her, her brows were raised in surprise that he had asked. "I feel like every day . . . every day I wake up and I might be someone different. And I don't know if that person is good or bad or a fool."

Daniel chuckled ruefully. "That sounds somewhat better than waking up certain of who you are, and wishing you were otherwise."

She sighed. "There is always something in the way of happiness, no?" She shrugged. "All this talk made me think. Well, I'm always thinking, but it made me think *more.* I'm sad because the man I thought loved me did not. Not the *real* me. But perhaps that is asking for too much when I'm not sure who I am myself. I know this babble makes me sound like a child."

She looked up at him and the vulnerability in her gaze moved through him fast and clean, like a blade.

"There's nothing childish about it," Daniel replied quickly. "We're always told that we have to know who we are and what we stand for. When I returned from my imprisonment and forced labor, the thing that seemed to bother everyone the most was that they no longer knew who I was. 'You've changed,' they'd say in this disappointed tone, and I never knew how to respond. Of course, I had changed!"

He sucked in a breath and lowered his voice. "Of course, I'd changed. But they wanted me to smile, and sleep through the night, and act as if nothing had happened. To talk of the war and freedom, but not to talk about the truth of slavery. It's one thing to read it in a pamphlet and another to hear it over dinner."

He expected her to offer him pity, but she was silent for a moment. "I think that's what people usually want. The pleasantries, based on what they consider pleasant. I *know* it's what they want because I gave it to them and they were never disappointed with me. If you look at a person, at how they look at you and speak to you, you can see what they expect and then give them that. And then they are content."

"But are you?" Daniel asked. The life she described sounded miserable. He thought of the first thing he'd noticed about her, how she was always watching and reading the room. "I must say that this trait is quite useful for a detective, but perhaps not the best adaptation for everyday life."

Janeta made a sound something like a chuckle.

"I was not happy. And it's horrible to say that I'm happy right now, but I am. My father is imprisoned and this country may destroy itself, but I feel different. More sure of myself." She smiled at him and there was nothing of the temptation she'd used when talking to the Russians, or the coy intelligence she'd used on the ship's lieutenant. It was an honest smile, and that was more enticing than any of her others. "Maybe this is the most me I've ever been."

He pulled out the piece of wood he whittled at when he needed something to do with his hands. "Do you regret it? Joining the Loyal League because your lover asked you to?"

"No," she said. "I regret that I had reason to join. I regret my father being imprisoned. But I don't regret this." She yawned, her lush lips parting before she covered her mouth with her hand. "I think I may be able to sleep now."

"Good night," Daniel rumbled.

He listened to her footsteps as she headed toward the wagon. Janeta said she knew how to make people happy when she spoke to them. He wondered if that's what the unfamiliar feeling in his chest might be.

Chapter 13

Janeta had never plucked a chicken before. She had never killed one, either — Shelley had figured that out when Janeta dropped the fowl she'd been handed with a shriek and grabbed her skirts. The small woman had taken it up by the neck and given it a quick, sharp swing, amusement on her face, before handing the carcass over to Janeta to be plucked.

Now Janeta sat with a dead chicken in her lap, panic rising in her as she tried to formulate a reason why she couldn't give Shelley what she needed. More importantly, why she wouldn't know this simple act of homemaking. She was good at lying, but this was so basic, like not knowing how to comb one's own hair — Janeta had figured that out quickly enough, though she still sported snarls that she hoped weren't detectable. They'd have to be cut out when she had time to deal with such matters.

There were so many things she'd never had to give thought to before leaving, like how her food was prepared. She could cook basic things, but she'd never had to do the dirty work of plucking or skinning, let alone actually killing the poor creature that would become her meal.

Moses sidled up beside her, a dubious expression on his small brown face.

"Want some help, Miss Janeta? Cook showed me how to do it real fast back home."

"Thank you, *chiquito,*" she said helplessly.

The boy grabbed the bird and began plucking dexterously, small hands flying as he explained what he was doing, just as someone had obviously explained to him. Janeta grinned, but the sudden realization of *why* such a young boy possessed this skill pulled her mouth down.

He was a slave. This small, beautiful, friendly boy who was afraid of monsters was owned by someone, and likely only knew how to pluck chickens because it served his master that he knew such things. Moses looked up at her, one hand gripping the chicken, the other full of feathers, and nausea roiled through her as she remembered that little girl who looked like her in the cane field. That girl, all the children and the adults on the plantation, had been owned by someone: her father.

Papi is a good man. He didn't know better. If he had known, he would not have made his living this way.

She held out her hand for the carcass, trying not to let her dismay show.

"You are such a good, helpful boy, Moses. Thank you for teaching me. I will do the rest now."

He beamed with pride, handing the chicken over to her before rejoining the other children, who played quietly alongside the wagon.

She began plucking again, and though she was at least making progress, she was nowhere near as fast as him. She was disappointed with herself, but she didn't let it show, and the tears she blinked away weren't from frustration, but from shame.

She was slow because her family's slaves, the people dark like her but whom she hadn't been allowed to mix with, had taken care of that work for her. And she had left Palatka, full of guilt and anger, to help make sure those people would *always* have to take care of others. That hadn't been her intent, of course, but she wouldn't lie to herself any longer. If she aided the Confederacy, she may as well slap shackles around Moses's wrists herself.

How could she be part of this? Why had she not given this thought before she'd left? Because if she had, the lies that held up her very identity, variable as it was, would have come crashing down. Perhaps it should have come down earlier, before she'd built over two decades of selfhood on who she wasn't instead of who she was.

Papi had never been cruel to her like Augustus and Jim's father. The brothers were the result of a similar union, though their skin color would have gained them more acceptance from Sanchez family friends than hers had. Would their father have married their mother if it'd been allowed in the States, as it was in Cuba? Did it make a difference in the end, when both of their fathers still owned slaves? The man refugeeing these slaves owned his love and his own children. He forced them to work for him. The thought sent Janeta reeling.

Had her mother truly been the only one to capture Don Sanchez's attentions? Had Janeta been his only *princesa*? She thought again of the girl in the cane field.

"She looks like me, Mami."

She began plucking furiously, focusing on the awful feel of feather tugged from flesh instead of the nausea threatening to overwhelm her. She could never be sure, but that fact made it worse. In her last weeks, her mother had ranted and raved, and no one had known what to do. She'd wasted away in her bed, refusing to eat, murmuring in Spanish and a language that sounded like the whispers in the slave quarters.

Iya ran mi. I tried so hard, iya.

"Did that chicken do you wrong before it met its maker?"

Janeta looked up and felt how her expression was contorted by grief and anger. She forced her features to smooth out as she looked at Daniel, standing just a few feet away. He'd been more open since they joined with the refugees, like the wails of his nightmare had bled some of the bitterness out of him, releasing it up into the gray morning sky.

He'd had longer conversation with Jim, Augustus, and the other refugeeing slaves, had talked freely and not resorted to barbs and anger, though he had gone quiet from time to time. He'd touched her arm, even joked with her, going along with the lie that they were an item.

She hated how much she liked that lie.

She had fallen asleep after their discussion the night before, cursing herself for saying too much, for fooling herself along with everyone else. But Daniel had been more open, and she wondered if that was what he'd been like before he'd been kidnapped.

"This chicken said something rude about the state of my dress," she replied, a smile curving her lips despite the turmoil in her mind. She glared at the carcass and gave it a shake, drawing a chuckle from him.

"Well, then it brought this aggressive de-feathering on itself." He sat beside her and held his hand out. "Let me."

She was confused, but she passed over the surprisingly heavy carcass and he took up where she'd left off. He wasn't quite so good as Moses, but a sight better than her.

"Did you sleep well?" he asked.

She'd been in the back of a wagon crowded with children and supplies, but her answer to him was honest. "I slept better than I have in some time, after speaking with you."

He chuckled and shook his head. "Good to know my conversation induces slumber."

She was opening her mouth to explain when he glanced at her, mischief in his eyes. Daniel was joking again, perhaps even flirting. Her pulse sped up.

"Last time it was you who fell asleep. And used me as a pillow I might add." She was struck then by how even though he'd held her at arm's length, he'd still fallen asleep against her. It had likely been because of pure exhaustion, but . . . She remembered sitting still, barely breathing as he dozed against her. That had all been forgotten after the attack, but now she remembered — vividly. It seemed Daniel had forgotten, too.

He pressed his lips together and she saw just the quickest flash of his tongue.

"That is true. I guess we're about even," he said. His voice was lower than usual, and something flickered in his eyes. She knew what she would have said if they were really a couple, or really flirting.

No, to be even I'd have to use you as a pillow.

But the mere thought of that sent all kinds of ideas tumbling through her mind. Ideas she shouldn't be having.

"This is a nice way to travel," she said suddenly, then immediately backtracked. "Well, the destination isn't nice, and neither is the reason for the journey. I just mean —"

"I got what you meant, Sanchez," he said quietly, his gaze on the chicken. "It's not my usual style. I prefer being alone."

She thought about his crushed soul. She thought of how he'd chuckled quietly when Jim had told a long-winded tall tale earlier as they'd set up camp, then seemed to catch himself mid-laugh, as if such simple joy wasn't allowed to him.

"Right," she replied, her ideas stopped mid-tumble. "Everyone has their preferences, I suppose."

That was an assumption on her behalf, since she usually tailored her preferences to whoever was in her vicinity.

Daniel sighed and brushed feathers from his thigh. "But I have to admit that perhaps companionship isn't the worst thing in the world."

She had been speaking of their newfound travel mates, but could he mean her, too? And their discussions?

No. He'd been sharp and cagey with her just two nights before. His newfound sense of humor hadn't been sparked by her, and she shouldn't care if it was. She was still untangling what Henry had really been about and didn't need to start feeling warm about the neck for the next man who happened to show her kindness. Especially a man who would hate her if he ever knew what her intentions had been when she joined.

"No, it is not." She sighed, and shivered a bit against the breeze. "I don't think I shall ever get used to this cold. I nearly froze through last night."

Daniel didn't respond for a long moment. "I should apologize again, for the other morning. I'm not going to sleep again tonight. I can't risk everyone here."

Had he not slept at all while keeping watch? Janeta was struck by how easily he decided to forego his own comfort.

"Do they happen often? These nightmares?"

"No, but I never can tell when they'll strike. That's part of why I preferred not having a partner. No one to endanger, and no one to look at me with pity when I woke myself squalling like I was still in a crib."

His voice was losing its lightness, like the bile was rising up in him again, clawing itself back up his throat to blot out his good feelings. She thought of how he'd listened to her talk about herself the previous night, how he hadn't judged her.

"Well, it's not like you wet yourself," she said absently. "I did that a few months back."

"Pardon?" His voice was strangled, but not by bile. She didn't think so at least.

"It was so hot, and I drank an entire pitcher of water before going to bed. I can sleep rather soundly sometimes, and well . . ." She didn't know where to go with the outrageous lie that had pushed itself out of her mouth to head off his despair. "I suppose the two of us make a fine pair. One who cries like a baby, and one who pisses like one."

When she turned to him he was staring at her wide-eyed. A tuft of feathers clung to his beard, and the shift of it just before his laughter shook it loose sent a surge of pleasure through her, almost as much as the sound that followed it. Daniel had a fine laugh, low and quiet, and his eyes crinkled at the corners, the crow's feet like irrigation ditches on the plantation but carrying mirth instead of water, which was no less vital.

She allowed herself to laugh, too. They were pretending after all. That they were a couple. That she was a Loyal League detective. That she wasn't hopelessly tangled in a knot of her own making. She couldn't think of Henry, or her father, or her true mission now. Not amongst these people. So she laughed and then grabbed the chicken from Daniel, pulling out the last of its feathers and holding it up.

"You finally done with that?" Shelley called out. She was smiling, too. "Come on and bring that bird over here."

Dios, *I'm tired of pretending, but this part? I don't want this part to end.*

Daniel stood, taking the chicken back

from Janeta with a bow before conveying it to Shelley. Janeta followed, in search of a task she could complete without assistance. Shelley set her to cutting up some wrinkled potatoes and withered carrots, and she did, only nicking herself once.

The chicken had crisped up nice and brown, dripping its juices down over the vegetables to mask their age in greasy goodness, and the sun had set, when the sound of approaching hooves startled them.

"Children, get in the wagon," Jim said. He'd been smiling a moment before, but now his face was blank. His lips pressed together into a blanched line as the children darted off, looking back longingly at their dinner.

Daniel came to stand beside Jim and Augustus, and Janeta began to walk toward him when he fixed her with a gaze shrouded in his familiar coldness. "Go mind the children with the women."

She thought of what he'd said to her when she'd tried to wander into the woods, and didn't argue, though she did pull out her guns as she settled into the wagon, peering out as three men in tattered gray rode up. These were men who, in another time, would have begged work outside of the Sanchez's Florida farm. Now they were infused with the confidence of uniforms and guns and dominion.

"What you doing out here?" one of the Confederate soldiers said. He looked to be of the lowest rank, the kind of man she'd have passed the note still braided up in her hair. A shiver ran down her spine when she saw how he regarded Daniel and put his hand on the gun at his side. His gaze slid to Jim and Augustus, wary. Could he tell?

"We just refugeeing some slaves," Augustus said. His voice had a different tone, a kind of aggressive but friendly confidence, and Janeta wondered if he wasn't imitating his father. She wasn't an expert at American grammar, but she was certain his words were meant to be vague. He could have meant they were the slaves, or that they were in charge of the journey, and both were true.

"You got some proof of that?" the soldier asked.

Augustus searched about in his pocket with his hand and pulled out a folded paper. The soldier took it and read, slowly, brow creased. His fingers caressed the butt of his gun and Janeta's heart began to pound. Sweat broke out on her brow as she remembered the bullets hitting the pook turtle — even the thick metal hadn't been impenetrable, and the canvas of the wagon would pose no threat.

These men, they can do anything to us. And no one would know. And if they did know, few would care, apart from a slave master worried over his losses.

That she couldn't even imagine Henry mourning her loss was a realization she would deal with later.

The tense silence stretched out. She could faintly make out the man's lips moving as he read slowly and silently. Daniel, Augustus, and Jim stood still, but the flickering firelight danced across their clothing.

"All right. Looks about true, and even if it weren't, ain't no place for darkies to escape to. They'd follow that North Star right into the muzzle of a Rebel rifle."

He handed back the paper as the other soldiers laughed.

"That's a mighty fine dinner, though," another of the men said. "Shame to waste it on darkies."

Janeta's momentary relief quickly veered into anger. The hungry children shuffled behind her, and she gripped her pistols.

"We got kids to feed," Augustus said in a low voice. "Master said we got to keep them in good condition on account of he don't want no slaves he can't fetch a good price for."

The soldier shrugged.

"Well, we's got orders to commandeer food and all that might be useful to us. Although, now that you mention it, maybe some little darkies would be more useful than chicken and taters. Chicken can't shine up my shoes and fetch my breakfast."

Janeta closed her eyes and prayed. She prayed for lightning to strike the man. She prayed to open her eyes and live in a world where she hadn't been blind to such monstrous acts, but when she blinked them open, nothing had changed. Nothing at all, except the sickening rage that filled her.

This wasn't fair. In no world could this be seen as fair. But this was reality. The world she had lived in, with pretty porcelain dolls and lacy dresses, was the fraying fantasy stretched thin over the ugliness, and it had been ripped irreparably.

"If it's to help the Rebs, of course you should take the food," Jim cut in, trying to sound pleasant.

"You're damn right," the soldier said, seemingly annoyed that his chance to take it by force had been undercut by the offer. "We're fighting to keep these darkies out of the clutches of the Yanks. Ain't no way in hell they should eat better than us. Bring us some drink, too."

The soldiers all dismounted — they didn't mean to just take the food. They would sit and enjoy it. Jim and Augustus moved away, but Daniel stood still, his back hunched and his shoulders stiff.

"Shoo, boy. The men are having dinner now," one of the soldiers said, knocking his shoulder into Daniel as he passed him. The soldier was a full foot shorter and scrawny — Daniel could have easily smote the man from existence. But the soldier didn't even think that a possibility worth considering. His friends had weapons and would be happy to use them.

"Over here, Cumberland," Augustus called out.

Daniel didn't move for a long moment and the Rebels stared at him. Finally, he turned toward the brothers and walked stiffly away.

The soldiers laughed and ate noisily, singing "Dixie" and other Confederate songs. Janeta had used to accompany Henry on piano as he sang in his slightly off-key voice. The memory made her sick. Had that been her? Really?

The children began to whimper, and she assisted Shelley in shushing them. Moses crawled into her lap and took the edge of her coat's lapel into his mouth. "I'm hungry," he mumbled around the material.

She ran her hand over his head and sighed. "It will be all right," she whispered. "Stay quiet now."

He nodded into her collarbone and Janeta glanced toward the fire. The men were finally standing. Augustus and Jim walked over, their expressions blank. The soldiers were looking toward the wagon now. One took off his hat and scratched his head, and another burped loudly. Jim shook his head, and the soldier started to get agitated.

"If you want another chicken, we can give you another 'un," Jim said. "But that's all you'll get."

One of the horses made a soft noise, and Janeta saw a shadow move against other shadows near them.

"Says who?" the soldier who had demanded the dinner asked.

The shadow stopped moving.

" 'Cause I'm fighting for my country, and that means I get recompense." His gaze slid toward the wagon again, eyes large and covetous, and Janeta's blood chilled. She understood what the soldiers wanted now. The same thing the *Yanquis* who had cornered her in her own home had wanted.

What Henry had sweet-talked her out of.

She settled Moses on the floor and pulled out her pistols again. Her hands were shaking too badly to handle knives.

"Are there monsters?" Moses asked.

"Shhh, little one. Go sit with the others." He scrambled across the wagon, where Mavis and Shelley stared wide-eyed. They couldn't see what was happening, but they seemed to have guessed. Unlike Janeta, they had probably been tensed for this as soon as the men had arrived. They hadn't been taught that Confederate soldiers were gentlemen, that they fought to keep women safe.

Suddenly, there was a loud whinny and one of the soldier's horses reared up before running off into the darkness.

"Aw, shit, that horse's got the supplies!" one of the soldiers shouted. "Didn't you tie him, Amos?"

"I did! I swear I did!"

The soldiers ran to the remaining horses, jumping into their saddles, and took off after the horse that had run off. They left nothing but dust and silence, and the lingering residue of their lecherous intent, in their wake.

Janeta didn't put her guns away, not yet, but she allowed herself to take a deep breath, filling her lungs after the shallow, anxious gasps she'd sipped while watching terror unfold. She'd already figured it out before Daniel reentered the circle of firelight, but still, something warm and proud and victorious pulsed through her when he appeared, resheathing his knife. He didn't look like he was savoring his hoodwinking the men, though. His face was drawn as Augustus and Jim confronted him.

The three men conferred for a moment; then they all approached the wagon.

"Don't much like traveling by night, but I believe it's best we break camp," Augustus said quietly. *"Now."*

He didn't meet Janeta's searching gaze as she hopped down. Shelley hurried down to help load the wagon around the children; then they all got a move on. Daniel walked behind the wagon, gun at the ready and gaze searching the dense forest, as they slowly passed down the road. The mule took a plodding pace in the darkness, guided by moonlight, but it was better than veering off the road or attracting attention by lighting the lamp.

Janeta hopped down from the wagon to walk beside Daniel.

"I hadn't planned on sleeping tonight anyhow," he said. "But you should."

"I'll stand guard with you," she said quietly.

She wanted to be near him and she didn't know why. It was different from when Henry had rested his hot gaze on her and taken her hand beneath the tablecloth. She felt odd, like she might cry or might scream if she didn't say what she needed to.

"Daniel?" Her voice shook.

"Sanchez?" His was flat — he didn't want to talk.

She reached out, bare fingers cutting through the cool night air because she'd dropped her gloves in the darkness of the wagon, and placed her palm over his heart again.

"You are a good man." Her words came out trembling, but she pressed on. "I know you do not trust easily, but this is something I would never lie about."

She felt his sharp intake of breath in the swell of his broad chest beneath her hand. She dropped her hand then, but she didn't leave his side.

They walked in silence broken only by the slow roll of wagon wheels, and together they listened for Rebels in the silent Mississippi night.

Chapter 14

Daniel awoke with no recollection of when he'd fallen asleep.

He'd kept watch for two nights after their dinner had been plundered before Janeta had finally forced him to lie down, reminding him that if any Rebels or slavers were to ambush them, he'd be of no use if he was so exhausted he could be knocked over with a feather. She'd said she would stand watch with Augustus as Daniel slept, but he was slowly growing aware of a weight behind him. On him.

He couldn't see her, as he lay on his side, but she had both arms wrapped around him, and her head rested on his shoulder. She held him tightly — protectively — as if she wouldn't let him go no matter what.

It was improper, her lying with him like that. It was absurd, how he wanted to stay and let the comforting warmth of her body continue to seep through the fabric of his coat. It was dangerous that he imagined rolling over and molding himself around her, fantasized what would happen if her eyes fluttered open and that smile of hers curved her lips.

It was *frightening* that he felt safe like this, that his first thoughts weren't terrible memories, that his first sound wasn't a strangled cry but a suppressed groan.

He'd been celibate since he'd returned from slavery, and during his enslavement he'd thought only of returning to Elle. He had many reasons to never let anyone close again, but Janeta's nearness was tempting. Not because he'd lusted after her, though want simmered in his veins, but the heat of her body pressed against his reminded him that there were good things in this world — pleasures as small as the feel of another person's heartbeat keeping time with your own — and he was trying so very hard to forget.

There, on the hard ground with the early-morning mist of a Mississippi autumn swirling around them, Daniel could feel himself wanting not only Janeta, but goodness, and light, and laughter, and that terrified him. He knew all too well how easily those things could be stripped away from a person after taking root, ripping away the parts of your heart and soul that they had been grafted to.

In that moment, he knew why he'd been telling himself he could never be happy, apart from the fact that he didn't deserve it. Because happiness inevitably died, either taken by force or withered on the vine. He wanted no part of that imminent loss, and especially not with a woman like Janeta.

He *shouldn't* want it, at least.

"You awake?"

The voice was thin and high-pitched — Moses's attempt at a whisper. Daniel tilted his head back to find the boy sitting cross-legged in the dried grass with a large stick resting over his lap.

"Moses?" he whispered. "What are you doing?"

"Keepin' watch," Moses said proudly, his shoulders dropping back and his chest puffing out.

A very different emotion filled Daniel as he looked up at the slim, dark boy and the determination in his eyes.

"You should be sleeping," Daniel said gently.

"Ain't tired," Moses insisted. Then he yawned, and his determination turned to sheepishness. "Maybe a li'l."

The boy stood and Daniel expected him

to walk back toward the wagon, but instead he took three quick steps and dropped onto the ground before Daniel, snuggling into the space against his chest.

Daniel stiffened, buffeted by warmth and emotion on both sides.

"Daddy let me sleep like this with him and Mama sometimes," Moses said. "I hope they get here soon. They said they was comin' after us, but . . . I hope massa ain't sold them."

Daniel's chest went tight. Children were so resilient. It was easy to forget that as they laughed and played, they were beset by the same fears the adults faced, except they could do even less to counter them. They could only hope that the world would do right by them, hope with the strength of imaginations not yet fettered by chains, even if their bodies were.

"I hope they arrive soon, too," was all Daniel replied, but he threw his arm over the boy, who sighed and cuddled closer to him. The boy's head smelled both sweet and sweaty, and his chest began to rise and fall slowly almost immediately. How long had he sat there wanting to be held?

Daniel could ask himself the same, he supposed. Janeta shifted behind him, though she didn't awaken, but Daniel didn't follow them back into sleep. He stared off into the woods beyond Moses's head, listening to the sounds of birds and small animals. He accepted the soothing warmth these two people gave him, even if he couldn't accept that he deserved it.

Eventually, he moved slowly to stand, extricating himself from the two. As he pulled off his jacket he saw Janeta reach for him and then move closer to Moses instead. Her eyes did flutter open now, and she did smile; then Daniel dropped his jacket over both of them with a nod and walked off toward the trees.

He washed his face in the creek that ran by near where they'd set up camp, the bracing water jolting him fully awake. If it wasn't so cold, and the camp wasn't so close, he would have stripped down and washed completely. He still stank of the anxious sweat that had bathed him as he watched the Confederate soldiers settle around their campfire and eat the food meant for the refugeeing slaves. For the children.

He was embarrassed Janeta had been so close to him, had been able to smell his fear and anger and impotence.

He'd wanted to hurt the soldiers badly that night. He'd felt it like a pounding in his blood, driving him toward them, demanding they pay for the pain they so casually wrought by experiencing it in kind. Unfeeling Rebels weren't deserving of mercy, from either God or man. But hurting them could have had far more dire ramifications. Could he have killed all the soldiers quickly and cleanly? Or would one have shot wildly, perhaps hitting an innocent child, or run off and brought back more Rebs to bear down on them? He hadn't wanted to see Jim, Augustus, or any of the others hurt because he hadn't been able to control his anger.

His hands began to shake as he remembered the way the Rebel had looked down on him from his horse. Daniel had wanted to put fear into that man's heart, the same fear that resided in his own.

If he accomplished his goal in Enterprise, that soldier and others like him would know fear. And those like Daniel might feel a moment of vindication — the knowledge that men who did the devil's work weren't impervious to justice. As good as Janeta and Moses's warmth had felt, nothing would feel as good as vengeance. He needed to remember this. If he didn't, he might lose sight of why he'd joined the Loyal League, and the unique opportunity before him.

"Are you feeling rested?"

Her voice came from behind him, and though his thoughts were in a dark place, he felt his face warm beneath his palms and the corners of his lips curl up. He swiped the moisture from his beard and turned to her.

"I am. I couldn't help but notice that you were beside me when I awoke."

"Yes." A statement of cold fact divorced from the warm memory of her that Daniel would have to fight against now.

He waited for her to elaborate, and when she didn't, he sighed. "Why?"

"I was cold." She raised a brow, but her gaze was soft. "And you were so worried about . . . making noise. I thought perhaps having someone near you might drive the nightmares away."

Daniel had absolutely nothing to say to that. The ugly voice in his mind told him that he should be ashamed that she'd thought he needed her assistance, but he found that something else was crowding out the shame. Gratitude. It didn't batter into him like a wave, but filled him slowly, like a rivulet pouring into a basin that had been parched by drought.

In those first months back home after being freed, there had been a brief period where he'd thought that everything would go back to normal. Then the dark thoughts had come, and the nightmares that left his throat hoarse and frightened his parents and neighbors. His father would shake him awake, telling him to pull himself together, that men shouldn't behave in such an unbecoming way. There had been such fear on his father's face, and sometimes anger. Daniel couldn't blame him — Richard Cumberland was the child of formerly enslaved people. How it must have galled to see his son unable to bear for such a brief period what some were born into and departed into the afterlife from without experiencing otherwise. Daniel knew his father had been trying to help in the only way the old man had known how to, but at the time Daniel had grown sullen and frustrated.

"Can't you just be there for me? Without judgment? Without pity?"

The words had flown from his lips, and he'd apologized without meaning it. Then he'd told himself that it was too much to ask, that he deserved no such grace, and he'd set out to at least die with a purpose if he couldn't live with one. But Sanchez — Janeta — had given that grace to him without his even having to ask.

She *was* dangerous.

"Thank you," he said gruffly. "You didn't have to."

"And you didn't have to protect me when we were on the pook turtle, or carry Moses on your back yesterday though you were too tired to walk in a straight line."

Daniel made a noise, and Janeta shrugged. "Do not think of yourself as a burden. You're not," she said softly, and the words tore into that secret longing he thought he'd shielded from everyone. He wanted to believe her so badly that the hope was a heavy ache in him. "I did it because I wanted to, but also because you deserve it. You deserve to be cared for."

Somehow, they were very close together now, despite the wide stretch of land along the water; he realized they'd been taking small steps toward each other ever since she'd answered yes to his inquiry. Had she done it unconsciously, as he had?

Her lips parted and she looked up at him through those thick lashes of hers. Whether she'd done it unconsciously or not, she was aware of their closeness now, and she wasn't shying away from it.

His voice was rough when he spoke. "You take things any man should do and make them seem noble."

She shook her head and took another step closer.

"Don't you understand? That you think any man should do these things *is* what makes you noble."

She was so close that Daniel needed only to lower his head to capture her mouth with his own. That he even thought of such a scenario was a shock to him, but less so than the sudden certain need he felt for her. It wasn't just desire that made his skin pebble beneath her gaze. He didn't deserve to have a woman looking at him like this — like he mattered. Like she would have him know that he did.

Daniel wondered what it would be like to *feel* worthy of such an expression. Maybe he could pretend, just for a bit, since they were already acting. Just until they parted ways with the people who thought them to be a man and a woman who were intimate. He leaned his mouth closer to hers, or rather allowed it to go where it would if he stopped holding himself away from her.

She didn't pull back. She held her ground as he moved closer, her eyes wide and expectant. He was inches from her face when he saw something peeking through her frizzed hair. A sharp cream edge, like folded paper. It could have been anything, but something about it sent a shock of foreboding disquiet through him. The women in the Loyal League often hid notes plaited into their hair, where prying eyes — and fingers — rarely ventured.

"You got any dispatches to send out, Sanchez?" he asked suddenly, halting his forward motion.

"What?" The smile that had teased about her mouth twisted into a grimace of confusion.

He pressed on. "I was hoping to find a way to send some dispatches before we got to Enterprise, so if you have anything to pass along, you can give it to me."

"You really are an interesting man," she said in what he supposed was a joking tone. "I have nothing."

Her hand reached up to smooth over her hair, over the spot where he'd seen the flash of cream, and his stomach clenched.

"All right," he said as he turned and headed back to the camp, the mantle of humiliation and anger he'd temporarily shed settling over his shoulders once more.

He'd forgotten himself for a moment. Dyson had joked about how green Sanchez was when he'd assigned Daniel to partner with her, but she'd always impressed Daniel with her ability to adapt. He remembered her introduction to the other detectives, how she'd picked up so quickly on what people wanted to hear, and responded accordingly. She'd told him flat out that she knew what gave people pleasure and excelled at giving it to them, and she was likely falling into habit, if not something more nefarious.

No one would be kind to a man like me just for the sake of it.

Daniel reminded himself of that truth, and that he'd have to watch himself with her from here on out. He'd allowed himself to slip into emotion, but no matter how friendly she was, Sanchez was dangerous. At the very least she'd aroused interests that shouldn't be aroused, and that alone was enough for him to keep her at arm's length. He had plans, and he wouldn't be distracted from them by pretty words and a prettier smile, no matter how much he wished he could believe them.

CHAPTER 15

"We should get to Meridian by evening, if the fella I just talked to knows what he's about," Jim said. He dragged his feet a bit, scraping away the mud that clung to his boots from venturing into the marshy field beside the road, where he'd spotted a man at work repairing a plow. "Then you two can continue on your way."

Daniel sobered. He'd spent so much time spinning fantasies of vengeance against the South or avoiding fantasies of Janeta, he hadn't actually thought about how he would get to the man who was key to all of this: the British consul. The Russians said he was a lord, or close enough. Unsurprising. The British wasted much breath on the topic of their staunch abolitionism, but the wealth of their empire was drenched in the blood of slaves. Tea and sugar tasted quite fine with scones, but they didn't appear on the isles by magic.

He considered discussing the matter with Janeta, but he'd avoided her for most of the day. She'd gotten too close, and it would take time to repair the damage to his mental defenses, and to his ego. He'd allowed himself to think she might really . . . no. None of that mattered, even if embarrassment flooded him at how close he'd come to pressing his mouth to hers. Not just because he knew she couldn't possibly truly want him, but because given what he knew of her, she might have let him do it anyway. She knew that her greatest skill was seeing what people wanted, but he wasn't sure she was aware that her greatest weakness was wanting to give it to them.

Daniel told himself that using that weakness against her wasn't retribution for stirring feelings he wished still lay dormant. Her smile had abruptly fallen away the first time he had greeted her with coldness after their near kiss. He'd decided he would treat her as he had the other detectives before she'd come into his life. The behavior hadn't won him any friends.

"Paranoid fool don't trust his own shadow creeping up behind him."

Daniel didn't need friends.

His fellow detectives didn't understand. How could he explain a night spent toasting his own bravery that ended with him locked in a coffin, choking on bile and fear? How could he explain his behavior on the plantation, his attempts to improve the lives of his fellow slaves that had only made things worse.

He hated that he'd thought Janeta might understand. No one would.

His scalp was prickling and his chest was beginning to feel tight, and he needed a distraction to ward off what might become a shameful attack.

"What will you do when you get to Meridian?" Daniel asked Jim.

"Well, we'll set to work preparing the house for our father and the rest of 'em who will come down soon after. He's got an overseer there waitin' on us, to make sure we don't feel too free after traveling all this way alone, I suppose."

There was no anger in Jim's voice. There was nothing at all, and it chilled Daniel to hear a man speak of his own forced servitude so blandly.

"Do you . . . do you want to get free?" Daniel asked, the words heavy on his tongue. He didn't know why he asked such a thing, or why he spoke at all.

"What I want don't matter," Jim said

bluntly. "What I want don't change nothing."

"But if the North wins, or the Yanks take Meridian —"

"If the Yanks take Meridian, I'll think on gettin' free then." A deep furrow settled on each side of his frown before he spoke again. "He was supposed to free us, you know. Before this war talk started. He was lettin' me and Augustus work toward our freedom, or so he said. Then the talk of emancipation started up and something went wrong in his head. He said we was his, and he wasn't letting a one of us go now, even if we could pay him." Jim tugged at his ear, then wiped a hand across his mouth. "On the day we got word of the proclamation, things got real heavy. Like, the air got all suffocating. He was slamming stuff around and muttering and getting in the way.

"We got word that our neighbor didn't want to deal with the bother. He called his slaves together and told them they was free to go, who wanted to go. They left by night, 'fore he could change his mind and 'fore anyone else could hear and lay claim on 'em. My wife was born to that master, and coulda been free if she hadn't married me."

Daniel had heard of such occurrences — masters who had reacted with resignation even as the Confederates marched on toward their supposed God-given glory.

"We didn't say nothing, but you could feel that knowin' buzzing through everything and everyone. We *knew.* And he didn't like that one bit. Pulled at his whiskey all the next day, face all scrunched and miserable, then marched us all to the bank of the river. Made me go stand right along the edge of a bluff." Jim's voice was rough now, and it cracked a little at that; he cleared his throat. "The sun was setting, and it was hittin' that muddy water so pretty, but the air was full of evil. And his eyes and his heart was full of evil. He pulled out his gun and fired before I even knew what was happening. I felt a bullet go right past my head."

Daniel thought of his annoyance with his own father, how he'd felt the man no longer understood him, but Jim and Augustus's filial relations gave him new perspective. His father had hurt him, but not like this. He wouldn't be capable of such malice.

Augustus cut in, voice hard instead of his normal cheery tone. "He said, 'You darkies belong to me. And I'd rather line you all up and kill you 'fore I let some Yanks take you from me.' I thought he was gonna shoot us all right there."

"Why didn't he?" Daniel asked, chest tight

just from hearing this awful recounting. He knew why they showed so little emotion; this story was a shout that would start a landslide of emotion if they let it. They spoke low and slow to avoid being crushed by their own pain.

"Mama. Mama went to him and talked real low and sweet, and he lowered the gun and took up the bottle and walked off with her." Jim shook his head. "She tried to convince us to run while we was refugeein'. Said Augustus could take us anywhere if we cleaned him up and slicked his hair. But we can't leave her with him. I don't know what he'd do to her or the others if we did. So here we is."

Daniel sucked in a breath. His master had been indifferent to the lives of his slaves — he'd given all his power to his miserable overseer, preferring not to dirty his hands with such interactions. He'd begun selling them off rather than put time and effort into refugeeing, saying that he'd rather have money in the bank than have to worry about slaves running off or being taken by Northmen. That was how Daniel had ended up on a Richmond auction block. He'd thought his experience uniquely grotesque, but Jim and Augustus's lives further affirmed his shame at his own inability to move on.

Still, Jim's cynicism cut him deeply. He wanted to tell the man to live, to think of his future and that of his family, but Daniel had been unable to do either of those things himself. How could he demand it of another?

Augustus sighed, and as he talked there was color and light in his voice again. "If we get free —"

"When you do," Daniel offered. His throat felt tight with emotion, and he cleared it.

Augustus nodded. "When. I want us to get some land, where we can farm and raise animals and provide for our families. Someplace nice, with a school for the children and a church where we can praise freely. I don't think it hurts none to plan for that. It's not asking for a lot."

"No. No, it's not," Daniel said.

Jim scoffed. "You think they gonna just let us have that? It ain't a lot, but it's *something.* They want to take everything we have, brother. I wonder if we could ever take from them like they done took from us."

Finally, Daniel asked the question that had nagged at him since the Russians had revealed plans of Davis's trip to him and Janeta.

"I've wondered the same. What we could take from them. For example, Jefferson Davis, who so many of them revere. What if he was stopped before his government could do further harm?"

"Stopped? You talkin' 'bout killin'?" Augustus asked. "I don't think we should kill folk. Not our place to play God."

"But we're at war," Jim muttered. "Why is stopping one man playing God, but killing a whole passel of 'em just fine and dandy?"

"I don't like no kind of killing, Jim, but there ain't no honor in assassination. That's what you mean, right?" Augustus glanced at Daniel nervously.

Daniel sighed. "I mean no disrespect, but what honor is there in letting a man who works to keep you in bondage live?"

"Mmm-hmm," Jim said. "No one ever thinks about doing anything to honor folk like us. I can't say I'd be sad if someone helped usher Davis into the afterlife, and all of those Rebs we had to hear about every night. I wouldn't be sad if they was wiped from the earth. If ever there was a time for smitin' and such, it's now."

Augustus shook his head, stubborn. "Well, I think the Lord will decide that, just like He'll decide when and how Davis is to go. Like I said, anyone who takes it on theirself is playing God."

"Or maybe they're an instrument of God,"

Jim said, clearly frustrated. "We get to be that, too, sometimes, instead of just cursed, don't we?"

"I've always wondered when our people will have our own Exodus," Daniel said.

"Exodus?" Jim asked.

"In the Bible, when Moses led the pharaoh's slaves to freedom," Daniel explained, but he caught the look of confusion that passed between the brothers.

"Ain't never heard of that bit," Jim said. "It's in the Bible you say?"

"Oh, I thought you meant little Moses," Augustus said with a chuckle. "He is named after a Bible fella, that's right."

"That's what they call that Tubman lady, too," Jim said slowly, realization dawning on him. "The one who leads folk to freedom, and talk about the North Star. Patty from Winston's farm told me about her."

A terrifying realization struck Daniel; for many slaves, the closest they were allowed to literature was the Bible stories they were told — most couldn't read for themselves, and they received the stories from others. But not every part of the Bible suited the ideas of enslavement. It would be so easy to foster a belief of the Word in a group of isolated slaves, while hiding what the Word said about freedom from them.

"I'll tell you about Moses, leading his people to the Promised Land."

Jim and Augustus listened eagerly, and Jim's dourness fell away as Daniel described the parting of the Red Sea.

"Wait, that don't seem fair," he exclaimed after Daniel had spoken of how Moses never reached the Promised Land himself.

"No, but I think it fine to work for your people's freedom even if you never see it yourself." He touched the hilt of his knife.

Janeta appeared at Daniel's side then. "I think we may have to rest soon. The children have had too much water to drink. We know what that can lead to."

She winked at Daniel, reminding him of her confession from the other night. She stared at him, as if trying to will him to open to her again, but he gave her a curt nod. "All right."

She lingered, as if expecting him to say more, and when he didn't she awkwardly turned way and headed toward the back of the wagon.

When he glanced at Jim and Augustus, they were sharing a loaded look. Let them think what they wanted. They would be parting ways soon enough, and they had problems of their own to deal with. If he felt the slightest pang of regret that he hadn't been able to smile and continue the playacting of a loving couple with Janeta, well, it wasn't the worst thing he had dealt with.

Chapter 16

Janeta hated the gulf of anxiety that opened up in her when she knew someone was cross with her. It was the fear of that gulf that drove her to twist and change herself into whatever pleased people most.

She'd felt she owed her family because, even though she had always been told otherwise, her reflection proved that she was indeed like the people working the fields, and serving, and cleaning, and everything else that required labor. She'd felt that she owed something to everyone who treated her like she wasn't, who saved her from a life of hardship.

So she gave them what she could of herself, and that had amounted to . . . everything.

She shrugged off any self-pity. She was free. All that had been asked of her was to make sure she was capable of charming everyone so thoroughly that they wouldn't begrudge her it. It was no hardship compared with the hardship of a life in the cane fields. After all, she could see what people wanted — all she had to do was fit into the mold they'd laid out for her.

Papi had wanted a doting daughter who clung on to his every word and made him feel like a great man. Her sisters had wanted a good, obedient girl who pretended her skin wasn't as dark as the slaves'. Henry had wanted a woman seductive but coy, exotic but familiar, fiery but submissive. And Daniel? He'd just wanted her to leave him be. He'd said that from the start. So it shouldn't have hurt when he'd retreated back into his cold, unsmiling behavior.

But it did. It cut her much more deeply than should have been possible.

That was just further evidence that Janeta Sanchez knew nothing. She'd thought herself brave and determined when she'd set out, but these days she felt like nothing more than what she truly was: a shell, filling itself with whatever was needed to please the people around it. Daniel had likely sensed that; after all, it was only when she'd tried to be herself with him, or what she thought to be herself, that he'd pulled away.

She'd tried talking to him in a friendly way after that morning at the river, and when that hadn't worked she'd tried to talk Loyal League business, and after that she'd tried desperate flirtation. He'd avoided her every time, and she'd eventually given up, keeping close to Shelley and Mavis and avoiding the women's pitying glances.

The truth of the matter was at hand: she had failed. She couldn't get information for Henry, and she no longer wanted to. She couldn't make Daniel want her help. She should just leave, but how? She'd have to find a telegraph and hope the message got to Henry, and then what? How would she get back to Palatka? How would Henry respond to her failure? How would Papi?

She hugged her arms around herself as the wagon jolted over the hole-pocked road.

"We'll be there soon," Shelley said, misinterpreting Janeta's agitation, and reminding her that there were people with bigger issues than being a spoiled, foolish *princesa.*

Shelley, Jim, Augustus, and the others would all be put to work. They would be in an unfamiliar town with people who might treat them even worse than what they had grown used to.

"I'm sorry," Janeta said. "That we're almost there."

"No need to be sorry. It is what it is." Shelley stroked the head of the child that lay curled in her lap. "We gon' be free soon enough. I know it. And folks like you are helping us to do that."

Janeta startled and Mavis laughed.

"Oh, of course we knowed you wasn't just two Negroes wandering the woods for no good reason in times like this. We talked to other folk like y'all before."

Shelley lowered her head shyly. "Wish I was brave enough to do that."

Shelley had misread her again. Janeta shook her head. "You're so much braver than me. Both of you. Truly. And . . . and . . ." She closed her eyes and swallowed, then opened them and met Shelley's gaze. "And I am going to do my best to help put an end to this war. For the North. For you."

Tears welled in her eyes and she dashed them away. Those words were — that *vow* was — a refutation of everything she'd promised to do when she'd left Palatka. They were an abandonment of her father. But she could help him in another way — she could help Daniel get useful information from this Englishman, and maybe from Jefferson Davis himself, and she could ask the Union to show her father clemency in return. Henry had told her there was only one way to free her father, but she was realizing that Henry also told people what they wanted to hear — and he'd wanted more in return than acceptance. He'd wanted to aid and abet very bad men.

It struck Janeta then, what she had circled and circled around even after admitting to herself that Henry had never loved her: he wasn't just helping bad men; he *was* one.

"Well, if you say I'm brave, I'm not one to turn away a compliment," Shelley said with a trembling laugh.

"You are. And even if you weren't, you would still deserve to be free. If there's something I can do to help that, then I will."

Janeta was so used to saying what people wanted to hear that she wasn't sure if her words were true or simply meant to make herself or Shelley feel better. All she knew was that, for the first time in a long time, her words didn't feel like a lie. For the first time maybe ever, she felt swayed by more than love for herself or her family or a man. Her chest filled with something — an overwhelming desire to be better, to do more.

She thought of her mother, broken by the lies she had told herself and her daughter and anyone who would listen. Janeta would no longer break herself trying to shape herself into other people's desires.

Janeta Sanchez was a fool, *insensata,* but even a fool could do the right thing.

Homes began cropping up along the road, many abandoned or damaged, and fields that had been cleared of their harvest or hadn't been tilled for some time and lay fallow. It was only after passing several empty barns that Janeta realized there were no animals to be seen besides the mule that pulled their wagon. And though there were houses, there weren't many people, though she could feel the gaze of strangers from darkened windows.

War had touched these people in a different way than it had in Palatka. There had been skirmishes outside the town and on the river, but the struggle for control had been a matter of numbers and not force, with the goal occupation and not destruction. The *Yanquis* who approached her home generally had done so while feigning civility; they'd smoked cigars with her father and drank his rum, while eyeing his fine daughters. Even when they'd led him to the stinking prison, they'd done so with regretful looks.

The area they passed on the way to Meridian had not been given such courtesy; it had seen heavy battle. She'd heard Daniel talking to Jim: after Vicksburg, the land had been fought over in a game of tug-of-war. Soldiers from both sides had likely taken food and supplies from the people here, and likely more.

She would have felt untainted pity for these people at some point — already poor and having lost more than they could possibly ever regain. Back home she had helped organize food and clothing to be sent to those in nearby towns. But now she had to wonder how she would be greeted here were she to knock at one of their doors and try to talk as if she was their neighbor, let alone their social better.

Janeta shook her head; she didn't have to wonder. She knew. Her assistance wouldn't have been given a welcome with open arms, as she'd received from the refugeeing slaves. As they reached Meridian's main street, she felt a heaviness in her chest knowing that she was leaving Jim and Augustus and Shelley and Mavis — she couldn't even think of Moses and the other children.

"Are you gonna come visit us? After mama and everyone else come?" The little boy's eyes were round and hopeful as they unloaded from the wagon, and Janeta did what had always come so easily. She told him what he wanted to hear.

"Of course, we will come visit you! Daniel and I will not be here long, but we will see you before we depart."

She glanced at Shelley, who was staring at the ground working her bottom lip with her teeth.

"That would be something," Shelley said. She looked up and her own eyes were glossy. "Would be something even better if old Abe sent some more of the boys in blue round here, but to hold the line this time."

"Don't know for sure nothing is better or worse until it happens," Jim said with his usual cynicism before turning to Janeta and Daniel with worry in his eyes. "You sure you both gonna be all right?"

Her chest squeezed because she realized then that, though they were enslaved, Jim and Augustus had some power imbued by the color of their skin and how people perceived it. They'd offered more than companionship for the journey — they'd offered what little protection they could. And now they were worrying over whether Janeta and Daniel, free people, would suffer its loss.

She swallowed a sob. She couldn't ever allow herself to forget that she had once agreed to help the men who wanted to keep Jim and Augustus and Shelley as their property, forever. It shamed her, but she would use that shame as a guiding light.

"We will be," Daniel said. His voice was flat and he couldn't quite make eye contact as he shook each person's hand. He turned toward Janeta, so she saw the painful surprise on his face when Moses's arms went around Daniel's legs.

The boy looked up with a serious expression. "Don't worry none, Mr. Cumberland. *I'm* gonna protect everyone from the monsters now."

He held up the stick he had been toting around since the Rebel soldiers had come to the camp, displaying it with the same fierce pride Daniel had displayed when he'd shown the boy his knife upon their first encounter.

She expected Daniel to keep up the quiet, withdrawn demeanor that had eclipsed his sunny behavior — and their near kiss. Instead, Daniel smiled and picked up the boy and seated him on his shoulder. Moses's squeals of delighted laughter echoed over the group.

Daniel's voice was deep and rough when he spoke. "Moses has very bravely offered to protect you all from monsters, but I request that you all protect each other. Can you do that?"

"Yes!" The other children swarmed around Daniel's legs as he swung Moses down.

"Well, then I guess we'll be off," Daniel said. "Take care of each other."

"Y'all do the same," Augustus said. Then their friends continued down the road. Shelley peeked out from the back of the wagon and gave an abbreviated wave.

Janeta didn't understand why it was so painful to walk away from these people. They had only spent a few days together. She'd met hundreds of people in the parlor of Villa Sanchez. She was used to saying goodbye. But this was the same glancing ache she'd felt when Lynne and Carla had gone off on their mission, leaving her with Daniel. She was leaving people who accepted her at face value, and seemingly liked her as she was. And she was being left with Daniel, who had frozen her out. If she hadn't known true cold before, she certainly did now.

"Time to see about this Roberts fellow," Daniel said. He walked stiffly and wouldn't even look at her. They passed an older Negro man in front of a general store who cast a suspicious eye toward them, and then went inside the squat building.

Janeta looked around them: it was an average main street, lined with small businesses and horses and people milling about, like she'd seen both in Santiago and Palatka, but everything seemed ominous.

The townspeople going about their daily business glanced at her and Daniel and whispered behind their hands, or actively glared at them. One man spit his tobacco in an arc that landed in a dark mass on the ground right beside her foot; she had to force herself not to gasp.

A sheen of sweat broke out over her skin, raising the chill bumps, and she shivered. She remembered what her mother had told her when she reached adolescence, hunching over to avoid the stares of strange men and sneering women. *"Chin high, shoulders back, remember that your father can crush any of these fools who look down their noses at us."*

Janeta adjusted her posture. Her father wasn't there to help, though, and she had a very bad feeling about the people around them.

She tugged Daniel's sleeve and he stopped without looking at her.

"I think maybe we should head back the way we came," she said.

"Why would we do that? We've already dallied longer than we should have."

"Because I don't think we are welcome

here," she said.

Daniel sighed. "See, this is why I didn't want a partner."

Janeta felt a flare of anger. "Why? So no one would tell you when you were acting like a stubborn ass?"

When he finally looked at her his gaze was blank and she shivered again.

"No," he said. "Because you think I care about a welcome."

The approach of footsteps made both Daniel and Janeta turn their heads. She was already frightened and so upset at Daniel's change in behavior that she wanted to cry or scream or both, and the sour-faced man standing before them was surely not going to improve her mood.

"What business you got around here?" the man asked. "Where's your master?"

His cheeks and nose were red, as if he'd been drinking recently, or drank so often that it was his natural complexion. His eyes glinted with amusement, but not the kind that would bode well for her and Daniel.

"We have no master," Janeta replied, trying to keep her voice bordering on insouciant and respectful. "We are here seeking out Brendan Roberts."

"Oh, are you now?" The man asked in a mocking tone. "On what business?"

Others were ambling up to join their initial interrogator, curiosity and annoyance and mischief on their pale faces. Janeta knew what they were thinking. It had been ingrained into her for her entire life, even if no one had said it aloud.

Up to trouble. Up to no good. Got to keep them in line or there'll be chaos.

She glanced at Daniel, at the way his face had gone blank and expressionless. She knew that beneath that mask he was bound by fear. Fear that clung and restricted like the knots of scar tissue on his back. It didn't matter if he hated her — she would say anything to stop the anguish that caused him to cry out into the night and cut himself off from the rest of the world. She would tell any lie, because lies were all she had to give him.

"The man asked you what business you're here on," one of the new arrivals to the scene said, his eyes narrowed.

She sucked in a breath, straightening her spine and looking down her nose at the man. "The business of the royal family of Spain, by way of Cuba."

They looked at each other, then burst out into laughter.

"You darkies expect us to believe you're here on *royal* business?"

Their laughter continued, stretching out well past comfortable until the keening barks transformed from jest into threat. Janeta had perhaps pushed too far, but she couldn't let doubt creep in. She had to play this just right, or she'd put Daniel in even more jeopardy.

"We are Cubans, sent here to report back on this American war and how the people of the South conduct themselves," she said haughtily. "The queen would know from her own subjects whether the Rebels are worthy of aid when she might use the funds to cultivate her own interests in the Americas."

The expression on the man closest to her wavered between anger and fascination. "Well, look at this one talking all fancy." His gaze cut to Daniel. "And what about you, boy?"

"Yo soy Daniel. Soy Cubano," Daniel said, his eyes still blank. *"Un día seré libre."*

Janeta suppressed her shock at his words and turned back to their interrogators. "He doesn't speak English."

"What should we do with 'em, Wil?" one man asked another.

"You have two choices," she cut in. "You can continue to insult me and my traveling partner, and we have received many insults in this country that supposedly wants aid from Spain, or you can take us to Roberts and let him decide whether we are worth laughing over."

The man named Wil slid his cold gaze over both her and Daniel. "I think we have a sight more choices than that, honey."

Janeta should have been angry or frightened, but she was suddenly very tired. Life was difficult in ways she had never imagined while coddled by her family. She couldn't move freely without threat, she couldn't speak freely without ridicule, and all because her skin was brown like her mother's had been.

When she was a child, Janeta had sometimes wished she could wash the brown hue away so that she looked like her father and sisters and their family friends. It was only after Mami had passed that Janeta had grown fond of the golden umber of her skin in the looking glass. Her mother had always walked with her head high, and Janeta realized now why that was — because people were always trying to push her head down, to use her as their stepping stone. Janeta understood her mother less as she grew to know herself more, but of one thing she was certain — Benita Sanchez had done what she thought was necessary to give her daughter a better life. She hadn't wanted Janeta to experience this disrespect — the type of humiliation that seemed to be one commonality in the vast American experience.

"I was told someone was inquiring as to my whereabouts?" a crisp British accent cut in. Janeta glanced over and found the slave who had been watching them with interest a few moments earlier standing beside a man whose clothing announced his wealth and whose bearing served as a reminder. His face had a hangdog look about it, and his dark hair was a bit unkempt, but his eyes were sharp and his gaze darted between her and Daniel.

Janeta watched him closely. She'd need to know how to proceed.

"Just these two darkies messing around," one of the men who detained them said in annoyance. "We didn't want to bother you none. Probably just runaways spreading some lie to get away from work. You know how lazy they are."

There it was — Roberts's lip curled slightly in disgust at the word *darkies,* before quickly schooling itself back to drab calmness. He should have been used to such a word, and it was surprising that he didn't embrace it. The Russians had wanted to know what this man was about, and they suspected he was helping the Confederates, but all Janeta could hold on to was the crumb of evidence his behavior had given her.

"We are envoys from Cuba," she said calmly. Her accent was already thick, but she leaned into it. "And we have much to report to the government of Spain about the abominable treatment we have received at the hands of these proud Southerners."

His brows raised, but his expression remained unreadable. "We've already been robbed of most of our belongings, which is why we seek your aid, and now we must be subjected to threat and harassment? If you thought the Trent incident caused problems for the North, that is nothing on what troubles our treatment will bring for the South, and for Britain, if you refuse our call for aid."

Roberts looked at them for a very long time, and Janeta was certain she had miscalculated, that she had ruined everything. What would happen to her? She had some vague idea given how the man named Wil had looked at her. And Daniel, what would become of him? She doubted he would go willingly into enslavement once again.

Finally — finally — Roberts gave a curt nod.

"Ah yes. I had received word that there were two Cuban envoys in need of assistance somewhere in my territory. Come along, then." He looked over at the group of men and clapped his hands together. "Gentlemen, thank you so very much for making sure these two weren't up to anything nefarious. I'll take them into my care now. And do come by this Sunday after church for tea as a token of my appreciation."

"Really?" The men looked even more pleased with themselves, though they had done nothing to merit either thanks or reward in Janeta's opinion.

Roberts turned and bade them follow him, and Janeta started after him. She pulled up short when Daniel's hand closed over her wrist.

"Are you mad? You're agreeing to go with him?"

She glanced at him. She had been focusing so hard on Roberts's reaction that she hadn't checked in with him. There was no time for delay, though. "We don't have much choice here, Cumberland."

"You should have discussed this with me before making such outlandish claims."

He was right, but embarrassed frustration welled up in her. "Maybe I would have if you hadn't been pretending I didn't exist for the past two days."

Daniel didn't have anything to say to that, apparently. She tugged her arm away gently and followed Roberts, who was at the very least playing along with her scheme.

Up ahead of them, Roberts reached his carriage and his driver opened the door and ushered them inside. Janeta clambered in and settled into the seat, the familiar opulence jarring after her weeks on the road. The clean, comfortable interior reminded her of everything she'd left behind in Palatka, and also of the recent time spent in the back of the wagon with Shelley and the others. Her throat clogged with emotion as the two very different experiences overlapped.

Daniel settled beside her — she could feel the tension rolling off him. He was so tense that he seemed likely to snap. She hadn't thought of how hard this would be for him when she'd decided to try this wild gambit. She could apologize later. Now she had to focus on Roberts.

Roberts slid in and pulled the door shut; then the carriage pulled off.

"Are you both comfortable?" Roberts asked.

"Yes," Janeta said. Daniel didn't speak.

"Good." Roberts reached casually into his pocket and pulled out his pistol, training it on them. "Now tell me who you are and what you want."

CHAPTER 17

Daniel fought the nausea roiling his stomach and the cold sweat beading at his temples. If he had traveled this far, gotten this close to Roberts and the proximity to Davis and the Sons of the Confederacy that he could bring them, only to fail, he would never forgive himself.

He shouldn't have ignored Janeta. He should have developed an actual plan other than getting to Enterprise and finding Roberts — he shouldn't have fallen back on the isolationism that had sustained him since he'd joined the Loyal League. No matter his feelings for Janeta, he'd carried himself back to the Deep South, done the slavers' job for them, and now they were in a situation he might not be able to get them out of.

Pain throbbed in his head, but there was no time for steeping tea or calming his nerves. His palms rested on the knees of his dusty trousers, but maybe he could slowly inch it down toward the hilt of his knife and . . .

Roberts tutted. "Both of you do please lift your hands up toward the ceiling of the carriage. Like that. Excellent, thank you."

Daniel glared at Janeta out of the corner of his eye. What had she been thinking, coming up with some foolish tripe like that? She could have said they were slaves, or freed people, or tradespeople perhaps, but envoys sent on behalf of Spain? It was outrageous. He'd known that she was not from the same background as him or most of the other detectives in the 4L, but that she didn't think to lower herself and had instead decided to raise her position spoke volumes about the difference in their lives before the League.

He'd known getting stuck with her would be the end of him, but he hadn't thought she'd bring about their demise in such a foolish way.

"Who sent you?" Roberts prodded. "Certainly no one professional. I know Stewart has been obsessive about me, but I doubt you're from the Northern intelligence agency, with that bumbling story."

Daniel almost concurred, but kept silent.

Janeta huffed. "Honestly, this is an outrage. As soon as I'm able to reach a telegraph —"

"As soon as you reach a telegraph you'll . . . send a message to the Queen of Spain? Is that correct?" Roberts smiled and brushed a bit of his overlong hair back with his free hand. "Forgive me, I know that in this day and age anything is possible, but I'm quite certain you're lying. Because you are lying, you are a direct threat to me. This is a new carriage and I've learned the unfortunate way that blood is somewhat impossible to get out of fabric, and the smell is even worse. So. The truth?"

He gestured with the gun in a circular motion, urging them on. The move was so seemingly careless, as was Roberts's demeanor, that Daniel tensed to spring at him, but as soon as he moved the slightest bit the gun was steadily trained on him.

"You. Cumberland was it? *¿Quieres decirme la verdad?*"

Daniel knew that *verdad* meant truth, but he wasn't certain about the other words. In fact, his entire vocabulary had narrowed down to one word. Two syllables.

Escape.

He knew what this man could do to them, and death wasn't the likeliest option. Daniel refused to be enslaved again and he wouldn't let it happen to Janeta — she wouldn't survive it. She'd be broken within a week, and not because she was weak but because enduring such sudden cruelty was a shock to any system.

"I'm American," Daniel said slowly. Deliberately. "I was given information about certain happenings in this area and I wanted to look into them. This woman is someone I met along the way and who decided to accompany me. If you are planning something untoward, she deserves no such treatment and she should be released."

Roberts smiled. "Do you think I would really just let her go?"

Daniel returned his smile. "No, but I had to make the offer. Now that you've refused it, you are accountable for any ill that falls upon her. You will pay dearly if she's hurt."

Janeta huffed again; it seemed her frustration with him was greater than her fear. "Excuse me?" She shifted her glare from Daniel to Roberts. "I would like to join in this battle of wits. I will also hold you accountable for anything that happens to *him.*"

Roberts's gaze slipped back to Janeta, and Daniel resisted the urge to growl at her. He was *trying* to distract from her. Why was she so intent on joining the conversation?

"Are you his mistress?" Roberts asked bluntly.

"No, I am his friend. And I will not stand by and have him threaten you on my behalf when I'm perfectly capable of threatening you myself. You will pay dearly if he's hurt."

For a moment, Daniel wasn't thinking of escape. He was thinking of the tone of Janeta's voice. He'd heard her mimic conviction and outrage when she'd shouted at the men trying to detain them. This was different. Her voice was high and sharp and dangerous; she was not faking her anger. What she had just said was real. *Verdad.* She was half his size and Roberts had a gun pointed in her direction, and yet she defended him like he was worth the trouble. He'd doubted her, withdrawn from her, and she still tried to protect him.

Could this really be an act?

Roberts chuckled and leaned back in his seat, the gun resting in his lap but still trained across the carriage.

"I suppose I might relax a bit. Given the amateur nature of this conversation, I'm going to guess you weren't sent to kill me."

"Not unless we have reason to," Daniel replied.

"People have any number of reasons for wanting to kill me. A couple of months back there was word that a Yankee was sniffing about because he knew I was helping the Confederates break the blockade and make ties with Europe. A few weeks ago, there was the man who knew that I was secretly a spy for the North out to undermine the Southern cause. Americans are terribly excitable. It can't be good for the circulation." He gave a long-suffering sigh.

"Which is true?" Janeta asked, because of course she would ask.

Roberts shrugged. "Both? Neither? Why would I tell two strangers in firm alliance who've told a preposterous lie in the service of ascertaining my whereabouts?"

Janeta rolled her eyes. "*Dios mío,* is it really so preposterous? I'm starting to take offense."

"Preposterous, but brilliant in its own right." Roberts grinned. "I gather you were trying a pared down Polish duke ploy?"

Janeta crossed her arms over her chest in response.

Roberts nodded. "The Southerners *do* have a rather pathetic attachment to the aristocracy, much to my benefit, but this is a society rooted in slavery. Such a ruse has worked a few times before, but I'm rather certain that, like most morally dubious attempts to get over in America, one has to be white for such a caper to succeed."

Daniel realized something as he took in Roberts's casual demeanor and frank tone — he wasn't talking down to them. He wasn't rude like Hooper of the pook turtle, or aggressive like the soldiers who had invaded their camp, or the men who had surrounded them in the town. Despite having a gun drawn on them the whole time, the consul spoke to them as equals.

It was likely a trap, but one that was effective. Daniel's heart rate was slowing, and the pins and needles at the crown of his head began to dissipate. He was by no means comfortable, and he didn't trust Roberts, but he was beginning to think that things were perhaps different than the Russians had suspected. He couldn't tolerate any additional suspense, though.

"Well, what are you going to do with us?" Daniel asked.

"I really don't enjoy killing," Roberts said with a frown. "Nasty business, that."

"I do enjoy it," Daniel retorted, drawing himself up so that his head nearly brushed the ceiling of the carriage.

Roberts stared at him, gaze narrowed, his perpetual grin fading. "No. No, you don't."

Daniel tried to hold the man's gaze, but it was too knowing and worse, too kind. He huffed and turned his head toward the window. "Whether I do or I don't, I won't sit idly by while you decide whether to murder us."

"I'm not going to murder you. I just said I don't enjoy killing, and what is murder but killing? Do pay attention, Cumberland."

Roberts ran a hand through his hair and sighed. Then he put his gun away. "I find you both to be infinitely less tedious than these Southerners and their grasping affectations. Will you join me for supper, and we can discuss exactly what business *the Queen of Spain* has with me?"

Daniel felt Janeta's hand touch his arm, gently. "We do not have to, if you don't want to."

Oddly, Daniel found himself intrigued instead of anxious. And besides, Roberts hadn't offered to let them leave. Daniel would rather not push against that figurative door and find it locked until he was sure he'd be able to kick or blast his way out.

"I wouldn't mind supper if you're offering it," he said. "It's difficult to kill on an empty stomach no matter how much you enjoy it."

Roberts brows raised and he chuckled. "Ah, you have a sense of humor. Splendid."

Daniel was confused, his head still hurt, and he wasn't sure what lay ahead of them, but at the very least if they were to die, they would die well fed.

The carriage turned and the jolting gait of the wheels over bumpy road was suddenly smooth.

"Ah, we've nearly arrived," Roberts said, peering through the window. "You both are being quite the sports about being held captive."

Captive.

Daniel remembered the last time he'd been taken to the home of a white man against his will. His temporary calm evaporated in an instant and then there was only head-rattling, heart-pounding fear, so sudden and vicious he thought he would be sick. His heart hurt, and he was certain he would die if he didn't get out of the carriage right then. He leapt up without thinking, hands bracing himself against the side of the swaying carriage.

"What the devil?" That was Roberts, alarmed. Daniel was searching for the latch on the door. He had to get out. He had to get away. Or he'd — he'd —

He punched at the door.

"No, put your gun away," Janeta cried. "He is not himself! Stop the carriage!"

Daniel tried to follow the conversation, but he couldn't breathe. He remembered the wood grain of the coffin digging into his fingertips, the fruitless kicking and punching at the wood and how he'd kept thinking, *Just one more blow and I will break through,* but he never had. Instead, he'd soiled himself and screamed impotently into the rag stuffed into his mouth.

His hands went to this throat.

"Daniel? Daniel!"

Janeta. He would fight his way out. He had to, for her. Just one more blow and he would break through.

He was already beginning to fall back into his seat, but he lashed out with the greatest swing he could muster.

He couldn't let her be captured, too. He couldn't . . .

A sharp, acrid scent flooded Daniel's nostrils, the smell burning through the haze in his head and jolting him awake. Awake?

Oh no. He remembered leaping from his seat as memories had assailed him, of needing to escape the small space, of struggling for breath.

How many times must I relive my former humiliation and create new ones?

Shame and anger and the certainty that he would never escape the grip of his past engulfed him as he opened his eyes. He lay on a comfortable cushioned seat, and above him was a wood slatted ceiling painted an intense blue that he at first mistook for the sky. The air was still cool, and when he turned his head he could see the expanse of a well-kept lawn beyond the edge of a beautiful wooden porch.

"Daniel!" Janeta again. That was what she had last said in the carriage, and now they were at Roberts's estate. Daniel sat up woozily, his head pounding.

Roberts sat across from him, his mouth turned up into the barest smirk. "You should have told me you were so famished you were likely to pass out. I would have asked Richard to get us home with some haste."

"I —" Daniel swallowed thickly.

"No need to explain," the consul said. His gaze darted to Janeta, and Daniel understood that Janeta had told the man *something.* He hoped she was as good a liar as he'd thought her to be because if this stranger knew of his past, his pain, and his weakness, he would have to leave. But when Roberts's gaze returned to Daniel, it wasn't filled with pity or disgust. In fact, his eyes held the same droll amusement that they had in the carriage. "I knew the smelling salts would be of use one day. Thank you for making carrying them worth my while."

"Thank you," Daniel said. He felt out of sorts and woozy, but tried to regain some semblance of dignity.

"Well, I suppose you two want to wash up. I certainly do. My servants will see you to your quarters and provide you with fresh clothing. After all, I'm sure the Queen of Spain wouldn't want her envoys walking about tattered and smelling of donkey." He clapped, then stood and executed a quick bow. "Maddie, can you see after them, please?"

An older Negro woman who had been hovering near the door approached.

"Right this way." She bowed her head, wrapped in brown fabric that matched her clean poplin dress.

Daniel's head was still spinning and he felt like he'd been kicked by the donkey he stank of, but he pulled himself to his feet. Janeta came to his side, slipping her arm through his.

"I owe you an apology," Daniel said darkly. "I treated you as if you would hold me back, but I am the one who has needed constant coddling on this journey."

"I think we have different definitions of coddling," she said. "I meant what I said. You are my friend. Perhaps I don't deserve a friend like you, but I will make sure that you know you deserve a friend better than me."

Daniel didn't answer, but he squeezed his arm against his body, pressing hers close to him. He hadn't thought himself in need of a friend; he hadn't given thought to what he needed in some time. Wanting was dangerous enough; *needing* could be deadly. Both left you open to disappointment, which seemed a mild word for trauma that could raze your spirit and salt the earth afterward. But that's what his enslavement had been to him — a bone-deep disappointment that the country he needed to believe in, one where he and his people might be truly free, had been an unobtainable fantasy.

But he was already a broken man. Could indulging this one need sink him any lower?

"You overestimate what I deserve," he said. "And underestimate what your friendship has meant to me today. Thank you."

Janeta didn't have a chance to answer. She was asked to follow the female servant, and Daniel was asked to follow a man named Michael who waited near the entrance of a washroom.

"Do you need to be shown how to use the bath, sir?"

Daniel thought the man was jesting, but

then he glanced into the room. A large zinc tub encased in a wooden frame was against one wall. Another wooden frame stood perpendicular and a metal shower head fitted to a spigot.

"This home has heated water. The toilet is on the other side of the bath, sir. You turn on the water here, the soap is here, and you can leave your clothes there and I'll fetch them for washin'."

Daniel examined the craftsmanship of the wooden case and ran his hand over the zinc basin before shedding his filthy clothes. He used the necessary, marveling at the lavishly appointed water closet as he did. The room had fine wallpaper and a large window to let in the sunlight. And when he finally turned the spigot and stepped under the warm spray? Delight. Pure, unabashed delight filled him. The water was hot! And plentiful! It rained down on him, leaving his hands free to scrub and lather and wash away the layers of sweat and grime.

It was odd, but as he scrubbed and soaped he felt like he was stripping away his anger and despair. Even as his hands passed over his raised scars, he didn't get pulled into an awful memory, but thought instead of the future. What would their time here achieve? Why was Roberts so eager to allow them to stay? Why was Janeta so good at pretending she cared for him?

Only time would tell.

For these fleeting few moments, he didn't worry about it. He let the water slap into his hair and neck and back, and stared at the tiled wall until his mind went blissfully blank.

Chapter 18

Janeta sat at the guest room's dressing table, being attended to by an enslaved woman as she had been for most of her life, and hoped she hadn't made a terrible mistake.

They still didn't know for whom Roberts worked or what his goal was. The Russians had painted him as a danger, and perhaps he was, but their private conversation had shown that they didn't know for certain. He seemed cordial enough, but he might be the enemy, and even if he wasn't, that didn't mean she could trust him. People in the Loyal League had trusted *her,* after all.

She hadn't told him Daniel's secret, had instead pulled another lie from her seemingly endless sack of them. She had feared *El Viejo del Saco,* but she had become her own version, peddling lies instead of naughty children.

Janeta had called upon something she'd heard Henry talk of. A friend of his who had answered the first call for Confederate troops, who had gone to battle barely trained and come through alive and relatively unscathed, but with a mind that occasionally slipped back to the battlefield.

She'd told Roberts that Daniel had soldier's heart, as Henry had called it, unable to tell the difference between the present day and battles of his past. That wasn't false; more and more Janeta was realizing that what she'd been taught was the natural order of things was a type of warfare, with more casualties than anyone would ever be able to count.

After Daniel had struck the consul in his last attempt to save himself — or was it her he'd wanted to save? — before he passed out, Janeta had expected Roberts to have them hauled off to jail, or to serve his own justice for the insult. A Negro man striking a white one was enough to merit any harsh treatment Daniel received, in the eyes of the law. The price for such an action was supposed to be so high as to deter others from even thinking of it.

Roberts hadn't sought to hurt Daniel. He'd nodded understandingly and sent his driver for Maddie and the smelling salts, and to pass on word to chef that there would be two more for dinner. He'd taken another glance at Janeta and asked him to tell Michael to lay a fire in the parlor. He'd prodded at his sore cheek but hadn't commented on the blow otherwise. She didn't know what to make of him.

She winced as Maddie tugged at her matted hair; Janeta had tried her best to clean it, but had given up in frustration and fatigue.

"I can take care of that," Janeta said, awkwardly reaching up to take over for the woman. *"Gracias."*

Maddie huffed a laugh but kept working. "Oh, I think you done about enough to this head of yours. Ain't no trouble to me. What's this? You got something in here."

Maddie passed Janeta the remains of the note that she'd braided into her hair what felt like forever ago. Janeta held the wad of paper tightly in her hand, a reminder of the deception she was capable of.

The edge of the note had once been sharp, but was now a soggy and useless mass. Her words would be indecipherable now, and she took some comfort in that. A shiver went through her thinking of what she had initially set out to do when she arrived at that cabin in Illinois. Of whom she had wanted to do it for. She had agreed to spy for the Confederacy to save her father and please Henry, and she wasn't sure if that had been the order of importance in her mind at the time she'd agreed to do it.

She'd already been spying before she left Palatka. Why? To win smiles and caresses and sweet words from Henry. That was what had gotten Papi into trouble. And now Papi sat rotting in a prison, if he still lived, because Janeta had discovered new convictions, new people she wanted to win smiles from. She'd reinvented herself, she who lied as easily as the snake had to Eve — she was now shedding the skin given to her by slave owners and rebels and seeing what was beneath. It seemed she was always becoming a new person, though. How could she be sure that who she was now was who she would be tomorrow, or the next day?

Panic fluttered in her chest and she closed her eyes.

I am Janeta Sanchez. Descendant of slaves and conquistadores. I am a member of the Loyal League, partner to Daniel Cumberland, and I will complete the mission assigned to me.

Yes. She couldn't be sure of the future, but this version of Janeta was as real as any of the others had been, and she didn't need to know the future for that to matter. She did need to know one very important thing, though.

"Maddie? Why is Mr. Roberts being kind to Daniel and me?" she asked carefully.

"Oh, he's just a nice man, I suppose," Maddie said, tugging at a snarl in Janeta's hair. She reached for a small jar of hair oil.

Janeta tried a different route. "Should we be worried about our safety?"

"From Mr. Brendan? Oh no. He won't hurt y'all. He's not like the other white folk around here. But then again, y'all ain't like the Negroes around here, so I guess I should ask the same: should we be worried about *his* safety?"

Janeta paused. She wasn't exactly sure what was going to happen. The Russians had told them about a secret meeting with dangerous Rebels, but Roberts treated them kindly. He'd spoken candidly about the South and its racism. Could the same man also be planning to help Europe overthrow the North?

Your father married your mother. Did that mean he thought all slaves should be freed?

"We mean Mr. Roberts no harm," Janeta said truthfully.

Maddie nodded as she finished the second of two cornbraids. She'd left most of Janeta's thick hair out, and gathered the ends of the braids and the remaining hair into a bun.

"He's a good man," Maddie said, securing the bun and then standing. "Different, and not just cause of that accent. He been here . . . two years now? I been made to work in Enterprise all my life, and I ain't ever been treated better. The day he go back to England is gonna be a sad day for me and Michael."

Janeta would pass that information on to Daniel. She didn't know how he would feel about Maddie defending Roberts, but the woman had little reason to lie.

"I'll bring you to supper," Maddie said.

Janeta followed her through the hallways decorated with expensive floral wallpaper and detailed wood molding. The hallways were immaculately clean, but some of the rooms held large crates that were either in the middle of being unpacked or loaded.

The house was smaller than her father's Santiago estate, but larger and more opulent than Villa Sanchez in Palatka. The large paintings, fine furniture, and modern light fixtures were somewhat extraordinary, as had been the hot water taps in the washroom; the house was in the middle of nowhere but had all the latest features of a modern home that her older sisters had sighed over with their friends.

When she entered the dining room, she wasn't prepared for the unexpected sight that met her. Roberts was dressed the same and still sported a red mark on his face from where he'd been grazed by a fist. Daniel was nowhere to be seen. That's what Janeta thought at first before she realized the handsome man talking to Roberts *was* Daniel.

He hadn't worn rags during their journey, but he was now dressed in fine trousers and a clean tan shirt, with a matching brown vest and jacket. His hair had been trimmed and he'd shaven the wild beard that he'd sported since she'd met him. Janeta had already thought him an attractive man, but there was something about being able to see the strong jut of his jawline and the sharpness of his cheekbones that drove home the fact that Daniel was not only beautiful on the inside. Not to her. He looked younger and less troubled and, damn him, Janeta's face was hot and she could not pull her gaze from him.

A beard was just hair, to be shaved and regrown, but seeing Daniel without his seemed somehow intimate. She could suddenly imagine him as the idealistic young man, eager to study law, running a knuckle along his jaw as he pored over legal documents. She could see the man he had been before cruel fate — no, not fate, humanity — had crushed his soul. Perhaps he had wanted her to see this.

No, don't be foolish. He simply wanted to be appropriate for a meal in a place such as this. Or to be free of uncomfortable facial hair.

Daniel's gaze caught on hers as Roberts talked to him, and though he nodded and replied, he didn't look away. His brows raised, ever so slightly, and she realized she was standing and staring. She made her way over to them, trying to gather the thoughts that had been scattered by Daniel's change in appearance.

"You look different," she said to Daniel after they'd both stood and greeted her.

He ran his hand over his smooth cheeks and Janeta's cheeks flushed warmer.

"Is that the polite way of saying you prefer me with the beard?" He seemed to enjoy the fact that he'd been able to surprise her.

"Not at all, though I suppose this will take some getting used to," she said. Her gaze sought the floor between them, as she was suddenly unable to look at him. His eyes had always been lovely, but now they seemed larger and deeper, the warm brown more apparent.

"I'm sure I'll be unkempt again within a

few days' time," he said. "Enjoy this while you can."

He grinned, a full-on charming grin that made her breath hitch in response. She was grateful that he had been distant and rude when she'd first met him. Even then, she'd felt the inklings of attraction. Now, she saw how things could be between them. Joking and subtle looks and not-so-subtle attraction. She knew things with Daniel couldn't last. Perhaps they had a day or two, or even just those few minutes before Roberts did with them what he wished.

She absorbed the warmth of his smile like the rays of the equatorial sun.

"I believe I will," she said.

They took their seats at the large table and the servants brought out the first course, a hearty autumn stew. Janeta wondered what Augustus and Jim and Shelley would have for dinner that night. She also thought about the fact that the only dark faces she had ever seen at her father's table were her mother's and her own, yet Roberts had welcomed them to share his own supper.

"Now that you've had a chance to eat a bit, I'm going to be unbearably rude and ask what exactly it is you want of me. This week is a busy one, with an important delegation arriving at the house in just a few days. I don't have time for espionage games and banter. I don't have much time at all. None of us do."

His brow creased.

Janeta looked at Daniel, who dabbed at his mouth with his cloth napkin.

"Are you aiding the Confederacy?" he asked bluntly.

Roberts didn't even flinch. "That depends on whom you ask. I am the British consul in Mississippi. Some believe it is my job to increase relations between the South and England. To ensure that trade relations and access to cotton and tobacco are not unduly affected. To pressure other European nations to also recognize the brave and valiant Southern forces."

"I am asking *you,*" Daniel said flatly.

Roberts took up a spoonful of stew and chewed politely before answering. "No, I am not aiding the South. I am the British consul in Mississippi. I believe it is my job to convince Britain to cut relations with this abomination of a society for the good of the United States and the world. I believe that there is nothing brave and valiant about owning other humans, and that it's the job of all civilized nations to soundly reject the core beliefs of the Confederacy."

Roberts had maintained a mild demeanor since they'd met him, but Janeta saw anger flash through in his response.

"Why?" she asked. "Why do you care?"

She had allowed herself to be misled for so long; Roberts's clear-eyed condemnation shamed her.

"I care because as long as slavery is sanctioned in this world, either directly or tacitly, we are a doomed species. There is no hope for progress, no hope for a world of peace and prosperity, if some men are allowed dominion over others for as arbitrary a reason as skin color."

Daniel held his spoon but didn't eat. It rested against the vegetables in his bowl. "Do you believe financial means to be a better indicator of worth? I was told that you're an aristocrat, so you'll understand if I'm a bit skeptical of your support for the downtrodden."

"I was born into wealth, yes, and trust me when I say that I know where it comes from, and it's not the backbreaking labor of *my* ancestors. I don't believe that an accident of birth makes me worthier of anything. A guillotine perhaps, if I look to my French compatriots across the channel."

Janeta put down her fork and knife. "Are you saying then that you are for the Union?"

"I am saying that I am against slavery and any government that supports it. As President Lincoln has made his Proclamation, that is an indicator that they're the side I would like to prevail in this war. But those are my personal feelings. My professional ones are this: Great Britain, despite its foul past, is currently an abolitionist nation. Yet the Confederacy sways my people to their cause. I have been working to show that this Southern government, a gutter trap for all the worst leavings of this fledgling nation, must not be acknowledged. That to do so would be shameful and lowering."

Janeta didn't know what to think. His words lifted her spirits — an ally! — but she knew better than anyone that what a person said was not necessarily what they believed. She had been guided to the heart of the Loyal League with the express purpose of finding out their secrets and revealing them to Henry, who would then pass them on to the Sons of the Confederacy. She had changed her mind, but she had been in cahoots with those who wanted to snuff out one of the only hopes for the Union — for people like her — to persevere. Could she really take Roberts at his word?

"This is an interesting revelation," Daniel said. He took a sip of his water. It was strange how his bearing had changed. He'd had a rough, slightly combustible air to him since they'd met. He'd seemed to get some thrill out of shocking his fellow detectives with his flaunting of the rules, and Janeta by occasionally following them. But here he was, seemingly comfortable debating with a British aristocrat. "If this is the case, why must you hide your true intentions?"

"I suppose I could ask you the same," Roberts retorted. "But I already gave you my answer. I am the British consul in *Mississippi.* It's much more efficacious for the people I encounter daily to believe I am for their cause. The things they tell me — the casual cruelty and inveterate laziness of their characters revealed in everyday conversation — provides the most damning evidence that I can relay back to Parliament. And when people believe you are on their side, they will tell you anything."

He looked over at Janeta and she was stricken by the way his gaze lingered on her.

No. There is no way he can suspect. He is in the middle of nowhere. He's likely never even heard of Palatka, let alone me.

His gaze slid away, leaving a residue of fear covering Janeta's fine, clean clothing and her shiny new convictions.

You are a fraud, the voice in her warned.

Daniel should trust Roberts more than you.

"That the people here believe I am for the South is why President Davis will be stopping here for dinner in a few days as he makes his way back from out West. And this is why some people who are very invested in the South strengthening their relationship with Europe will be attending our meeting."

"Will there be representatives of other European powers at the meeting apart from you?" Daniel asked.

Roberts raised a brow, affronted. "*I* am the supposed link to stronger European relations. The British are not known for giving away our power easily."

For Davis. And the Sons of the Confederacy.

Janeta pushed her food around on her plate and when she looked up, Daniel was watching her with keen interest. She looked back down at her stew.

"So. Out with it," Roberts said. "Are you with Furney Bryant? Daughters of the Tent? Or is it the 4L?"

Daughters of the Tent? Janeta wondered how many groups there were working to undermine the Confederacy. How many networks large and small, toiling in secret and hunted by Rebels and never given proper due for their bravery. She didn't answer him, though, and neither did Daniel.

Roberts lifted a shoulder. "I'm quite good at finding out things people would rather I didn't. It's not my personal talent — I have agents who work at that. My talent is seeing the potential in others and putting it to use. You don't have to tell me who you work with, for I will know soon enough. But you both have potential, likely currently harnessed by someone else, and don't seem to wish *me* harm."

He looked at Daniel, and Janeta saw a flash of cunning in Roberts's eyes. "I do believe if you stay for the meeting things will be even more interesting. By the way, neither of you bothered to ask me what those organizations were, so might I assume I'm on the right track? Oh, the next course is arriving. Let's save this dreadfully boring talk for later."

Janeta had barely eaten her stew, but she let her bowl be taken away as she stared at Roberts. For the first time in her life she couldn't get a read on another person, and not because she was letting herself be deceived. If this Roberts was as good at getting information as he'd pretended, if he found out why she had originally joined the

Loyal League . . . her heart heaved painfully in her chest.

She had already lost everything, including all that she'd been taught about herself. Now she might lose Daniel and the Loyal League, too.

Daniel had been right about her not knowing what true cold was; early November in Mississippi surely wasn't anywhere as cold as Massachusetts, but Janeta still shivered beneath her cloak as she walked through the garden, which was likely resplendent in summer but now boasted shades of dull green and brown. It was apparently colder than usual, and rain and wind had shaken the leaves from the trees. The fading leaves that littered the ground gave the bleak landscape a hint of color, but the lack of brightness and sunshine filled Janeta with a longing for home.

Home.

Mami and Papi laughing. The brilliant green of a palm leaf, the chattering of birds and frogs, the smell of the ocean wind, and the incredible blue of a summer sky in Santiago. More than that, she longed for her innocence, for a time before she'd known slavery was wrong and that she'd had some part in that wrongness.

No. She would never want to be that ignorant again. If she had never left Cuba, she would have never learned about who she was and who she might be, and she would never have met Daniel. Now that she had some quiet, that hurt to think of, too.

She looked up, suddenly yanked from the depths of her musings, and there he was.

Daniel sat on the porch in just his shirt, cupping a mug of something warm and steaming in his hands. He was watching her; she had no idea how long he'd been there.

"Aren't you freezing?" she called out, unable to hide her disbelief, and because she needed to do something with the silly burst of giddiness that exploded in her at the sight of him. She began making her way to him, keeping her steps measured.

He chuckled, lifting his shoulders as she approached. "I'm a New Englander, Sanchez. I'm overdressed right now."

She scoffed, then stood awkwardly before him as she reached the steps leading to the porch.

He was still looking at her as if she were a great distance away, or as if he was searching for something within her. "Seemed like you were walking off some worries. Penny for your thoughts?"

Fear seized her.

"You offer too much. A Confederate dollar would do," she said as her shoe hit the first step. She paused and looked up at him, imagined telling him what she had been thinking of. His warm brown gaze would ice over and his full lips would pull into a sneer.

She would lose him someday soon, and it ached so much more than it should have. More than Henry's deceit, more than her longing for home.

"I was wondering what life would have been like if I had never left Cuba," she said, starting up the stairs. That was close enough to the truth. "I would not have learned many things if I'd stayed. I —" She could tell him a little maybe. "I grew up on a plantation. For a long while, I was taught that I was not like the people enslaved there. And I believed it. And if I had not joined the Loyal League maybe I would have always believed it."

She expected him to make a remark about how foolish she was, but he simply sipped his tea and nodded.

"Sounds like you must have had some hard realizations then, huh?"

"Honestly? Some days I don't even know who I am. I try to remember who I was, but that person no longer exists. And I don't want to be her anymore, anyway." She cautiously sat beside him — cautious because now when she was close to him she felt like being closer, like she couldn't be close enough. *Tonta.* "I suppose that now I'm trying to figure out just who it is I *want* to be."

He laughed and shook his head. "It's that simple is it?"

"Maybe. I hope so. And even if it's not simple, I don't have much choice." She rested her elbows on her knees and leaned forward, staring out across the lawn. "You can't live in the past, so you have to choose what you can of our future."

He cleared his throat. "When I was kidnapped into slavery, they brought me back to the farm and introduced me to the other enslaved people and I was completely at a loss. What was the damned correct salutation for that? I was frightened and angry and frustrated. I didn't understand." He sighed and rolled his cup back and forth in his palms. "Why did they do the work? Why did they treat the ignorant overseer like a god? Why didn't any of them *do something* to stop this, instead of just working themselves to death for nothing?"

A familiar anger was in his voice and when Janeta looked at him his eyes were closed. She finally understood something — the anger and hatred and fury she had read in his eyes that first day had been correct, but she'd mistakenly thought he hated everyone. No; Daniel Cumberland hated himself.

She placed her hand on his forearm and he let a sigh slip out and opened his eyes.

"I tried to talk sense into the other slaves. I tried to reason with the overseer. I started secretly teaching the children their letters. And one day, one of them got caught. Winnie."

"*Ay Dios,* no," she whispered. Her grip tightened on Daniel's arm. "You didn't know —"

"I knew. I studied law, remember? I knew that it was against the law, but I also knew that it was wrong. I was so sure of myself that I was reckless. I paid for it, as you've seen, but Winnie?" He tensed beside her. "She was nine, small for her age. A wisp of a girl. And Finnegan beat her as viciously as he beat me. And to teach the other children a lesson, he took his boot to her fingers."

Tears welled up in Janeta's eyes. She tried not to cry; this was his pain, not hers. But she thought of his wails into the night. How gentle he could be with others while being hard with himself. She'd thought herself good at giving people what they wanted, but Daniel had crafted a much more convincing façade than she ever had. He'd convinced others that he didn't care for their esteem, when that was a lie. He simply didn't think himself worthy of it.

She slipped her hand down his forearm and clasped her fingers around his palm. He didn't let go of his mug, but he loosened his hold to allow her hand more contact with his. She stared at him, trying to figure out what he needed. Absolution? Forgiveness? No.

"Sometimes we do things that we think are right, and others get hurt because of it," she said. "My father is imprisoned because I was passing along information. He is older and sickly and imprisoned. Because of me. And . . . I've done worse. So I can't tell you to forgive yourself for what happened. I can't say that it's all right." She paused, struggling to find the right words in English. "The only thing we can do is try our best not to hurt others again. I think that is reasonable. And maybe not to treat ourselves worse than we would treat our enemies."

She looked at her hand clasping his because she was afraid to look at his face. Afraid he would ask her what that "worse" she had done was.

"Janeta."

She had to turn her head toward his; that request had been in the way he said her name, and she couldn't deny him.

His gaze roamed over her face, searching, and a wry grin had replaced his frown. His beard was starting to grow again and she wanted to run her hands over the stubble. To pull his face close.

"And to imagine I was upset at being partnered with you. Perhaps I ought to give Dyson more credit. And you should give yourself the same." His face was so near and his body was so warm in the cool afternoon air. "You're new to this world, in more ways than one, but when it comes down to it, your instinct is to do good. That counts a lot more than any of your sins, I'd think."

She sucked in a trembling breath and nodded. His words filled her up with hope, and suddenly she was longing again. Not for home, or for the past, but for a future where she could lean into him and take more of his warmth, and give it to him, too. Giving and taking — it happened so naturally between them.

When he finds out . . .

As if summoned by her sudden anxiety, Roberts stepped onto the porch, a letter in his hand.

"There's been words from one of my contacts that the Sons have been active in town over the past few days. I imagine they're doing a sweep before the meeting takes place. The men sniffing about said they were Home Guard when asked, but they would have been local if that was true. Just letting you know." He pointedly didn't look at their hands. "Beautiful day out. I'll be in my office if anyone needs me."

Daniel stood. "I'd have a word with you about sending a letter or two."

He looked back at Janeta before following Roberts inside. The sound of their heavy tread disappeared into the house and Janeta hugged her arms around herself. If Roberts truly was a collector of information he might find out her awful secret. If members of the Sons of the Confederacy were arriving, they might know her for who she was. There were so many reasons to reveal the truth to Daniel and only one that she didn't: she had lost everything she knew, and she didn't want to lose him, too.

Chapter 19

Daniel didn't understand this kind of wealth. The sitting room with its fine furniture and delicate wallpaper and lavish decorations made him uncomfortable. He focused on the grill over the fireplace; it was perhaps the only object in the room he could truly feel at ease with.

His family had been well-off compared with many other Negro families, but they hadn't led lives of luxury by any means. His father had worked with his hands, a blacksmith, and Daniel had come up at his side. When he'd decided to leave working with his hands and try his turn at law, Daniel had thrown himself into his studies with fervor while still assisting his parents as much as he could. He'd never had the pleasure of lazing in a parlor as big as his family home, waiting for work to fall into his lap.

It was maddening.

The only thing he could think of to pass the time was to seek out Janeta, but that wouldn't do. Without the stress and travel that had marked the majority of their partnership to distract him from his distinctly unwanted feelings, any time spent with her was dangerous. He liked the way she looked at him. He liked that she had opened up to him on the porch the previous day, and hated that she still held back on the most important things.

He'd wanted to kiss her as she held his hand, to feel her lips against his. He didn't regret sharing his experience with her, but he wasn't a fool. Things had changed between them, or maybe what had been there right from the start had finally been allowed to surface. He knew what could happen if they were given enough time alone now — he'd been imagining those scenarios in great detail. How soft her skin would feel beneath his hands. How she would look up at him with those deep brown eyes of hers. He'd been imagining and desiring and, worse, starting to think that maybe he was allowed to do so. That he was worthy of being desired in return.

"You're a good man," she'd said as they'd walked behind Jim and Augustus's wagon, voice urgent, as if she might will him to ac-

cept her words as truth.

It scared him, the possibility that he wasn't broken and unworthy. Or that he was, and the only one who would begrudge him it was himself.

He thought of Dyson, and Logan, and Carla, of Jim and Augustus and Shelley — all the others who had suffered and were dealing with that suffering in their own way, but who'd still had some measure of faith in him. Of his parents and friends who had tried to help him, though they hadn't known how.

The voice in his head that often shouted him down and pointed out his flaws was still there, but another voice was growing stronger. One that whispered of how things had been for him once and how they could be in the future. One that heard the ugly recriminations ricocheting in his mind and said weakly, but defiantly: *No. I am good. I am worthy.*

The fact that he was thinking of a future at all meant something had shifted in him. Maybe it was like Janeta had said: people were always changing. If he never went back to being the affable and naïve Daniel Cumberland, that was just the way of the world and not evidence that he deserved to suffer.

He huffed a sigh just as Maddie passed by

the parlor door, carrying a stack of folded linen. He jumped to his feet and made his way toward her.

"Maddie?"

She slowed her pace and looked back at him over her shoulder, but she didn't stop. He wasn't sure, but he thought he caught censure in her gaze. He jogged to catch up to her.

"*Miss* Maddie?" he said, remembering his manners, and when she glanced up at him the censure was gone and she seemed pleased. She stopped walking at the foot of the stairs and paid him her full attention.

"How can I help you, Mr. Cumberland, sah?"

"I was wondering if you might point me toward Mr. Roberts's office?"

"I'm heading that way," she said. "Come along now."

"I can take that for you if you'd like," he said as he started up after her, but she shook her head.

"If there's two things in this world I carry well, it's laundry and secrets," she said. "Certainly don't need help from you, though I appreciate you tryin'."

Daniel sized the woman up: older, proud, with the regal gait of a woman who wouldn't be bowed by circumstance.

"Do you find yourself carrying secrets often, Miss Maddie?" he asked quietly.

She glanced at him as they reached the top step, and gave him a smile that made him understand she'd brought many a man to their knees in her youth and probably still could.

"Mr. Brendan's office is the first door over on the left. Good day, Mr. Cumberland sah."

She kept walking, leaving him behind, and Daniel decided to ask Janeta about her interactions with the woman later. Something about her had caught his interest, and maybe Janeta had sensed something as well.

"Can I help you?" Roberts asked without looking up from the paper he scratched at with a quill when Daniel presented himself.

"Yes, I need something to do. Sitting and staring at the wallpaper might be of interest to aristocrats, but it's not to me."

"Can you not find a darkened alcove in which to pass the time with your fellow envoy of the Spanish throne, as any good houseguest would?" He was jesting but probing, which Daniel understood but didn't appreciate. He adjusted the cuff of his shirt.

"I'm not sure Ms. Sanchez would care for

your assumption of her character. I certainly don't."

Roberts pointed at a stack of correspondence without apologizing. "Read those. Summarize each one in a written sentence or two. Tell me if it's something of importance and indicate whether I need to read it myself. Obviously, if you discover something of major import, you can just bring it to me."

Insecurity suddenly nagged at Daniel. He remembered when he'd returned home and attempted to return to his studies. How he could no longer focus — how he no longer cared. He'd let down the abolitionist lawyer who had taken him on as an apprentice; he'd heard the chatter asking what the man had expected by taking on a Negro, whose intellect wasn't made for handling such work. He'd hurt the chances of any of his brethren who would attempt to study law in his town after him.

"You're going to trust my capabilities?" he pushed. "Not even going to ask whether I can read or write?"

Roberts didn't speak for a moment — Daniel wasn't even sure he was listening. Roberts wrote with intensity, brow furrowed. When he finally looked up a moment later, his gaze was sharpened by annoyance.

"If you couldn't read and write and wanted to work, you would have asked Maddie or Michael, not me. You came to my study because you wanted to do something that one attends to in a study. I suppose you can lay a fire if you don't feel up to the task. Or you can take this and stop distracting me."

He held up the packet of letters and gestured toward a smaller, less ornate desk facing the window, and Daniel strode forward and took the bundle from him. Roberts immediately returned to his work without so much as a "thank you." Daniel went over to the desk assigned to him and tugged it carefully away from the wall, turning it so his back was not to Roberts or the door.

"Very well. I shall busy myself with your busy work," he said, summoning his resolve as he took his seat. He'd once sat at a desk every day, but it seemed strange now.

Roberts looked up from the next letter he had begun to write.

"Busy work? No, there are matters of grave importance tucked in with the invitations from anxious mothers wanting to thrust their daughters at me, though I suppose those mamas imagine their invites are matters of life and death. I need you to pay attention and to take the work seriously, but you seem like a man for whom that won't be a problem. A man who can work *independently.*"

Roberts nodded firmly, then turned decisively back to his own work.

Daniel first sorted the paper by quality of material. The clearly reused paper and scraps of wallpaper he set into one pile, the fine, thick paper he set into another. That was one preliminary step to sorting foreign and domestic, given the impact the war'd had on access to paper in the South. He took up one letter and read through it once, glancing up sharply every few moments. Roberts had entrusted him with this?

He took up the clean sheet and the pen on his desk and wrote his first summary:

> One. A report from Lord Russel detailing a contentious meeting of Parliament in which a speaker on the behalf of the Confederacy made a stirring argument that would have won over the crowd, if he had not then been thoroughly refuted by information passed along by the consul in Mississippi.

Daniel had known things were precarious, but not that those sympathetic to the South had such reach as to be able to take the floor of Parliament. Enclosed was a newspaper clipping detailing the man's near success and how at the last moment it had become his national shame.

Daniel moved on to the next crisp, cream paper.

Two. Rose Greenhow, known Rebel spy currently taking refuge in Europe, is said to have met with the Emperor Napoleon himself, and secured his promise of aid for the South. He plans for French expansion in Mexico and therefore seeks to be on good terms with the Confederacy.

Daniel skimmed through some of the shabbier looking letters then. Like Roberts had predicted, many were invitations for tea or to dinner from mothers lamenting their lonely daughters, though one caught his eye.

Three. Appeal for aid after an encounter with a strange man supposedly searching for Roberts's residence. Man did not give his name, though he was dressed in fine clothing. A slave who led the man to Roberts never returned to his owner. Some believe the slave ran off, but his master believes he was killed and requests assistance.

Daniel's blood chilled. The slave may have run off, but something about the strange visitor had disquieted the slave owner enough that he would write to Roberts. Even the toughest government detective and most seasoned members of the 4L gave members of that particular society a wide berth.

Daniel had sought them out.

Something pricked at him, and he placed the quill down and looked at Roberts.

"You say you don't intend to kill us but —"

"I never said that," Roberts said blithely. "I said I don't want to. I fully intend to if either of you gives me reason. I don't think you will, though."

Daniel couldn't even grow agitated at that. The man was odd, and either too honest or too skilled a liar. Daniel would play along.

"If you don't *want* to kill us, why are you allowing me to read all of your correspondence, including what seems to be private governmental information?"

Roberts kept writing.

"I am a man short on time, Mr. Cumberland." He groped about on his desk with his free hand, then held out a folded paper.

Daniel walked over slowly, taking it to read for himself.

> My dearest Brendan,
>
> I have held Secretary Seward at bay for as long as possible, but unfortunately, you will be recalled. The uncouth lout rails and rages and doesn't understand that he hurts his own cause! Much will be lost on both sides when you return home, and I can only hope that this war comes to an end soon thereafter. I can give you a month; after this meeting, you must return home immediately or lose the protection of the Crown.
>
> Yours,
> Lord Russell

"You are leaving?" Daniel asked.

Roberts's grip on his quill tightened, but his voice was level when he spoke. "While I do hope for the North to prevail, if they do it won't be because of Seward. He's a bull in a porcelain shop, crushing those who might help him to proverbial dust under his hooves."

"Why can't you just tell him that you are for the Union?" Daniel asked.

"Because I am not. I am for England, as

is proper and expected for a man of my position." Roberts sighed and placed his quill down. "I have explained myself to this numbskull repeatedly, with many, many a suggestion that while I cannot express pro-Northern sentiment, I am most certainly not for the South. Any man with a dash of sense would have taken my meaning, but Seward's surety of my ill will to the North, or some devolution in the American wit, has rendered him incapable of reading between the lines.

"Thus, after the meeting, I shall bid these shores farewell and return home. I will do what I can from England, but it will certainly be much more difficult than being here. But if I can use this meeting to gather the requisite information, then I will have done more than I thought possible when I arrived in this dismal backwater."

Roberts gave him a put-upon grin and a resigned sigh, but Daniel could see the fury and frustration in his eyes. He wasn't good at dissembling, which made Daniel . . . not trust him, exactly. But feel slightly better about whatever this strange alliance was between them. He still had to question his motives, though.

"Being short on time doesn't quite explain this carelessness," he said.

Roberts raised a brow and regarded Daniel with a suddenly steely gaze. "Carelessness? I didn't think that was the case, but perhaps I was mistaken about your capacity."

Daniel swallowed and dropped the letter onto the desk before walking back to his own. "This meeting. Sons of the Confederacy and Jefferson Davis himself. All under one roof. You're leaving anyway — why not poison them all and be done with it?"

The sharp laughter from Roberts startled Daniel. He'd thought the man was pointing out his foolishness, but he'd apparently found Daniel's take truly entertaining.

"Mr. Cumberland, yes, I did think about poisoning their tea in a moment of great frustration, but I decided that it would be abominably impolite in addition to a declaration of war. One that would solve nothing."

"What do you mean it would solve nothing?" Anger constricted Daniel's breath suddenly. It was easy for Roberts to say such a thing from his mansion with hot water and plumbing and gas lighting, where even in the throes of war he still had tea and supper and tobacco. "Ridding the world of men such as these would solve a great many of *my* problems."

"Would it?"

Daniel sucked in a deep breath. How dare he talk down to Daniel. How dare —

"When we carried you from the carriage, I felt the scar tissue on your back," Roberts said somberly. "I am going to say this in complete seriousness and please don't think I'm making light — slave masters have been whipping slaves for generations. They've been *killing* slaves for generations. Has all of that pain and all of those deaths stopped the Negro from desiring freedom?"

"Of course not," Daniel bit out. "We are human and want to be free."

"Exactly. Freedom is an idea. But the supremacy of the white race is another idea, a twisted and warped notion of gaining strength from the subjugation of others, and you can no more kill that by poisoning a handful of men than you can stop hope by whipping a slave."

Daniel had no reply. This man was wrong. He spoke in hypotheticals because he had no idea, and could never begin to imagine suffering such as Daniel had known.

"I've angered you." Roberts stood and walked over to the fireplace, throwing another piece of wood onto the flames. "I did not mean to. Please, I'd love to hear why you disagree."

Of course, Roberts could discuss this logically; it wasn't his humanity up for debate.

"By your logic, the North should have just surrendered to the South instead of fighting," Daniel said. "What's the point if you can't kill an idea, after all?"

"No, no, no, that's not what I said. I said you cannot kill a man in place of an idea. You can fight against an idea, as the North is to some extent, and you can defeat it. The Emancipation Proclamation did more damage than the Gettysburg, Sharpsburg, or Chattanooga campaigns."

Daniel scoffed and when he spoke his voice was constricted by rage. "That half-assed token attempt at baiting the South? It was a weak nod to abolition driven by politics, not passion, and it's conditional. When you can say a man is free here but not there, that's not true freedom. The Rebels don't care about that proclamation except wanting to spite it."

Roberts opened his mouth to speak, shut it, then seemed to find what it was he wanted to say. "The damage done wasn't in telling the Rebels that their slaves had to be freed. It was in telling the slaves that they *could* be freed. By order of law. Do you think there's any going back from that for a people who have been waiting for a miracle and working to make one for themselves and their families? To my knowledge, freedom being granted seemed like an impossibility, and yet it has happened. The impossible is possible. Ideas are not immortal — they can be killed by newer and stronger ones."

Daniel gripped his hands together in his lap. His fingers flexed, the muscles at his neck tightened, and he felt he couldn't control the expressions his face was making.

He tried to school his expression to something resembling calm.

"I don't believe I'll be swayed by the words of a white Englishman who gets to leave this country and never deal with its inherent evil again. If someone were to get rid of Davis, in a public and terrible manner, the South would know fear. It would puncture this puffed up pretense of grandeur they've created. If you aren't up to the task, just say so, but don't hide behind these false notions of justice and an America that doesn't exist."

Roberts nodded a moment, then rubbed at his chin.

"That doesn't exist *yet.* You are still in the cradle as a country. Not even one hundred years have passed since Yorktown! There remains plenty of potential in this American experiment; hope is not lost, Mr. Cumberland."

"This country is young, but steeped in an evil as old as time. And sometimes evil only speaks the language of evil, and the only force that can stop it is one driven by a matching hatred. I cannot *hope* while men like Davis blithely rend the country in two and rip away the possibility for a better future."

Roberts chuckled ruefully. "All I will say is that if someone was to get rid of Davis they'd be doing his opponents a favor. And his generals, too. It would certainly be a shock, but while the mourning clothes were still starched, men with more common sense and political prowess who've been waiting to harness power would step into the empty space he left behind. I'd be worried indeed if anything were to happen to dear old Jeff."

Roberts didn't understand that all his talk of killing ideas actually fit perfectly with what Daniel had planned. To many a Southerner, Davis was a rallying point for their cause. His politics didn't matter, and neither did his prowess. He was an idea, and Daniel would smite that idea, lectures from an Englishman be damned.

Daniel stood. "I believe I'll go find Sanchez."

He didn't interrogate why he wanted to be with her instead of alone when the property was large enough to provide him with the latter. Maybe he would tell her his plan now. Or maybe he wouldn't. That was the thing with detectives: they tended to keep secrets, even when they shouldn't.

Roberts nodded. "Thank you for your assistance. Feel free to return later if you wish. I can use all the help I can get."

Daniel gave a terse nod and stalked out.

He had his own mission and a few words from Roberts wouldn't change his mind. Someone had to pay for all of this, didn't they? For his pain? For the pain of his people?

Daniel had already learned he could rely on neither God nor the law to pass judgment on evil men.

He'd do it himself, and take the consequences as they came.

Chapter 20

Janeta wanted to leave.

She didn't know where she would go, but the familiar wealth of Roberts's home, and the time to reflect on all that had passed since she'd left her own, assailed her resolve and her growing sense of self.

She felt like one of the ruined daguerreotypes she'd seen in the back room of the photographer in Palatka, with the photo's subject blurred and seemingly several versions of themselves struggling to exist at once.

It was hard, not falling back into the mind-set of the old Janeta while being waited on and chastised when she tried to help. It was hard, looking at Daniel working in Roberts's office, handsome and smiling, engaged deeply in conversation with Roberts. He'd spent the last two days at work, and though he occasionally sought her out, he'd kept their conversations cordial. All business, as he described what he'd read in the missives, and what Roberts said. Meanwhile, she couldn't stop thinking of the comfort she'd felt when their hands had touched on the porch.

She had been foolish to think a man like Daniel would want or need anything from a woman like her. He was . . . substantial, like one of the marble columns that lined the porch of the house. Janeta was an overexposed photograph who could be blown away with a light breeze.

After smiling and faking her way through dinner, and learning even more about the Sons of the Confederacy, who would have benefited from her information if she'd sent it, she'd claimed fatigue and went to lie in her bed. Now it was Lord knew what time of night and she was wide awake. She pulled on the thick dressing gown she'd been given and tied it shut. Even with that and her sleeping gown, she still felt a bit of a chill.

She made her way down the hallway of her wing of the house and into the library she'd discovered while aimlessly wandering the halls as Daniel and Roberts worked. She'd always gone to the library at Villa Sanchez when she was upset — not because she particularly cared for reading, but because the rest of her family certainly did not. Their library was for show, a room to be used for the occasional business meeting. She could always be alone there, and this library was no different it seemed.

High shelves full of important-looking books written by men who looked like Roberts or Papi or Henry. A small cabinet for the alcohol — brandy here, not rum. A fine, thick carpet that sank beneath her feet, and two upholstered chairs before the fireplace, which was cold but occupied by a stack of logs.

Perfect.

She lit one of the candles on a low side table and placed it in front of the fireplace, then stepped back as far as she could across the room. She reached into the pocket of her gown and closed her fingers around the cold blade of a throwing knife.

This was what a library was to Janeta — a room in which she could do as she pleased without her sisters calling her wild or an embarrassment. She could read books in a parlor without censure, but this was something that had required more privacy, and perhaps the use of a leather-bound book as a target if there was no wood lying about.

She was a little rusty, but she didn't worry about missing as she considered the balance of the first knife, found the perfect equilibrium as she took aim at the log behind the glowing candle, and let the sharp metal fly.

Thwack.

Thwack.

Thwack.

Three lines of metal embedded in the log now reflected the candle's dancing flame, and Janeta felt some of her frustration loosen within her. She went and collected the knives and repeated the motion again and again, until her wrist hurt and her mind was cleared of everything but the feel of warm metal in her palm and the satisfaction of hitting her target.

"You've been holding out on me, Sanchez."

The voice came from the darkness as she collected the knives and began to slip them into her pocket. It so startled her that she gasped and whirled, knocking the candle over. Just before the flame guttered out she caught sight of Daniel, emerging from the shadows. His eyes had caught the light, amusement and curiosity in an orange glow before darkness fell.

"How long have you been there?" she asked. Her own racing heartbeat thudded in her ears and she felt on the floor for a candle, grabbing it though she had no means of lighting it again.

"I've been coming here the past few nights to read." His deep voice sounded from across the room, but moved closer to her as he continued speaking. "It seems something about these moldy books is very efficient at putting me to sleep. It's a shame I can't carry a library in my pocket."

He was near her now. She couldn't see him, but she could feel his presence. She was glad she couldn't see him. Glad he couldn't read the panic in her eyes.

"It's good that you've been able to sleep," she said quietly.

"But you haven't. I was more than a little confused to awaken to the sight of you throwing knives in a state of undress."

She'd forgotten that she was only in her sleeping gown. It didn't matter. That was the least of her problems and besides, she'd done much worse with Henry while wearing layers upon layers of skirts and frills.

But this wasn't Henry. It was Daniel. Daniel who had looked at her with such warmth as they'd talked over the past few days. Daniel who had every reason to hate her if he found out the truth.

"It's a habit. Something I've done since I was a child. It's comforting, in a strange way."

He chuckled, and the sound wrapped

around her in the darkness. She wondered what it would feel like vibrating against her skin and her eyes glossed with tears.

Tonta. Tonta.

"Your mama let you throw knives in the house?" he asked.

"No one knew. The library was always quiet. No one would judge me there."

"Library. Your home had a library. I take it this wasn't a corner of a room with books your mother collected while cleaning the homes of rich whites, like my family's."

He wasn't judging her, just stating a fact — one that made clear he understood she'd provided less details about her background than she could have. She'd known when she'd said it that it would jostle something in his mind, and begin laying down the foundation for a truth she couldn't tell him. She couldn't. How could she?

She had to.

"Yes, I grew up in homes not very different from this. Large, and staffed by slaves. I lived a lavish, pampered lifestyle that was the result of a wealth made from the work of those very same slaves."

He didn't speak, but she could feel his silence and all it might contain — judgment, anger, hate. It didn't matter. Lying was so easy to her, but the truth? If she was going to tell the truth, she was happy to do it in the dark.

"I am a spy, Daniel. I was one, rather. No, I still am, but not how I was . . ." She growled in frustration as the words piled up on her tongue. "*Odio este lengua feo!* I am not what you think, Daniel. I am a bad person. I —"

I can't tell him. I can't. Why? He doesn't have to know.

A sob trembled from her lips instead of what she needed to say. The darkness had provided her too much confidence. The sun would rise, soon, and there would be no hiding from Daniel's hatred of her.

"Janeta." Daniel was right next to her now, and she felt his touch ripple through the darkness right before his fingertips reached her sleeves. There was no anger in his grip on her arm, and that gentleness was what pulled a hiccupping sob from her. She remembered her first thought had been that he would be easy to take advantage of because he was alone and needed a friend. In the end, she was the one who needed him.

"Tell me." His voice was deep and smooth and encouraging.

"You will hate me," she said.

She waited for him to remind her that he

already did. Instead, he pulled her into his arms, holding her loosely so that she wasn't pressed against him.

"I thought the only thing I had in me was hate, but oddly enough I don't hate you," he said. "Not sure I can. I've certainly tried."

She let her head drop down and rest on his shoulder. He would push her away eventually, but she was pathetic enough to steal this comfort while she could.

"I am Cubana, descended of slaves and conquistadores," she said, finally. "My mother was a slave on my father's plantation, and he married her after his first wife died. I grew up doted on, loved, but reminded constantly, constantly, that I wasn't like *them* working the field."

His body tensed, but she plowed forward. There was no going back now, just like dawn couldn't be held back to keep the world shrouded in the safety of the shadows.

"I wasn't allowed to mingle with the slaves, and though there were free Blacks, my parents didn't associate with them. Then Mami died and we moved to Florida because that was easier than living in Santiago without her, I suppose. America was hard for me — I was always assumed to be a slave, or worse, my father's mistress." She shuddered at the memory of the lewd insinuations she'd overheard. "And then Henry started courting me, started telling me that I was beautiful just as I was. That I was beautiful *because* of what I was. When the war came, all he asked for in return was information. That didn't seem like a lot to give to be loved."

Daniel had stopped breathing as he listened. She could sense his stillness. She hurried to get out the rest.

"When my father was imprisoned by the Union because of information I provided Henry with, Henry told me to join the Loyal League. He said that finding out your secrets would help my father get free, and that there was some group, the Sons of the Confederacy, that would make sure of it." She tightened her fingers around his forearms. "I haven't told him anything. I know my word means nothing, but I swear —"

He sucked in a breath. "How could you even consider it? Betraying your own people?"

"I never *had* people." She tried to keep the tears out of her voice. "I only knew what I'd been taught, and what I was taught was wrong. And I'm *angry* because I believed it. I wanted to please everyone, but I couldn't. Now I know the truth — Henry used me. I can't free my father. I'll be kicked out of the Loyal League. And then there's you."

Her teeth ground together as her mouth snapped shut. She knew what to do to make him pity her. To make him soothe her. But she couldn't bring herself to say any more. She didn't want to manipulate his affection. She wanted what she couldn't have. She wanted him to love her as she was — willful and weak, brazen and broken, devious *y descarada* — of his own volition.

Impossible.

"You embarked on your quest to join the Loyal League with the intention of spying for the Confederacy. Is that all?" he asked.

She whipped her head up. She couldn't make out his features, just the vague shape of his head, but for some reason she knew he was grinning. There was amusement in his voice when there should have been anger.

"What?"

"Janeta, I'm no Ellen Burns, but I am a detective who's seen more than his fair share of action. Did you really think I knew nothing about this?"

Her head was spinning, spinning, and her knees buckled beneath her. Daniel caught her because of course he would.

"You knew? How?" She couldn't stop the

heaving sobs of relief that shook her body. Her hands clasped at his clothing and she came up with fistfuls of his shirt and held on for dear life.

He guided her to the chair in the darkness, seemingly feeling his way, and dropped her into it before perching on the arm beside her. He ran his hand over her hair, the soothing sensation calming her though she shook with emotion.

"LaValle, the man you first presented yourself to, suspected you because of intelligence he'd received from sources in Florida while tracking illegal importation of enslaved Cubans. He sent out a call for information, and as you know, the enslaved hear all. You traveled from Palatka in a coach driven by an enslaved man, and on a train with enslaved porters, and your contacts had enslaved people around them as they discussed how useful you would be to their cause."

Her chest hurt and she was having trouble breathing. He knew. He had always known.

"They paired me with a new detective with no training and no common sense because they know I won't show you any mercy."

Now she understood the meaning behind those words.

"Why." Her body felt heavy and her

tongue heavier. She didn't have the strength to make the word a question. "You could have . . . stopped me."

She should have been frightened right now, with his hand resting on her head, and his strength so much greater than hers, but she knew Daniel wouldn't hurt her as he could have. As perhaps he *should* have hurt an enemy spy.

"Well, you might have been useful to our Cause," Daniel said quietly. "I was tasked with watching you, making sure you didn't pass on information, and seeing what I could learn from you. Dyson assigned you to me because the Sons of the Confederacy were my particular interest — and because he thought I was a ruthless bastard who would do what was necessary to make sure you didn't threaten the 4L or the Union."

An unexpected, and ironic, flare of anger and betrayal rose up in her as she thought of his probing questions and his annoyance with her and his insistence on what a burden she was to him. Now she knew why he had been so extremely aggravated, why he'd treated her like a child he had to watch over. That had been his explicit task — to watch over her. To fool her into opening up to him. And to get rid of her if necessary. Perhaps his kindnesses had been false ones.

Perhaps he had used her just as Henry had — and as she had intended to use him.

She took back her previous thought: Daniel *could* hurt her. Not physically, but the pain in her chest was no less real than if he had pulled his blade on her. His words ricocheted through her body like buckshot, the implications multiplying. If everything she knew of him had been a lie, everything she had based her new truth in was, too.

Hot tears slicked down her cheeks. She tried to breathe, and managed somehow, though she felt as if she might rip apart the seams of the self she'd pieced together since infiltrating the Loyal League.

"What did you learn from me?" she asked. "Wait, I can tell you. That I'm a foolish woman who everyone pats on the head and allows to believe she might have some use in this world?"

Her voice broke on the last word and she raised a fist to her mouth to silence her sobs in the darkness. That fist couldn't stop her shoulders from shaking. Daniel's hand slid from her hair, down her neck, to rest on her back. He rubbed there gently, his large hand warming her as he soothed.

Soothed.

"I learned that you are an intelligent, caring woman who has the potential to be quite the Loyal League detective, no matter how you came to join." His hand circled slowly between her shoulder blades, loosening the anxiety there. "It's not like my intentions for joining were so pure. I'll be the last person to judge you."

"How can you not?"

Her words echoed in the darkness of the library, followed by the slide of the fabric of his pants along the arm of the chair. He moved in front of her.

"For what?" He made a sound of annoyance. "All right, I can't say spying for the Confederacy is something that should be overlooked. But you are the product of your family, and at the first opportunity to do the right thing, you did. I won't laud you, but I won't mark you as a lost cause, either."

Janeta wanted to scream. All the stress and all her fears — this wasn't how she'd imagined the revelation going at all. She hadn't thought through what would happen if he didn't hate her because that had seemed like an impossibility.

"I was so scared you would find out. And then I was scared you wouldn't. Because what I want —" She swallowed against her fear. "What I want is for you to know me, Daniel. But to know me is to know this terrible thing I have done."

"I know you, Janeta."

Janeta shook her head, but warmth was flowing through her. "No, if you did, you would know I don't deserve forgiveness."

"What exactly did you do that I should punish you for?" he asked, a familiar exasperation creeping into his voice. "I'm certain you didn't pass on any information."

"I didn't. But I was determined to." She couldn't let him brush this aside.

He sighed. "I'm sure you were. Luckily for us both you're a terrible detective."

Laughter bubbled up in her, pushing past the obstruction of fear and shame, surprising her.

"Both Dyson and me were counting on the fact that I have no heart." His fingertips brushed her cheeks as he moved from his perch on the arm of the chair, and she could make out the darker shadow of his bulk as he kneeled before her. "I was wrong about that. I have one, and it's beating so strong and steady I almost can't stand it. It's beating again."

His words grated from his throat, a painful confession, and she realized what had happened in the safety of the dark library. They'd opened themselves up completely in a place their vulnerabilities were less visible. But she'd already known Daniel had a heart. And he'd already discovered something good in her, too. They had already seen each other, could *see* each other even now, in the deepest, darkest night. That was as much a miracle as either of them being there to begin with.

She placed her hand against his chest again and spread her fingers.

"Daniel. I want to kiss you," she said. "May I?"

"I will never again prevent a woman I care for from doing what she wants. As long as it's not spying for the Rebels, that is." His voice rumbled out, deep and amused and moving closer in the darkness until the warmth of his breath caressed her cheek. "Kiss me."

She turned her head and heeded his command, but in the darkness her lips crashed into his nose. They laughed, the sound full of anticipation; they moved toward each other again, more slowly this time, and the laughter dissolved into groans of pleasure as their mouths connected.

She grabbed his face in her hands to hold him close to her, so that nothing could come between them — not even the velvet shadow of night.

His kiss tasted of the earth, something green and bittersweet — likely the tea he'd drank before bed. His lips moved against hers with a focused intensity that seemed to somehow match that taste, inexorable as nature itself. His tongue probed her mouth with such shocking intimacy that it made her body heat; she'd been waiting for their kiss since the morning by the creek, and it seemed he had, too.

There was a sensual hunger in the press of his lips and his grip on her arms. She moved her hands, stroking up past his stubble and over the tight curls of his hair, down to his neck. She was afraid to let him go, she realized; she decided she wouldn't.

He was moving, though, and for a moment she was afraid he would pull away, but his hands patted over the chair and then her body before he slid one beneath her thighs and one at her lower back and lifted.

She felt herself hauled up against his chest before he took her place in the chair and lowered her onto his lap. She hiked up her gown as she settled her knees on either side of his waist, and when she lowered herself the bare skin of her inner thighs brushed the rough fabric of his trousers, a shocking friction. He was still kissing her, and now that she was settled his hands began to roam. His palms explored her curves, coiling the want and need inside of her. She moved her hips, pressing herself against the hard length of him.

It helped that he couldn't see her and she couldn't see him. Henry had eyed her greedily in the throes of passion, and she had confused his insatiability for love. Daniel's hands moved carefully, as did his mouth, but the rest of his body was still and she knew that he held himself back. He wasn't using her to slake his desires. He was touching and listening and waiting.

She pulled her mouth away from his.

"It's all right. I've already . . . I'm not a . . . You don't have to be gentle."

Daniel knew she'd had a lover, but perhaps he'd forgotten with the way his hands caressed her like she was fragile porcelain.

He was quiet for a moment, and she jumped at the intake of breath before he began to speak. "Do you *want* me to be?"

His question was as soft as his hands on her body, and that he had even asked filled her with equal parts lust and happiness. It was bittersweet, this joy at a man considering her feelings, because she'd never realized it was something she could ask for. Something she deserved.

"Yes, please."

"Good." His voice was a whisper that grazed her ear as his mouth moved toward her neck. "I need you to be gentle with me, too."

Then the warm softness of his lips brushed down the column of her neck. He was barely touching her, but the friction of their skin and the caress of his breath sent a shiver of pleasure through her body. When his mouth hit juncture of neck and shoulder, he suckled and she gasped as sensation exploded through her body. His slow, soft touches shouldn't have sent heat racing through her veins, but there was something indescribably arousing in the way he treated her with such care.

And she wanted to return the favor. Daniel was a large man, and strong, but she would take him at his word — he needed care, too. She pressed the sweetest of kisses to his temples, ran her hands over his neck and the ridged scar there, then splayed them over his muscled chest.

"I want to feel your skin," she whispered. "Against mine."

His pectorals tightened and released beneath her palms and she felt the evidence of his approval of her plan surge against her apex.

"You can unbutton my shirt," he said. His fingertips slid to the front of her wrapper and pushed it down her shoulders, then returned to her loose-fitting sleeping gown, which she pushed down as well. She pulled her arms free and settled the material around her waist before feeling for his buttons with trembling fingertips.

Daniel had been still before, but now his hips rocked up against her, his trousers sliding against the hair at her mound, and his hardness pressing into the sensitive flesh within her folds.

Desire cloaked her, along with the darkness, and she moved her hips to meet his restrained thrust. Finally, she spread his shirt wide and ran her hands over his furred chest. He groaned when her palms slid over his smooth, flat nipples, so she retraced her path and he groaned again.

She slid her hand down over the ridges of his abdomen until her fingertips hit the clasp of his trousers. She paused.

"Do you want . . . this?" she asked. Her voice was husky and it trembled because her body was trembling, too.

"I want *you,* Janeta. All of you."

Relief flowed through her, the urge to thank him so strong she had to swallow it before speaking. It wasn't like that between them. He wouldn't want her to be thankful to him or any man, and that was why she cared for him. "I want you, too, Daniel."

"Not all of me," he said, and she knew that he would pull himself away from her if he was given the opportunity. She pressed her mouth against his, kissed him until he released a shuddering breath against her lips and opened for her.

"I want any part of you you're willing to share with me," she said. He kissed her hard then. Not roughly, but with an excess of emotion that he couldn't convey with a brush of lips. His palms slid over the bare skin of her breasts and stomach, and he groaned with the pleasure of just those touches.

Then her hands went to work at his trousers, and they both shifted and arranged themselves until his erection was wrapped in her hand, a few inches from her opening.

"Take me," he growled into her neck. "I'll give you everything. All of me."

For a moment she considered that these were the same empty promises Henry had whispered to her. Then his doubt spoke again, reminding her that he was as vulnerable as she was in this situation.

"I can only hope it's enough."

She didn't answer him, or soothe him with words. She couldn't make him believe how she felt with a well-turned phrase. Instead, she slid down onto his cock, taking him into her deep and fast, and when they both cried out in pleasure it was muffled by their joined mouths and dueling tongues.

He filled her so completely she almost fell apart at that first stroke, but then he took over. His hands at her waist held her steady against the deep, steady thrusting of his hips. She cursed the darkness now — feeling him was wonderful, but she wanted to see him.

She did the next best thing. She leaned her body forward, her breasts brushing the hair at his chest. She threw her arms around his neck and pulled their bodies closer. She took his mouth and when they kissed this time, it was a clash of warmth and heat and pleasure. Her sleeping clothes bunched between their stomachs, forcing a bend at her waist that increased the friction and slide of him inside of her.

"Janeta," he growled, turning his face into her hair. His breath came in heavy huffs that tickled her scalp. "Janeta."

His arms wrapped around her, trying to pull her closer. His entire body strained as if he would make them one.

"Janeta." There was pleasure and pain and hope and longing in the way he exhaled her name, and her climax took her without warning, seemingly compelled by the *need* in his voice. She clamped around him and he hissed his own release as he wrapped his arms more tightly around her.

They sat wrapped around each other, breathing heavily. Through the window she could see the first traces of dawn. They wouldn't be in the shadows for much longer.

"I suppose we should leave," Daniel said eventually.

Janeta drowsed with her head on her shoulder. "We have to wait for the meeting," she said.

"Look at you. A dedicated detective." He chuckled and she felt it all through her body. "I meant we should leave the library."

She felt a pang of disappointment until he pressed a kiss to her forehead.

"My room is closer than yours."

There was a playful desire in his tone, and it sparked a corresponding heat in her body.

"Then I'll follow you there, Cumberland."

They stood and rearranged themselves in the dark, but when her hand searched out his, there was no fumbling or groping. It was right where she expected it to be, even though she couldn't see it, and that was another surprising joy.

"Let's go," he said. They were both still for a moment and she realized he was waiting for her to proceed. She started walking, and so did he, and she hoped they were both leaving the darkness of their pasts behind them.

Chapter 21

"What will you do today?" Janeta asked, running the tip of her nose along Daniel's collarbone before nuzzling against his neck. It had only been three days since their time in the library, and it still shocked him how quickly he'd gone from avoiding touch to reveling in Janeta's.

But, perhaps better than the touch was the talking. Sleep was still somewhat elusive, and the dark voices hadn't loosened their grip on him entirely. But instead of lying alone with his own pain, Daniel could now roll to his side and find the glint of Janeta's eyes in the darkness. They whispered of things silly and serious, and when he heard the panic or pain she tried to mask, he reassured her as best he could.

That was all people could really do for one another, he supposed. Take care of each other during the bad times — and there would always be bad times — and make each other happy during the good. Would there always be good, though? Her question reminded him that he had come here with a plan, and it had not been lazing in bed with her.

He kissed the top of her head and moved from the bed in her room and began pulling on his clothing.

"The meeting may be taking place soon," he said, then halted. "The Sons of the Confederacy, Jefferson Davis . . ."

"Ah, *sí,*" Janeta murmured. "You know, I imagine I could get some information from Henry if I wrote to him. In retrospect, he was not a very bright man, though he managed to fool me. But perhaps that would be safer than whatever it is you have in mind?"

He could imagine her raised eyebrows though he couldn't see them.

"That might be helpful," he said. "Though you should check in with Dyson on that before making contact, lest he think you've changed sides again?"

"Again?" she asked carefully.

"I wrote to him before you confessed to me and told him that I suspected your sympathies had never been very strong, and were now firmly for the North." He'd also written to Elle — not out of some misguided pining, but because she was his friend, and he had a very specific goal in Enterprise, one that perhaps meant he would never get another chance to write to her again.

"You trusted me that much." It wasn't a question.

"Yes, Sanchez. Now you just have to trust yourself." He tried to sound jaunty and flirty and not like a man throwing up a distraction. He walked over to the bed and dropped a kiss onto her mouth. "I'll be working in Roberts's office."

"I thought I might try to check in on Shelley and Moses and Jim and Augustus," she said. "Maddie said she'd help me arrange some things they might need while setting up house and have Michael bring them over."

Daniel smiled. "Make sure you send a big walloping stick for Moses."

She laughed. "I hope we can see them before we leave."

Daniel didn't answer this time. He kissed her knuckles and strode out of the room. Lying had never been his strong suit, but silence certainly was.

Daniel sat at the desk in Roberts's office that had become his working space over the last few days and read through the final letter, another from this Lord Russell, who had been managing Secretary Seward's ego from London and attempting to make the man see reason where it came to the consul in Mississippi.

After days of going through the correspondence with government officials, he was frustrated. The men entrusted with the future of the country were stubborn, pig-headed, and shortsighted, often working at cross-purposes fueled by their own political ambition. Daniel had thought greed was their worst vice; it was unsettling to truly understand that petty squabbling and sheer ignorance were just as dangerous.

"I used to think America's youth was an asset, but we're not even one hundred years into this republic as you reminded me, and look at us," Daniel said.

Roberts laughed. "If you think that age improves the temperament of governance I invite you to visit Parliament sometime. Grown men coming to blows on the floor of government. I once saw a lord get battered over the head with a chair. Perhaps once you've ascertained your position as a lawyer it would make for a good research visit."

Annoyance flared that Roberts should mention this as if it were something so easily achieved.

"That dream is dead," Daniel said carefully. He'd told himself the same thing a thousand times over but now somewhere in his mind a voice whispered, *What if it isn't?*

"Well, what will you do when this war is over, then?" Roberts asked, and the question amounted to the same as a bucket of freezing water being dumped over Daniel. He didn't know what he would do. He'd stopped planning on a future, even after one had been presented to him by the men who had freed him. Even though he'd been granted life and liberty, to some extent, he'd forever ruled out the notion of happiness.

Could he ever live a normal life? Go to work, come home to a wife?

Janeta's image flashed into his mind, the feel of her warmth in his arms.

He blinked the memory away; he wouldn't deny that he cared for her, more deeply than he'd imagined possible, but though she had an admirable inner strength, she was a woman, not a foundation. She couldn't support the weight of his entire future as well as her own, and he shouldn't expect her to. He'd have to figure out whether he was capable of living before he thought about whether he could live with her. He certainly couldn't live *for* her. He'd already walked down that path once and it had led to self-pitying despair.

She also wasn't even American. Would she stay in this country now that she saw all the ugly cracks in the façade of freedom? Could he ask her to?

"I'm not sure," he said, shifting the letters around on his desk. He picked up the letter he'd sealed that morning, a second missive addressed to Ellen Burns just in case the other never reached her, and tapped a pointed corner with his fingertips. "I'll have to see how this war shakes out before I make any plans."

He expected Roberts to make a wry joke, but the man nodded gravely. The few days in the home with lavish amenities and stocked with food made it easy to forget that this war was not yet won, and that the South very well might take the day.

Michael entered the room, jogging over to the larger desk.

"A message come for you," he said, handing Roberts a slip of paper. Roberts's brow creased and he stood abruptly. When he looked at Daniel his gaze was serious.

"There's been a change in plans. President Davis was supposed to head down farther South and then circle back, but the railroad tracks got pulled up down the line. He'll be arriving here this evening."

Panic knotted the muscles in Daniel's neck. He hadn't forgotten about Davis's arrival, but he no longer relished it as he had when the Russians had first made his travel plans known. Back then, Daniel had thought that he had nothing to live for. Now he wasn't so sure.

He looked to Roberts. "I imagine you'll have to prepare."

"Indeed. There's also the fact that he will be bringing company with him. I will talk to you and Ms. Sanchez later about how we are to handle things." He gave Daniel a weighted look, but said nothing further before turning and stalking from the room.

How to handle things.

Daniel had been sure of how he wanted to handle Jefferson Davis — with the sharp edge of his blade. Even now, the thought of Davis traveling in the grandest style while Negroes had to constantly fear being stripped of their possessions, family, and freedom made his blood heat.

He tried to shake off the tension and anger as he left the office and searched the house for Janeta, finally finding her in her room. He was no stranger to her chamber, but he put on an air of distant professionalism as he knocked. He didn't know why he bothered; any 4L detective could tell you that servants saw and heard all. Everyone in the house likely knew of their dalliance, and that was the least of his worries.

The door to her room opened, but she didn't greet him with the enthusiasm they'd shared for the past few days. Her expression was somber and her eyes were rimmed with red.

"Have you heard?" she asked.

"Yes, it's sooner than we expected, and I realize I haven't told you what I intended to do once he arrives."

Because he'd avoided telling her.

Was this still his plan? Before he'd been focused on the possible benefits of ridding the world of Davis. He hadn't thought of the possible negative outcomes. He hadn't thought about surviving, or even wanting to.

"Arrives? What do you mean?" A ridge formed on her brow. "I'm speaking of Moses."

Daniel's blood iced over at the hushed way she said the child's name. He gripped the door frame.

"What's happened to him?"

He remembered Winnie tracing her letters in the dust, proud of her work. He'd shown Moses his letters, too.

"The overseer at the farm tried to hit

Shelley, or maybe something worse. No one really knows. It was the middle of the night, and Moses said that he was trying to stop the monster."

Daniel brought his other hand to his stomach, pressing in against the nausea that roiled there. No, not the letters but something else he had said mindlessly. "This is my fault."

"No, it is mine." Janeta pulled him into the room and shut the door. "Michael found out when he tried to deliver the package to them. Augustus and Jim interceded before the man could harm Moses, but they were all taken into custody. They're in the jail now, and there are strangers in town starting trouble and saying the only way to teach them a lesson is to 'string them up.' "

Daniel resisted the urge to clutch his throat, to feel the ridge formed by the rope that had slowly strangled him for hours while wearing away his skin. He doubted Jim and Augustus would be subject to that slow torture, but who knew what would happen to them before then.

It seemed that everyone he encountered met a bad end. He'd harmed Winnie and the other slaves, who'd suffered Finnegan's wrath. He'd done his fellow Loyal League detectives a disservice by fighting with anger instead of the hope he was incapable of. And if he stayed with Janeta, she would meet a terrible end, too.

You are poison, the ugly voice in his head reminded him, and nothing could drown it out, not even Janeta standing before him. *Poison has one purpose.*

Janeta stepped closer to him, her expression distraught. "We have to go to Meridian. We can go by cover of night and —"

"And what?" The coldness of his voice shocked even him. In his mind, his thoughts were scattered, scrambling and trying to find shelter — they sought refuge in the familiar darkness that had been with him since his capture.

He wanted to hold Janeta. He wanted to help Jim and Augustus and Moses. But he couldn't. He couldn't help anyone because he was selfish and a coward and a fool, and a bit of love wouldn't change that. Pretending otherwise would only lead to pain, and to Janeta being hurt, too.

"And help them," she said, clearly confused.

He could read the hurt in her eyes. She'd never been good at hiding it; that hadn't been her skill. But he wouldn't stop hurting her because if he let her think this was a good idea for one moment, she could run off and get herself killed.

"What makes you think you can help them? You have failed at nearly every level as a detective, but you think you can rush in and save the day?"

Her expression crumpled and her shoulders hunched, and Daniel hated himself even more. That didn't stop him, though. This was less frightening than the hope and light that had been set before him. It could be snatched away at any moment, because he was undeserving. He'd stamp out that light himself; at least then he wouldn't have to worry about someone else doing it for him.

"All you're going to do is cause them trouble. You're the pampered daughter of a slave master. Why should a few more Negroes suffering suddenly upset you?"

The tears flowed from her eyes, but where her gaze had been soft it now went steely.

"You know I read people well, even if I am a bad detective. I know exactly what I'm supposed to do here. Comfort you. Tell you that you're better than this and know the right thing to do." She shook her head and dashed the tears from her cheeks. "To hell with that. You're trying to hurt me? To push me away? You've succeeded."

Daniel sighed and flexed his feet in his

boots to make sure the floor was still solid beneath him. He felt as if the world had tilted sideways and he was clawing toward the only thing that made sense to him in his pain: vengeance. "Jefferson Davis and representatives from the Sons of the Confederacy will be here in a few hours. We don't have time for emotions."

She laughed, and the harsh beauty of the sound hit him like she'd thrown one of her knives into his chest. "*Dios mío,* that's amusing. I'm crying because I'm frustrated with your behavior, which is delaying me in saving our friends. You're lashing out because you're afraid. But please do tell me about how *my* emotions are the problem here, Cumberland."

He exhaled a shaky breath. "I may never have the opportunity to be this close to Davis again. Someone has to do what's right for our people."

Her eyes went wide.

"You're serious." The disappointment in her voice was almost like a balm, soothing the parts of Daniel's mind that told him he deserved no better. "You really suppose that chasing after Davis is doing what's right for our people when our friends are imprisoned? Because of us?"

Daniel shook his head, stepped back.

"Jim understands," Daniel said. "He knows that Davis has to be stopped."

"What about Moses? Oh." Understanding dawned in her eyes, and her lips formed a blanched dusky pink line as she nodded stiffly. "I see now. Our people are your means to an end. You want a reason to hurt someone, to make people hurt like you've been hurting. You'd rather do that than help."

Daniel walked around her into the room, his feet carrying him to the window because he couldn't look at her anymore.

"I'm doing what the Loyal League expects of me," he said as he watched servants preparing for the arrival of the President of the South. "I'm doing what no one else wants to sully their hands with."

"You're hiding. And you're *choosing* this. No one is making you do anything."

"You're right." He looked back over his shoulder at her. "I'm choosing to do my job as a detective."

"If I'm such a failure as a detective, then you'll accept my resignation." She began pacing around the room, gathering her bag. She drew out her pistols and examined them, pulled out her ammunition box and closed it securely before placing it in his bag.

"You can leave my room now." She didn't look at him. "Me and my emotions have to figure out how to help our friends, and you and your vengeance have your own logistics to attend to."

Panic clawed at Daniel's back and shoulders and neck. This wasn't what he wanted.

But it's what you deserve.

"Janeta." She paused and her shoulders hunched.

"I want to ask you to stay. I want to say I can soothe that hurt inside of you. I can't. I will be here for you if you need me, but I won't be a target for you to direct your pain at." She released a shaky breath. "Leave. I'm scared I won't be able to say that again. If you're going to be hard, be gentle about it. *Dejame tranquila.* Please."

Pain bloomed in Daniel's chest. He knew he should stay. They were partners. Friends. Lovers. And he cared for her. But she was better off without him. Everyone was. If he stayed, he'd be sealing her fate, just as he had for everyone else.

He stormed from the room, his mind full of darkness and confusion that he hoped would give way to clarity. He had an assassination to plan.

That was all he was good for.

Chapter 22

Janeta willed herself not to cry. That only a few tears escaped reminded her of how strong she was, not how weak. She'd survived losing Mami. She'd survived moving to a strange new world, being used body and soul by her lover, and watching her father be dragged off in chains.

Her whole life had been surviving as she knew best — she'd figure out how to make do without Daniel. This was what life was: swallowing bitter disappointment and smiling instead of retching it back onto the ground. Hoping there was some nourishment mixed in with the pain.

She'd sank down onto the edge of her bed as soon as Daniel had left the room, her travel bag clutched in her hand. She hurt for herself, but she hurt for him, too.

He'd said horrible things to her, and she couldn't easily forgive that. But he'd forgiven Janeta her worst transgressions —

against him, his country, and their people.

And she had recognized exactly what he was doing as he spoke to her. He'd found the words that would hurt her most and hurled them at her, aiming their sharp tips at her vital organs. It had been all the more painful because only someone who knew her well would have been able to hone in on those things. Daniel had said he knew her and he hadn't been lying, and he'd used that knowledge to push her away because it frightened him, his knowing her.

She'd seen the fear and confusion in his eyes even as he'd used the strength of their connection as a cudgel. It might have been unpardonable if it hadn't revealed so much about how he saw her, and how he saw himself.

She remembered how even in the safety of the dark library he'd been sure of his own lacking. She remembered how he'd cried out into the night in the Mississippi woods. And she remembered his face when he'd talked about his experience during his enslavement, and how he had made life worse for everyone around him. Daniel was a man who focused on the fact that he seemed to attract sorrow. And now the people they had just traveled with were in trouble.

Janeta brushed away the tears that welled in her eyes again. Daniel was hurting because he thought he'd hurt others. He was running toward what he knew: violence and pain and maybe death. And Janeta couldn't save him.

For the first time in a long time she allowed herself to think of her mother in those last days. How she had stopped eating and lost the will to live, and cried for her own mother in a language Janeta could not understand — she had understood her mother's pain, though. That had needed no translation, but she had been unable to do anything to fix it.

"You must be perfect," her mother muttered to her, twisting at her matted hair.

"I will, Mami," Janeta said. She pretended her mother didn't smell terrible and look like a skeleton and smiled brightly.

Her mother's bony fingers grabbed her by the face and, even though it hurt, Janeta didn't let her mouth pull down into a frown. She didn't want to upset Mami.

"Good girl. You must smile. You must give them what they want so they won't send you to the fields." The tears started again then. "My mother couldn't save me. Maybe I can't save you. I couldn't even save myself."

Her mother had cried and cried, and the

doctors had suggested she be sent to the sanitarium. Papi had decided against it, and one day Janeta had woken up to quiet — there had been no more tears from Mami, just the silence of the grave.

She had tried everything she could to save her mother. Toward the end she'd even begged her to leave her bed, falling to her knees and tugging at her hands as their slaves looked on with pity and judgment in their eyes. But whatever ghosts had haunted her mother were too numerous for Janeta to defeat without her mother's help. And whatever haunted Daniel was the same.

Her mother hadn't been weak, and neither was Daniel. They'd had their souls crushed by a world not worthy of them, and however much she wished it, Janeta was not enough to heal someone else's soul. Her love was strong, but it wasn't magic.

When Daniel had turned away from her, he had walked into his own lake of pain and submerged himself. She'd told him she would be waiting on the shore for him. She could only hope that he would return to her — not because she needed him or he needed her, but because he'd caught a glimmer of his own worth in the past few days. He needed to walk back to land for himself, of his own volition. She couldn't help him before that, as much as she wanted to. There were others who she could help, though.

She took a deep breath and stood from the bed.

She was Janeta Sanchez: daughter of slaves and conquistadores, former Rebel spy, disgraced 4L detective. She was a photograph that had just been developed, and the picture was of a woman who would trust in the abilities she'd been given. She was going to save their friends, with or without Daniel's help.

She began moving down the hallway with purpose, toward the front door and the unknown. Janeta had always done well at strategy games because she could often read people's minute reactions. This was a different kind of strategizing. She couldn't see her opponents, and might rush headlong into something that required subtlety.

She heard the sound of something being dragged as she passed one of the empty rooms and poked her head in. Maddie and Michael were somberly packing Roberts's belongings into wooden crates. Several wooden crates large enough for the ornate furniture stacked along one wall stood empty.

Janeta felt the stirrings of possibility.

"What is all of this?" Janeta asked politely.

"Mr. Roberts's belongings?"

"Yes," Michael said as he carefully wrapped glassware. "The rails to the South is all messed up by the Yanks, bless 'em, but we got to load 'em up and send 'em off North."

Inspiration struck Janeta. Cargo was cargo, was it not? If she could get to Jim and Augustus and get them inside the wooden boxes —

"It's not gonna work, girl," Maddie said, scrutinizing her. "They gotta open the boxes to check the cargo, and the way they load 'em is too dangerous besides."

"What do you mean?" Janeta tried to feign ignorance, but the woman wouldn't allow her to.

"You know that we know everything that happens in this house. You can't save those men with some half-cocked idea. But if there really is Sons of Confederacy around here stirring up trouble for your friends, then maybe I know someone willing to help you."

Maddie spoke with a surety that surprised Janeta, though it shouldn't have.

"Ever heard of the Daughters of the Tent, girl?" Michael asked calmly, still packing.

"No," Janeta said. "Wait, yes. Roberts mentioned them at that first dinner. Is it another secret organization?"

"Secret enough to get what needs to be done done," Maddie said. "We don't have time for all this messing about with handshakes and passcodes and 4L nonsense. Men are so tiresome with their ceremonies. Just get to work!"

Maddie sucked her teeth.

"You are a detective?"

Maddie shrugged. "I ain't no detective. I'm a woman trying to help her people working with other women trying to help their people. What are you?"

Janeta took a deep breath. "That. *Sí,* I think I am exactly that."

Maddie nodded firmly. "Well, then. Welcome to the Daughters of the Tent."

Chapter 23

"She's gone, you know." Roberts said the words casually as he took a sip of his brandy.

Daniel was pacing in agitation. "I know."

When he'd gone back to Janeta's room, her bag had been gone. He didn't know what he'd expected to find on the scrap of paper lying on her bed, but the short missive had lanced him worse than reading all of Elle's letters had.

I know you're a good man. You need to know you're a good man. Buena suerte.

Daniel had crumpled the paper, then flattened it and smoothed out the wrinkles before tucking it into his pocket. For someone who didn't care about connections, he was terrible at letting go of them.

"Do you know where she is?" he asked.

"Yes." Roberts took a sip of his drink and ran a hand through his hair. "Davis should be here by now."

Daniel stopped pacing and looked at Roberts. "You're not going to tell me?"

"If she wanted you to know she would have told you herself. Or perhaps you have some idea, and could go find her, but you are here instead."

Daniel ran the heel of his hand along his stubbled jaw. "I'm a detective working for an organization that has prioritized undermining the Rebels. If Jefferson Davis is going to be here, if the Sons of the Confederacy are going to be here, then I will be here."

"And how exactly will your presence undermine them, if I may ask?"

Daniel simply stared at Roberts. "These men have committed countless atrocities. They should pay for them."

Roberts laughed without humor. "Cumberland, I know you mean well, but this mind-set can only lead to ruination. I have yet to meet a politician holding high office either home or abroad who has not played a part in some atrocity or another." He held up his hand when he saw Daniel ready to leap in with questions. "I do not condone this. I simply ask whether you believe that every politician be made to pay? Because your current government in the capital has done the Indian tribes many a disservice, in addition to the abominable treatment of the Negro. Should they not pay? And who will make them?"

"I don't have time for your detached morality," Daniel bit out.

"I suppose not, since you've already made up your mind that you are the sole method of ending the Rebellion in the States. That no one else has thought 'oy, just kill him' in the history of civil wars before. I have to admire that kind of confidence."

Daniel stalked over to Roberts and looked him in the eye. "I will not be the jest of a white man with no stake in this matter."

"A smaller stake." Roberts held his gaze and lifted his glass to his lips. The bottom of it grazed Daniel's chin.

Daniel felt the ugliness rise inside of himself again, the same that had led him to lash out at Janeta. "Ah, let me guess. You fell in love with a slave girl, or had some poor abused friend who met a pathetic end at the hand of racists. Or you feel that you must save us because we cannot save ourselves."

Roberts's nostrils flared. "If one need have personal reason to find slavery abhorrent, that is abhorrent in itself. I despised slavery from the moment I knew of its existence. I do not think it belongs in a fair and just world, and I need no reason further than that to throw everything I have against it."

"Aren't you special?" Daniel sneered.

"Absolutely not. Well, yes, in other ways. I'm quite a good poet, if you must know. But because of this? No." Roberts opened and closed his mouth, a movement Daniel had seen when the man struggled to compose his thoughts. "I understand that this is personal for you in ways that I can never, ever understand. It must chafe to have me presume to know what you should or should not do. I do not. I would simply ask that you ask yourself *why* you are doing something, and who it will benefit, and in what way."

Roberts moved away from him, toward the window, and Janeta's words popped into his mind. *You need to know you're a good man.*

Though the room he was in was bright with late-afternoon sunshine, he felt consumed by darkness. He thought of the troubles he had caused at the plantation, with his fellow detectives, with Elle . . . his head snapped up.

Presumption.

He had presumed he knew what Elle wanted, and how enslaved people should behave, and what his fellow detectives really thought of him. And he had been wrong.

And now he was presuming to know how to fix the Jefferson Davis situation, but in truth he wasn't sure he was right. He'd sworn his Loyal League oath on vengeance instead of the 4L — Loyalty, Legacy, Life, and Lincoln — but he'd begun to think that perhaps vengeance was the true toxin — perhaps he was poisonous, because he carried that toxin in him. Perhaps the only one to suffer its effect was himself.

"Ah. The first carriage is arriving. Come along. I suppose you can make yourself scarce if you don't want to pretend to be a servant. Don't try that Cuban bit again — your Spanish is atrocious."

Roberts walked away and Daniel followed him in a daze. There seemed to be a tunnel before his eyes, and he stared at Roberts's feet so that he would know where to step. The man was talking, but it was a murmur blocked out by the beating of Daniel's heart and the buzzing in his head. Sweat broke out on his scalp and palms, and his body felt incredibly heavy and slow.

An image of Winnie being yanked away by Finnegan appeared in his head. Winnie's wide eyes and fear, and how she had looked to Daniel for help. Her family's anger, and her crushed hands.

Daniel dropped to his knees in the hallway, the tunnel before him narrowing to a pinpoint. He couldn't breathe — he felt like he was drowning. And though he thought often of the peace death would bring, a sudden and overwhelming fear filled him.

He didn't want to die.

He had so much to do. He had something to live for. Not Janeta, though she was a part of it.

Moses's face floated before his. That boy was the future of this country. Would vengeance and death serve the Moseses and Winnies of America? Would it serve *Daniel*?

Something bittersweet and frightening spread within his chest, filling his lungs, and maybe filling his soul, slowly inflating the crushed, useless thing it had become.

Hope.

Hope.

Just the slightest ray of light, but even a trickle of light when you've been shrouded in the deepest darkness was painful and overwhelming.

God, how had he missed it? All those men and women and children in Cairo? Jim and Augustus and Shelley and Moses. There was something in all of them that knew they deserved freedom. Some had taken it for themselves, some had been granted it, and most would only get free if the South fell.

For all his anger at Lincoln and for all the Emancipation Proclamation's faults — what Roberts had said the other day was true. It was an ideal. It was a flame in the darkness. And if enough people added their own kindling to that flame, maybe it would be more than that. Maybe it would light the way toward something more.

Would Jefferson's blood fuel that flame or douse it?

The same optimism that Daniel had once felt as he pored over legal cases, searching for the key that would unlock the shackles of his people, galloped through the arid plains of his soul, leaving a trail of verdant green. That trail of green sliced through him like a wound; it was too much, this desire to believe that hope wasn't futile.

He dragged in a deep breath and the darkness before his vision began to clear. As the hallway came back into view, Daniel pushed himself back to his feet. He felt slightly woozy but walked to the end of the hall and turned the corner. Roberts had gone outside, but Daniel didn't follow him. He entered the dining room and made his way quietly to the window, moving aside the curtain to glance outside.

Jefferson Davis was a few feet away, on the other side of the glass. Daniel was frozen in place. He had built this man up in his imagination, made him into a dragon that needed to be slain, but he was a man. Tall, lean to the point of gauntness, with hollowed-out cheekbones that made his clear gray eyes seem too large. The wave of his hair was rumpled by travel, and his expression was serious but kind as he talked to Roberts.

A Black man bounded up the stairs, eyes locked on Davis, and for a moment Daniel thought someone had usurped his plan. But the man was smiling, and when Davis turned toward the movement, he smiled, too. The man handed Davis a small box, which Davis took. He clapped the man on the back and said something; then both he and the man laughed heartily.

Daniel closed the curtain as the man, likely his coachman or valet, jogged back down the stairs.

He didn't feel anger or hatred or rage. Jefferson Davis was a man who would die like any other. His death would change something, but exactly what Daniel could not predict with certainty. His eyes burned with pent-up anger and frustration, despite his recent burst of hope. Killing Davis wouldn't stop men like Finnegan, but a man like Finnegan had hurt Moses and Jim and

Augustus. Janeta had gone to Meridian to save them because that was what a true detective would do. She was fighting for Loyalty and Life and Love. And maybe . . .

Maybe Daniel was toxic because he'd been more loyal to his hate — of himself, of his country — than he had been to life and love. He was still broken. He was still unsure of his worth. But there was someone in his life who had picked up the torch that would light the way toward the future, when she had little reason to. She'd accepted her faults and was working to fix her mistakes instead of running from them. Daniel needed to follow that flame in the dark.

Hate made good kindling, but hope burned much brighter. It flared up in him, that sensation he'd thought he'd never feel again.

He stood in the parlor, the murmur of the President of the Confederacy outside the window, and walked away from the idea that his only use in this world was vengeance, or that vengeance was only hatred and pain. Vengeance was happiness in a world that wanted to crush him. Vengeance was love in a world that wished him misery. Vengeance was stopping injustice, like what might be perpetuated against his friends.

He made for the stables to find a horse

that would carry him to Meridian, and Janeta, as fast as the newfound purpose now pushing at his back. He would follow her down that verdant path of hope because that was braver than continuing on the dark and craggy road through his pain.

He'd told Moses to be brave, and he would be, too.

CHAPTER 24

Janeta had ridden along with Maddie in the wagon carrying some of Roberts's items into Meridian to be shipped, sending sidelong glances at the older woman all the while.

"Why did you ask me to join you?" Janeta asked.

"Because you're my sister in the Cause," Maddie said plainly.

"I was a Confederate spy," she said. "I'm not any longer, but you should know before you place your trust in me."

"Girl, I told you that I know everything that happens in that house. Even better is what I say. You know more about these people than some of us do. We can always use someone who knows how these folk think because I surely don't most the time."

Janeta was past the point of warning people away from her, especially after witnessing Daniel's behavior, but it was hard, this brushing away of her crimes.

"Do you think I will be accepted?"

"Long as you don't do nothing foolish, like questioning my judgment of your character." Maddie gave her a narrow look and Janeta nodded. "Now tell me how you gonna save your friends?"

"I don't know. I've been trying to think, and if they're imprisoned, then I'm not sure what can be done." Papi was still in jail somewhere, and she hadn't been able to get him out either. Impotent anger assailed her, but she tried to keep her mind clear. "When they took my father, I thought about just blowing the prison up," she said with a bitter laugh.

"Hmmm." Maddie rubbed at her cheek like she was massaging a painful toothache. She stared at the crates in front of her. "That could work. That just might work."

"What?"

Maddie looked at her. "First thing you learn about being a Daughter — sometimes you gotta be subtle, and sometimes you gotta burn it all down."

"But where are we going to get dynamite? And if we do, how do we make sure no one gets hurt?"

A mischievous look glinted in Maddie's eyes. "Someone's gonna get hurt either way, child. Hopefully it won't be us and ours."

After the wagon reached the outskirts of town, Maddie and Janeta hopped down. They made their way to a house off the road, hidden behind a thicket of trees. A woman as old as Maddie opened the door, and her gaze leapt from Maddie to Janeta like flames from branch to branch.

"Sister?" the woman asked, and Janeta nodded firmly.

The woman stepped aside to let them in.

Janeta almost thought the dark-skinned man in the center of the room was sleeping, but there was something unnatural about his repose. She jumped back when she realized he wasn't asleep, knocking into Maddie.

"Annabelle here handles deaths. That's Jeremiah, gonna be laid to rest tomorrow."

"Oh," Janeta said, her heart still racing. She'd never seen a dead body before — she hadn't even been allowed to see Mami. She glanced at the man out of the corner of her eye.

"Why are we here?"

"Because when you dealing with a life-or-death matter, this is where you come," Maddie said. "Annie, you got any of that stuff we used for blowin' those tracks?"

"Sure do," Annabelle said, moving slowly

to the corner of her one-room house, kneeling, and pulling up a wooden plank that wasn't nailed down.

She groped around for a bit and then came up with her age-spotted hand wrapped around a bundle of dynamite.

Maddie elbowed Janeta. "You ready?"

Janeta wondered what Daniel was doing. If she would ever see him again. She wished that things had turned out differently.

"I'm ready," she said.

"Take the path through the forest instead of the main road," Annabelle advised as they passed out of her house, hopefully leaving death behind them. "Leaves you right behind the jail."

Janeta gingerly held the two sticks of dynamite that Maddie had given her, out as far away from her body as she could manage. Annie had mentioned something about the explosives being "volatile" and warned them not to trip as they made their way through the woods.

They were watching the jailhouse from the forest, having just arrived, and things didn't look good. A group of white men milled about, yelling taunts and demanding to be let inside to deal with the darkies. The sheriff came out and tried to placate them, but some were clearly inebriated and others just spoiling for a fight.

"These are the men left behind, looking to show just how brave and strong they are since they ain't decked out in gray," Maddie said with disgust. "Someone's riled 'em up good. Probably these Sons of the Confederacy bastards who been hanging about. I told Roberts they was up to no good and to just have the damn meetin' already, but he wanted to wait for Davis and now look."

"We need a distraction," Janeta said. "Maybe we should set off one stick elsewhere, then when they go to investigate, we can blow the wall here?"

Maddie smiled proudly. "See? I told you I was a good judge of character. Look at you, strategizing." She carefully took one of the sticks of dynamite, then pulled out a flint strike and handed it to Janeta.

"Aren't you going to need it?" she asked.

"No, I'm gonna head over to old man Watson's store. He keeps the wood stove goin' out back to make warm drinks this time a year. Blowin' that up will be payback for the time he accused me of stealing and beat me around the ears. I wasn't stealing, but he's gonna lose a lot more than a handful of grain now." Maddie grinned. "Once you hear the explosion, wait for 'em to run;

then light the stick and leave it at the base of the wall. Tell the people in the jail to stand close to the bars on the other side and cover their ears."

Maddie padded off into the darkening night. She'd explained her plan as if it were mundane, and not a prison break to release enslaved men; not the exact situation white men and slave-owning territories all over seemed to hope for, so they could have an excuse to react with violence. Janeta didn't see much choice in the matter though. She would not leave her friends' fate to chance, especially when there were already men who seemed intent on doing them harm. At a certain point you couldn't worry about future evil when present evil was unfolding before your eyes.

Janeta crouched in the forest and watched, looking around at the growing shadows and jumping at every rustle in the trees. She began to shake as she waited there. She began to doubt. And when a man lumbered up the bushes just a few feet away from her, she resisted the urge to run. He swayed as he fumbled with his trousers and pulled his penis out to urinate. Janeta wanted to look away, but she couldn't risk him spotting her while she was trying to be proper. She kept her eyes above his waistline, watching his face as it contorted with relief.

The acrid scent of urine hit her nose and she held her breath. He stared off into the distance as he relieved himself, but suddenly his eyes drifted in her direction and focused as his mouth twitched into a frown.

"What you doin' here, boy?"

Boy?

Janeta glanced quickly behind her and all she saw was a flash of dark fabric and broad shoulder, but she knew who it was. Daniel. He had come! But he was also in danger, as was their plan. All the man had to do was yell to raise the alarm and bring his posse of angry friends over, and they would all be caught. The Loyal League, the Daughters of the Tent, Roberts before he could return to England.

Janeta did something she'd practiced for as long as she could remember, the motion so familiar she could perform it without thinking. In fact, that's how it happened: without thought.

Her mind was still frozen with fear — it wasn't until the blade was pinched between her fingertips and her eyes squinted as she focused on the man's throat that she began to comprehend what she was doing. She shifted her footing to one with more balance as she squatted, and the man's gaze moved to her just as she let the blade fly.

It didn't thud like it did when she practiced with wood and paper — it pierced his neck with a sickening sound, familiar from the days of watching Roberto cut meat in the Sanchez kitchen. Janeta didn't move from her crouch as the man fell, gurgling quietly. Her mind was catching up with her body's actions.

She'd killed a man.

"Ted, what are you doin' back there?" one of his compatriots called.

Still Janeta didn't move.

"Janeta. Janeta. *Sanchez.*"

She realized Daniel had wrapped her in his arms.

"Careful of the dynamite," she said blankly.

Ted twitched a bit on the ground, but he wasn't blinking. He'd fallen away from the bushes instead of into them, and his sprawled body would be evident to anyone who came near enough. There would be no time to drag him into the shadows.

"Hey, Ted, I said what are you doin'?" Footsteps started to approach them, dry leaves crackling under boots.

"He's dead," she whispered. "I took his life, and they're going to find us anyway."

One of Daniel's arms released her and she

knew he was reaching for his knife. "Well, then more of them will die. I won't let them take you."

Then the night was torn by a deafening boom.

CHAPTER 25

Daniel had rushed to Meridian thinking he would have to save Janeta — inexperienced and untested Janeta — but here he was cradling her after she'd killed a man with more stealth and skill than Daniel had ever managed.

It was no surprise, now that he thought of it. She'd fought by his side on the pook turtle, after overcoming her fear. She'd walked into a den of Loyal League detectives with devious intent and won most of them over with a smile. She'd declared herself aristocracy and talked down to men who might have killed her just for looking them in the eye.

That Janeta had saved him was about right. But now she needed him.

"Sanchez. You all right?"

"I've been better," she replied faintly from beneath him. When the explosion had rocked the night, Daniel had thrown himself over her. She pushed her way up and he rolled off her. "Have the men left?"

He dusted off his hands. "Yes, they've gone to see what the disturbance was."

"Then let's go. We have to move now before they come back if we want to save Jim and Augustus."

This had been a plan. Her plan. He was impressed.

She started crawling toward the jail, then pushed herself to her feet and ran shakily toward the building holding the jail. She had a flint lock in her hand and she began striking it as she stood beneath the window. She handed the dynamite she had mentioned to Daniel, barely looking at him, and in that moment his heart was well and truly hers. She trusted him to do what she needed of him, without asking. She trusted him to support her, without second guessing her. She trusted him to trust in himself.

"Jim. Augustus? Step far away from the wall," she called out.

"Janeta?" Augustus's shocked voice rose from the cell.

"Yes, it's me," she said, her voice trembling as she finally produced a flame. Relief softened her features for a moment; then her eyes narrowed and an expression of devious determination settled on her face.

"I'm going to blow you out of this filthy place. Now step back."

Daniel loved her.

She began passing the flame over the dynamite's wick.

"Hold on, hold on. Don't blow nothing up yet." That was Jim.

There was silence for a while; then there was a creak in the room and footsteps.

Jim and Augustus and Shelley staggered around the back of the building, blood stains on their clothes. Two dark arms were clamped around Augustus's neck and two legs crossed around his waist.

Moses.

Daniel rushed over and gently pried Moses off the injured man before swinging him onto his own back. Augustus nodded his thanks and limped toward his brother.

"Sheriff left the key when he ran off," Jim said. "Now we should run off, too."

Someone hurried around the corner and Janeta reached for her knives but stopped when she saw the woman — Maddie. One of Roberts's servants, and apparently even more than she appeared, like so many of the women in his life.

"Let's go," Maddie said. They hurried into the woods, cutting through a stand of bushes and sharp, leafless branches that tugged at Daniel's pants and shirt.

Soon a thin path opened and they stuck to it as the forest changed from patches of swampy mud and back to hard-packed dirt.

"I didn't protect everyone," Moses whispered as he bounced on Daniel's back. "I failed."

Daniel adjusted Moses on his back. "No, I failed by letting you think that you had to. It's not your job to protect anyone. You're a child. You are to be protected."

"But —"

"No. What happened was wrong and it was *not* your fault. You understand that?"

Moses was silent.

"Do you understand that, Moses?" he asked a bit more harshly. He knew what guilt and anger and frustration did to a person. He wouldn't have Moses take on that load at such a young age.

Finally, the boy nodded into his shoulder, gripping Daniel more tightly with his spindly arms.

"I told 'em you'd come back for us," Moses said.

Daniel focused on the trail ahead of them. He almost hadn't come back. He'd almost let vengeance stop justice. He committed to memory the feel of Moses's small body clinging to his. He memorized the warmth of the boy's tears running down the back of his neck, and the hiccup of his quiet, relieved sobs. This was why he fought. *This* was what mattered.

Daniel would die one day, as all creatures did. He didn't have to chase death and destruction when he could chase life and love instead.

"We're almost there," Janeta huffed from behind him. Her hand brushed his arm. "I'm glad you figured things out, Cumberland."

"It took me long enough," he said.

"I've recently discovered that sometimes we figure things out when we most need to," she said. There was a smile in her voice, despite the danger they were in. He needed to survive, just so he could feel that smile against his lips once more.

There was a house in the distance, and Maddie ran to it, hammering at the door. "Hurry up, Annabelle!"

The door opened and an older woman opened it, her gaze calm as she took in the scene. "Gonna be a tight fit."

She turned and walked into the house and knelt close to a wall. Maddie did the same a few paces away from her, and they quickly began pulling up the floorboards, revealing a hollowed out space.

"Come on now," Maddie said, beckoning. One by one, the escaped prisoners slipped into the shallow hole dug beneath the house and crouched, and Maddie followed them. Finally, only Janeta and Daniel remained, staring at the small space between Shelley and Jim, then looking at each other.

"We can flee into the woods," Janeta suggested. Dread enveloped her at the alternative.

No. No, she wouldn't leave him. Not after he'd come back to her.

"The woods gonna be crawling with slave catchers and Homeguard," Maddie said in a low voice. "Get in here, now, girl!"

Janeta looked at Daniel, eyes wide and determination setting her brow.

"I'm no —"

Daniel leaned forward and caught her mouth in a kiss, cutting off her words and tasting her one more time. In case it was the final time. He cupped her face, tracing her jaw as her lips molded themselves against his.

He pulled away and looked at her.

"Get in, Sanchez."

He managed a smile as he took the dynamite from her, and it wasn't even fake. He'd just kissed a brave, bold, and beautiful woman, and she was looking at him like she wanted him to do it again.

"Don't do anything foolish, Cumberland."

Like fall in love?

"I'll save that task for you, Sanchez."

She slid into the last tight space of the hidey-hole and Daniel helped the woman named Annabelle replace the boards. He gave Janeta one last glance before placing the final board down. She was grinning up at him, but her smile faltered just before the board was settled into place. He hated what that image evoked, and the flicker of panic it woke in him.

"I got a place for you, too," Annabelle said. "Don't worry none."

She led him to a part of the room cordoned off with a curtain and when she pulled it back Daniel reevaluated his new outlook on life. Perhaps he *was* a cursed man.

Before him was a dead man on a table and three wooden coffins stacked beside him. The woman was an undertaker.

"Help me move these now," she said.

Numb dread trickled down the back of his neck as he helped her move first one coffin and then the other. She pried the lid off the bottom and largest — but not large enough — wooden box and gestured for him to get in.

He stepped into the box but couldn't bring himself to sit. His skull prickled and sweat beaded along his hairline and under his arms. He glanced at the dead man on the table, whose eternal home he was likely breaking in for him.

Outside there was the sound of hoofbeats.

"Lie down!" Annabelle commanded. "If they find you, they gonna tear this place apart looking for the others."

Daniel crouched, then lay down, though his mind howled in protest. His hands shook uncontrollably and he curled them into loose fists and pressed them into his thighs. He closed his eyes and fought the urge to jump up and run, everyone else's safety be damned.

He groaned as she fit the lid back onto the box, but it was only when he heard the slide of the other coffin being placed on top of his that the panic kicked in.

No. No. You have to get out of here. Push the lid off. Run.

It was torture. *Torture.* Everything in his body screamed for him to move, to break free, to do anything he could to be out of the small, cramped space. His breath started coming quick and heavy as memories of his days of confinement bombarded him. Of his inability to move, to breathe, to be *free.*

The urge to put his palm against the lid of the coffin nearly overwhelmed him, but he resisted. If he placed one palm there, he would place the other, and then he would push in a frantic effort to be free, and all would be lost.

He balled his fists harder, digging his nails into his palms to distract himself. Sweat drenched his body, and he fought against the scream lodged in his throat.

He thought of Janeta, bravely jumping to her feet and pulling out her pistol. He thought of her flinging her knife with deadly precision. None of that stopped the overwhelming terror, but it tempered it. He silently whispered her name, a prayer to get him through this torment.

Something crawled against his face. The air in the coffin began to grow humid from his shallow breaths and his body heat.

You have to get out, his mind urged. *You* have *to.*

Something Elle had told him after she'd refused his request for marriage flashed through his panic. *"You get something in your head and you're like a dog with a bone, even if that bone tastes bad and maybe doesn't even belong to you. What would happen if you used that stubbornness for something else?"*

Daniel took as deep a breath as he could muster and focused on the very good reasons he had to calm himself as he slowly released it. *Everything is fine. You can move your arms and legs. You can breathe. The box is not airtight.*

Panic still gnawed at him like voracious insects, but he reclaimed the thoughts cycling in his mind bit by bit.

If you try to leave the box now, the Rebels win. If you stay calm, they lose. You cannot let them win. You are strong enough to do this. Janeta thinks so. Moses thinks so. Ellen thinks so.

He forced himself to focus on the words of self-support as much as he had focused on the voice that had told him he was worthless, and though he was still swamped in sweat and mired in panic, the situation was tolerable, and tolerable was all he needed to survive.

Finally, there was a heavy knock on the door, the force and speed of it transmitting in advance that the men wouldn't be ignored and would, in fact, do as they wished. He heard Annabelle open the door, feigning surprise.

"Evening, gentlemen. What can I — oh!"

There were two sounds in succession: a hard smack, then Annabelle hitting the ground with a thud.

"What are you doing?" she demanded, angrily.

"Some darkies on the loose," a man's voice said. His words were punctuated by boot heels reverberating on the wooden floor. "They blowed up the general store and escaped from jail."

Another man's voice cut in. "It's what those men was talking about. You give darkies an inch and they think they can do anything they want. We shoulda strung 'em up soon as they got marched to jail, men, woman, and child."

Daniel was no longer thinking about how awful it felt to be trapped in a wooden box. He was focusing on the man's words, and the sudden and unignorable fury they inflamed in him. Daniel was always angry, but this anger he held on to like a lifeline. He would not let these bastards find him cowering and afraid. His fists loosened and his mind focused, his calm driven by sheer spite.

"I don't know nothing 'bout no escape," Annabelle said in a voice steady but full of anger. "You busted up in my house, disrupting me laying a body to rest, and I don't know nothing."

"You think we don't know how people

sneak through here? Yeah, those men told us that, too," the other voice said. " 'I thought this was a Rebel town,' he said. 'But you got darkies sneaking around making trouble, like they smarter than you.' "

Annabelle sighed. "Now, Hiram, I knowed you since you was a boy. You gonna listen to some strange man who come to town making trouble? You gonna raise your hand to me and hurt me on account of them?"

"Yeah, I knowed you. Living out here alone doing who knows what devil work with your dead bodies. They say you get up all kind of hoodoo. That man said women like you even make poison to kill off white folk, and potions to make the slaves rebel."

"Now, I don't mess with none of that," Annabelle said with a dark chuckle. "Neither of you would be here if I messed with any of that, believe me."

"That a threat, darkie?" This was a new voice. It was more poised. More in control. "See? You let them talk to you like this, and that's why Clark County men are seen as nothing but weak and spineless wastrels, no better than a Northman."

Daniel grit his teeth. This was one of the primary strategies of the Sons, agitating and riling up poor white men whose tenuous pride was so easily wounded and whose intentions so quickly turned deadly.

"I wasn't threatening nobody," Annabelle said, but there was fear in her voice now that a total stranger had entered her home. "What I look like, threatening Hiram and Bill?"

Daniel's agitation grew and grew, but there was nothing he could do. If he tried to free himself from the coffin, he'd make such a commotion that they'd hear him before he could make his way from below. If they killed him, they'd kill Annabelle, too, and search the house more.

Tears of frustration squeezed from his tightly shut eyes, and his fist unfurled to grip the dynamite he'd taken from Janeta.

"Go look behind the curtain," the man said.

Daniel fumbled about, contorting himself so that his hand might reach the pocket in the inner lining of his jacket. Trying to move reminded him that he barely had any space to do so, but he fought his panic. He couldn't ignore his fear, but he could beat it.

I'm stronger than fear.

"There's coffins in here," Hiram shouted.

His fingers closed around the box of matches he'd been trying to find, and he eased them out.

"Well, search them," the commanding voice said, laced with annoyance.

The footsteps approached and the panic buzzing in Daniel's brain went silent. All his attention was focused on the feel of the match in his hand and his attempt to light it against the box balanced on his stomach. He stopped breathing.

He scraped it against the sandpaper, once. Twice. The match flared and then died.

The coffin shook as they pried open the one above it.

Daniel sipped in a breath and attempted to strike a new match, but his hands were damp and the damned match wouldn't strike; he tried until he was sure he'd rubbed away any part of it that would be useful, and then pulled out the third and final match.

The bottom of the coffin above him scraped against the lid of his.

He struck again. Once more, twice — *dear Lord, this is my last chance* — and then it flared triumphantly. Hope in the damned darkness, indeed. He lit the short fuse as the men pried at the lid. He had no idea how quickly or slowly it would burn, but he had no choice.

He didn't want to die anymore — oddly after so many months of longing for it, he resented this conclusion to his time on earth — but he would do it for everyone in that hole beneath the house.

For Janeta, who had only just begun to find herself. She couldn't die yet, and he wouldn't let her.

The lid began to be pried up. This was it.

He sucked in a breath, eyes on the sparks coming off the dynamite's wick.

As soon as it lifted the tiniest bit, Daniel sprang forward. He was a big man, something that had been touted as a benefit as he stood on the auction block, and he used his size and the element of surprise, pushing up hard.

He gripped the lid of the coffin as the men stumbled away in shock. He took the briefest second to relish the look of shock on their face — to them, Daniel was the dead come back to life. They weren't entirely wrong.

He held tightly to the coffin lid, the dynamite held against it with his right palm, and used it to push the men back, back out of the room. He didn't look at their faces any longer, only seeing pale pink blurs in his single-minded focus. He pushed them into the other man, another pale blur above a suit of black, pushed them out the door and into the night, the hiss of the dynamite's fuse driving him forward.

Everyone in the hole was in danger. If he failed, they would all die. Or worse, be sold back into slavery or punished for starting an insurrection. Daniel could not allow this.

He threw all his weight into the wood, knocking the men to the ground outside the door.

He still held the dynamite.

The wick burned low, but not low enough. Or was it? Daniel had no idea when it would go off.

The men were beginning to stand, and one of them was reaching for his gun.

Daniel lobbed the dynamite forward, and it tumbled end over end, leaving a trail of sparks in the dark night. Then the small dots of beauty expanded to a flash of light and heat and sound. Daniel flew backward, backward, backward, with no thought on his mind, but the heat on his lips making him think of Janeta.

CHAPTER 26

Everyone in the hidey-hole flinched as the shock of Annabelle hitting the floor reverberated through the boards brushing their heads.

Janeta had already reached for her guns as the men harassed Annabelle, as they spoke to her with contempt to make themselves feel big.

Rage simmered in her as she listened to them try to make Annabelle do as they wished, whining and complaining about what was owed to them as they tried to take power from others. The contempt in their tones heeled like trained dogs when the third man showed up, but they lost none of their angry entitlement.

Janeta grit her teeth. That her and her friends should be hiding like rats. That Annabelle should be hit like she was nothing to nobody. How could anyone think that this was the proper order of the world?

Janeta had lamented how easily she swallowed lies to believe that her life had been deserved, but she wasn't the only one.

Men like this roamed America, seeking to claim every part of this land for themselves like the plague of locusts the *padre* in church had talked about. She was sure these men sat at mass every Sunday and heard the same readings, but did they realize they were the harbingers of the end of all that was good? Were they oblivious, or did they know, and relish in that designation?

"There's coffins in here!" one of the men called out.

"Well, search them," their leader said.

Fear pushed Janeta's rage to the back-burner.

She couldn't imagine what state Daniel was in, enclosed in a coffin. But those men were going to find him. She gripped her guns, the weapons that had been given to her mother in case of slave rebellion. Perhaps Mami would be proud that that was exactly what they were being used for — rebellion. Janeta would never again smile and make herself small and grateful for being treated like a human, and she wouldn't allow these men to touch Daniel.

She shifted as if to stand, but Maddie grabbed her arm hard, then squeezed in warning. Janeta tried to tug away and Maddie's grip tightened. She knew what it meant.

You cannot go to him without risking all of us.

Janeta sat still, body tensed and tears stinging her eyes, listening to the drag of wood and the thump as first one coffin and then another was placed on the floor. She waited to hear the man she cared for executed. There was no other possibility — it was three to one, and Daniel could not lurk in the shadows and strike as he had with the soldiers who'd taken their food. Even then, his victory had been one of ingenuity and not brute strength.

Tears slipped down her cheeks and Janeta shook her head, unwilling to believe harm could come to him. Daniel had survived so much. He would survive this, too.

Then there were shouts, and not from Daniel. A heavy tread thundered overhead, pushing forward behind stuttering, shuffling steps that had to be the other men. The sounds were moving toward the front door.

Daniel was fighting back, and judging from the tumult, he was winning. There was a brief pause, and silence. Had Daniel won that easily?

Her heart leapt — and then the house

leapt, shuddering as a blast shook it.

No, no, no.

Maddie's grip loosened on her as they were all jostled and something slammed to the boards above them. Ears still ringing Janeta crouched with her hands against the boards above her, pushing and pushing to no avail.

She had to get to Daniel.

"Something's fallen over the boards. Help me," she begged.

"All right," Moses's voice floated to her, and tears sprang to her eyes.

"Thank you, sweet boy. All of us need to do this."

The others shifted around her, and she could sense their blooming panic as the smell of smoke drifted faintly through the cracks in the floor. What if the roof had come down on them? What if they couldn't escape?

"Everybody, let's push on the count of three," Maddie said calmly, taking the situation in hand. "Dig your heels in and give it all you got. One. Two. Three!"

Janeta strained, her feet digging into the cold clay ground. They all pushed up, as if lifting their hands in prayer, and though it had been difficult for Janeta alone, with their combined forces the boards moved as the blockage rolled away with a thud. They pushed aside a couple of the boards completely, debris raining down on them, and Janeta coughed as she peered up into the once-tidy room.

Smoke hung in the air, and splinters of wood. And when she turned her head, she saw what had weighed down the door — Daniel's body. His face and scalp were burned, and from this angle she couldn't see if he was breathing, but he was much too still.

"Daniel? Daniel!"

He didn't move. Janeta placed her guns down and braced a hand on the board in front of her, trying to hoist herself out.

"Daniel!"

The pressure on her arms eased, and she realized that the others were lifting her from below, an unasked for kindness, like so many she had received since she'd set out on this journey. She stowed that memory away — she couldn't take it for granted even though horror prickled her scalp and was beginning to numb her senses.

She stumbled up onto the floor and crawled toward Daniel, vision glazed over with tears. He didn't move. A living man's head wouldn't be turned at that angle, either.

She gagged, once, twice, but kept crawling.

"No. No!"

Her hands gripped his charred shirt and rolled him over. He was dead, indeed, but he wasn't Daniel.

Morbid relief flowed through her. What had the man's name been?

"Jeremiah," she said, flopping back onto her bottom. "Oh God, it's Jeremiah."

"Did you really think that was me, Sanchez? I have about a foot and fifty pounds on the unfortunate fellow."

Daniel was alive, carrying Annabelle from the other side of the shack. Bloody, burnt, and annoyed, but very much alive.

She didn't know how he had survived. She only knew that for one awful moment, she had known a world in which Daniel no longer existed, and that wasn't a world she wanted to live in.

"*Milagro.* You truly are a miracle." Her voice caught, and happiness filled her.

"I'd say I'm just stubborn." He had the nerve to smile, though he winced and limped a bit.

"And thank goodness for that," Annabelle said, gingerly rotating her wrists and wincing.

"What do we do now?" Janeta asked; then

she saw motion through the smoke behind Daniel.

"Daniel, get down," she said. "There's someone behind you."

Daniel dropped to his knees and Janeta grabbed and raised her gun.

"Daniel? Are you in there?" A voice called out from where the shadows moved. It was a woman's voice, husky and low. Then she said, "It's me. Elle. Show yourself."

"Elle?" The surprise in Daniel's voice was evident. "What are you doing here? How did you find me?"

The woman stepped into the room, a pistol in her hand and her gaze sliding over the room. She was smaller than Janeta had imagined, this woman who Daniel had loved and lost.

"I'm a detective," she said, then looked over her shoulder as if searching for someone. "We were tracking Davis and got wind of a very familiar-sounding man claiming to be an envoy from Cuba. Malcolm is with me, so please no one shoot the next white man you see when you step out of the house." She turned to face them. "He's got a wagon that we really should all get onto right now. This explosion is going to attract attention, Daniel."

"You should be proud," Daniel said, still

smiling. "I learned that from you."

"I was always proud of you, friend. But let's save the reunion for later."

Janeta had already begun pulling the others up out of the space under the planks, feeling a bit embarrassed as she watched the scene. Soon everyone was assembled and they jogged out to the wagon, driven by a large man whose face was mostly obscured by a beard.

"Load them up please, Ellen. I'd rather not have to fight tonight if I can charm instead."

"Fine, fine." Her gaze darted from Daniel to the man. "Daniel, this is my husband Malcolm. Malcolm, Daniel."

Daniel limped over and shook Malcolm's hand. "I hear she's been keeping you on your toes."

"Every day," Malcolm said. "And thank you by the way. For my brother."

"Thank you," Daniel said. "For me."

Janeta didn't know what they were talking about, really, but the two men nodded. She was about to climb in the back of the wagon when Daniel took her gently by the elbow. "By the way, this is our fellow Loyal League detective, Janeta Sanchez. My partner."

He said the word partner awkwardly, but with emphasis.

"Actually, I resigned from the Loyal League, but I'm still your partner, I suppose. Maybe you should come over to the Daughters of the Tent."

"Oh, I *like* you," Elle said, greeting Janeta but also herding them all into the wagon and pulling the curtain closed. She knocked twice on the wood; then Malcolm pulled off, the amble turning into a brisk pace. She settled next to Janeta in the dark of the wagon. "Thank you," she said quietly.

"For what?" Janeta asked.

"For taking care of my friend," Elle said. "I'm happy to see a smile on his face. If we all survive the night, remind me to tell you embarrassing stories from our youth."

"Ellen," Daniel growled. But in the darkness his fingers slipped gently through Janeta's, and she clasped her hands around his.

"That's right," Elle said. "I won't need the reminder." She turned to talk to Jim, who sat on the other side of her, giving Janeta and Daniel some privacy.

"Are you all right?" Janeta asked him, squeezing his hand back. There hadn't been time before.

"Perhaps," he said. "Let's see what the night brings. And the morning. And the afternoon. Maybe we can see that together

— what the future holds."

He squeezed her hand. She squeezed his. They didn't speak anymore because they shared their own language in the dark, and understood each other perfectly.

Epilogue

December 1863
Cairo, Illinois

Janeta watched Daniel as he slept. It was winter in truth now, winter in the North, but she was not cold. Daniel was beside her. Daniel who had risked everything for her and their friends. Daniel who loved her.

She tucked the moth-eaten woolen blanket under his chin as she slipped away from the cot they'd been allowed to use while visiting their friends, who were about to leave the camp for free life in the North.

She ran her fingertip over the smooth line in Daniel's eyebrow, the artifact of one of several burns he'd received from the blast that had saved them. His body was a map of scars detailing what this country had put him through, but she hoped that he remembered that all of them were memories of his bravery too.

His eyes fluttered open and he tilted his

head up and dropped a kiss onto her wrist.

"Good morning, Sanchez."

"How do you do, Cumberland?"

"Better than I ever imagined," he said, and she knew that he meant it. "And you?"

She turned her head away from him so he couldn't see her eyes. He knew her too well. And he'd been there when Lake had provided her with the intelligence they'd received from Palatka — her father was alive, but his imprisonment was no mistake. He'd been partners with men illegally shipping slaves into the country from Cuba, despite the decades old ban.

Part of her had been relieved that she hadn't doomed him to prison; part of her wished she had never known. But their wealth in America had come from somewhere that wasn't a sugar plantation, and she'd never questioned it. The wealth that had kept her and her sisters in finery.

Her sisters refused to respond to her letters, which hurt, but there was nothing to be done but bear the pain and hope that it would diminish with time, or that they would grow with it.

"I am not all right," she said to Daniel instead of lying. "But I will be."

"We can help each other," he said carefully. "I think we work together very well."

He tugged at the back of her shawl and pulled her down onto his chest.

"I think we do, too," she said. "I'm not sure if my fellow Daughters will approve of me courting a Loyal League man. They think you all are much too showy."

"I hope you don't have to get their approval. I hope this war ends, so there's no need for detectives or Daughters. That it ends, and we're all free."

He'd told her he hoped to take up law again. Up North. And he wanted her to come with him, if she desired. If they made it through the war.

She tangled her fingers with his and dropped a kiss onto his jaw before settling against him. "Go back to sleep. We have a long journey ahead."

The war wasn't over yet, and the Sons of the Confederacy seemed determined to win it for the South, even as the North gained power and won more territory.

She would fight until the end for this new land of hers. For this new love of hers. For her people. And for herself.

As she closed her eyes and drifted to sleep, she thought of her mother, laughing and beautiful before she was crushed by the world. Janeta wished Mami could see how perfect Janeta was, just being herself, and that she had been perfect, too.

She smiled as she slipped into a dream, one filled with hope and love.

ACKNOWLEDGMENTS

I would like to thank the Kensington Publishing staff from top to bottom, but particularly my editor, Esi Sogah, and art director, Kristine Mills-Noble, for helping this series and its covers to shine (and to Esi for putting up with my randomness). Thanks to publicist Lulu Martinez for being a great advocate of the series and pushing it hard. I'd also like to thank Norma Perez-Hernandez for being one of the first readers/cheerleaders, assisting with my rusty español, inducting me into the BTS Army (along with Michelle), and always making me feel like I can do anything. Special shout-out to Paula Reedy for dealing with my page-proof changes because I know being a production editor is a hard and often thankless job.

I'd like to thank Janet Eckford, Maya Frank-Levine, and Kit Rocha for advance reading and advice along the way, and all of my RAPTORS (rawr!!!) for reminding me that I would eventually finish, no matter how hard and unlikely it seemed.

Random thanks to Ryan Coogler for helping break my writer's block with his amazing film. Obviously he is completely unaware of this, lol, but sometimes one form of media can help you put together the mess of final puzzle pieces for another.

And huge, huge thanks to you, the readers, who read and review and reach out to tell me what the series means to you. Thank you!

AUTHOR'S NOTE

Writing any book has some level of difficulty, but among the books I've written thus far, *An Unconditional Freedom* is lovingly called "the book that broke me." That's not exactly accurate — it was the world that existed as I tried to create Daniel and Janeta's story that broke me.

When I first started this series, America was seemingly on an upward trajectory, despite still struggling with the whole "liberty and justice for all" thing. When *An Extraordinary Union* came out, it was alongside surging White supremacy, with neo-Nazis and Confederates being given glowing profiles in national newspapers, which led to them taking to the streets with torches. If you've read the book before reading this (I know some of you skip to the back of the book and I will not judge you [too much] for that), then you know this book was about a man who believed in

America and was grievously wronged by it, a man who was unable to process his trauma in a country that was still hurting people like him while also expecting them to help right the wrongs baked into the foundational bricks of the country.

As I was writing this book, it seemed that every other day brought a new story about a Black man or woman being killed by police. As I was writing this book, opening social media meant seeing the casual cruelty of the current government's policies. As I was writing this book, I couldn't help but succumb to sadness and defeat because what promise could I make a character like Daniel about America, knowing that in 2018 it had reverted back to everything he feared? How could I give him a happy ending in a country that was so set against him having one?

I became depressed and despondent at several times during this book. I stopped and started, and couldn't bring myself to push toward the end. There were several individual things that allowed me to finish the book — films, books, articles — but maybe foremost among them was one I watched with Betty Reid Soskin, a ninety-six-year-old park ranger and author of *Sign My Name to Freedom: A Memoir of a Pioneer-*

ing Life, and Luvvie Ajayi, author of *I'm Judging You.* Soskin said something that resonated with me deeply:

"There's still much, much work to do. But every generation I know now has to re-create democracy in its time because democracy will never be fixed. It was not intended to. It's a participatory form of governance that we all have the responsibility to form that more perfect union."

It reminded me of something that I had already known but had been buried under the relentlessly growing pile of awful news: Daniel's happily ever after didn't mean that America had to be that perfect Union as I was writing the story. It is in the *possibility* of perfection, in finding a community of like-minded people who share similar goals and work toward them, together. I wish that things were different. I wish the injustices chronicled in the Loyal League series were truly in the past. But wishing only gets us so far. I hope that by the time this is published, America is moving in a better direction. Whatever the situation is, I hope that you, dear reader, have found a way to exercise your rights, to participate in our democracy, and that you have found the community that will fight alongside you. We can't all be daring detectives, but we can all do *something,* no matter how small, to make the future brighter for every American.

SELECTED BIBLIOGRAPHY

The following is a selection of the books, theses, and articles used to research this novel:

Abbott, Karen. *Liar, Temptress, Soldier, Spy: Four Women Undercover in the Civil War.* New York: HarperCollins, 2014.

Foreman, Amanda. *A World on Fire: Britain's Crucial Role in the American Civil War.* New York: Random House, 2011.

Jordan, Robert Paul. *National Geographic Society's The Civil War.* Washington, DC: National Geographic Society, 1969.

Lause, Mark A. *A Secret Society History of the Civil War.* Champaign, IL: University of Illinois Press, 2011.

McPherson, James M. *Battle Cry of Freedom.* Oxford: Oxford University Press, 2003.

Pinkerton, Allan. *The Spy of the Rebellion: Being a True History of the Spy System of the United States Army During the Late*

Rebellion, Revealing Many Secrets of the War Hitherto Not Made Public. New York: G.W. Carleton & Co., 1883.

Pratt, Fletcher. *The Civil War in Pictures.* Garden City, NY: Garden City Books, 1955.

Tucker, Phillip Thomas, editor. *Cubans in the Confederacy.* Jefferson, NC: McFarland & Company, Inc., Publishers, 2002.

Van Doren Stern, Philip. *Secret Missions of the Civil War.* Westport, CT: Praeger, 1959.

Ward, Andrew. *The Slaves' Civil War: The Civil War in the Words of Former Slaves.* Boston: Mariner Books, 2008.

ABOUT THE AUTHOR

Alyssa Cole is an award-winning author of historical, contemporary romance, and SFF romance. She's contributed to publications including *Shondaland, The Toast, Vulture, RT Book Reviews,* and *Heroes and Heartbreakers,* and her books have received critical acclaim from *Library Journal, Kirkus, Booklist, Jezebel, Vulture, Book Riot, Entertainment Weekly,* and various other outlets. When she's not working, she can often be found watching anime with her husband or wrangling their menagerie of animals. Visit her at alyssacole.com.

The employees of Thorndike Press hope you have enjoyed this Large Print book. All our Thorndike, Wheeler, and Kennebec Large Print titles are designed for easy reading, and all our books are made to last. Other Thorndike Press Large Print books are available at your library, through selected bookstores, or directly from us.

For information about titles, please call:
(800) 223-1244

or visit our website at:
gale.com/thorndike

To share your comments, please write:
Publisher
Thorndike Press
10 Water St., Suite 310
Waterville, ME 04901